COLLECTED WORKS OF
ALEXANDER LANGE KIELLAND

CONTENTS

NORSE TALES AND SKETCHES

TALES OF TWO COUNTRIES

NORSE TALES AND SKETCHES

TRANSLATED BY
R. L. CASSIE.

INTRODUCTION

Encouraged by the great and growing popularity of Scandinavian literature in this country, I venture to submit to public judgment this humble essay towards an English presentment of some of the charming novelettes of Alexander L. Kielland, a writer who takes rank among the foremost exponents of modern Norse thought. Although these short stories do not represent the full fruition of the author's genius, they yet convey a fairly accurate conception of his literary personality, and of the bold realistic tendency which is so strikingly developed in his longer novels.

Kielland's style is polished, lucid, and incisive. He does not waste words or revel in bombastic diffuseness. Every phrase of his narrative is a definite contribution towards the vivification of his realistic effects. His concise, laconic periods are pregnant with deep meaning, and instinct with that indefinable Norse essence which almost eludes the translator— that vague something which specially lends itself to the treatment of weird or pathetic situations.

In his pre-eminence as a satirist, Kielland resembles Thackeray. His satire, although keen, is always wholesome, genial, and good-humoured.

Kielland's longer novels are masterly delineations of Norwegian provincial life and character, and his vivid individualization of his native town of Stavanger finds few parallels in fiction.

In conclusion, the writer hopes that this modest publication may help to draw the attention of the cultured British public to another of the great literary figures of the North.

R.L.C.

A SIESTA.

In an elegant suite of chambers in the Rue Castiglione sat a merry party at dessert.

Senhor José Francisco de Silvis was a short-legged, dark-complexioned Portuguese, one of those who usually come from Brazil with incredible wealth, live incredible lives in Paris, and, above all, become notorious by making the most incredible acquaintances.

In that little company scarcely anybody, except those who had come in pairs, knew his neighbour. And the host himself knew his guests only through casual meetings at balls, *tables d' hôte*, or in the street.

Senhor de Silvis laughed much, and talked loudly of his success in life, as is the habit of rich foreigners; and as he could not reach up to the level of the Jockey Club, he gathered the best company he could find. When he met anyone, he immediately asked for the address, and sent next day an invitation to a little dinner. He spoke all languages, even German, and one could see by his face that he was not a little proud when he called over the table: Mein lieber Herr Doctor! Wie geht's Ihnen?'

There was actually a live German doctor among this merry party. He had an overgrown light-red beard, and that Sedan smile which invariably accompanies the Germans in Paris.

The temperature of the conversation rose with the champagne; the sounds of fluent and broken French were mingled with those of Spanish and Portuguese. The ladies lay back in their chairs and laughed. The guests already knew each other well enough not to be reserved or constrained. Jokes and *bons-mots* passed over the table, and from mouth to mouth. 'Der liebe Doctor' alone engaged in a serious discussion with the gentleman next to him—a French journalist with a red ribbon in his buttonhole.

And there was one more who was not drawn into the general merriment. He sat on the right of Mademoiselle Adèle, while on the left was her new lover, the corpulent Anatole, who had surfeited himself on truffles.

During dinner Mademoiselle Adèle had endeavoured, by many innocent little arts, to infuse some life into her right-hand neighbour. However, he remained very quiet, answering her courteously, but briefly, and in an undertone.

At first she thought he was a Pole—one of those very tiresome specimens who wander about and pretend to be outlaws. However, she soon perceived that she had made a mistake, and this piqued Mademoiselle Adèle. For one of her many specialties was the ability to immediately 'assort' all the foreigners with whom she mingled, and she used to declare that she could guess a man's nationality as soon as she had spoken ten words with him.

But this taciturn stranger caused her much perplexed cogitation. If he had only been fair-haired, she would at once have set him down as an Englishman, for he talked like one. But he had dark hair, a thick black moustache, and a nice little figure. His fingers were remarkably long, and he had a peculiar way of trifling with his bread and playing with his dessert-fork.

'He is a musician,' whispered Mademoiselle Adèle to her stout friend.

'Ah!' replied Monsieur Anatole. 'I am afraid I have eaten too many truffles.'

Mademoiselle Adèle whispered in his ear some words of good counsel, upon which he laughed and looked very affectionate.

However, she could not relinquish her hold of the interesting foreigner. After she had coaxed him to drink several glasses of champagne, he became livelier, and talked more.

'Ah!' cried she suddenly; 'I hear it in your speech. You are an Englishman!'

The stranger grew quite red in the face, and answered quickly, 'No, madame.'

Mademoiselle Adèle laughed. 'I beg your pardon. I know that Americans feel angry when they are taken for Englishmen.'

'Neither am I an American,' replied the stranger.

This was too much for Mademoiselle Adèle. She bent over her plate and looked sulky, for she saw that Mademoiselle Louison opposite was enjoying her defeat.

The foreign gentleman understood the situation, and added, half aloud: 'I am an Irishman, madame.'

'Ah!' said Mademoiselle Adèle, with a grateful smile, for she was easily reconciled.

'Anatole! Irishman—what is that?' she asked in a whisper.

'The poor of England,' he whispered back.

'Indeed!'

Adèle elevated her eyebrows, and cast a shrinking, timid glance at the stranger. She had suddenly lost much of her interest in him.

De Silvis's dinners were excellent. The party had sat long at table, and when Monsieur Anatole thought of the oysters with which the feast had begun, they appeared to him like a beautiful dream. On the contrary, he had a somewhat too lively recollection of the truffles.

Dinner was over; hands were reaching out for glasses, or trifling with fruit or biscuits.

That sentimental blonde, Mademoiselle Louison, fell into meditation over a grape that she had dropped in her champagne glass. Tiny bright air-bubbles gathered all round the coating of the fruit, and when it was quite covered with these shining white pearls, they lifted the heavy grape up through the wine to the surface.

'Look!' said Mademoiselle Louison, turning her large, swimming eyes upon the journalist, 'look, white angels are bearing a sinner to heaven!'

15

'Ah! *charmant*, mademoiselle! What a sublime thought!' exclaimed the journalist, enraptured.

Mademoiselle Louison's sublime thought passed round the table, and was much admired. Only the frivolous Adèle whispered to her obese admirer, 'It would take a good many angels to bear you, Anatole.'

Meanwhile the journalist seized the opportunity; he knew how to rivet the general attention. Besides, he was glad to escape from a tiresome political controversy with the German; and, as he wore a red ribbon and affected the superior journalistic tone, everybody listened to him.

He explained how small forces, when united, can lift great burdens; and then he entered upon the topic of the day—the magnificent collections made by the press for the sufferers by the floods in Spain, and for the poor of Paris. Concerning this he had much to relate, and every moment he said 'we,' alluding to the press. He talked himself quite warm about 'these millions, that we, with such great self-sacrifice, have raised.'

But each of the others had his own story to tell. Numberless little touches of nobility—all savouring of self-denial—came to light from amidst these days of luxury and pleasure.

Mademoiselle Louison's best friend—an insignificant little lady who sat at the foot of the table—told, in spite, of Louison's protest, how the latter had taken three poor seamstresses up to her own rooms, and had them sew the whole of the night before the *fête* in the hippodrome. She had given the poor girls coffee and food, besides payment.

Mademoiselle Louison suddenly became an important personage at table, and the journalist began to show her marked attention.

The many pretty instances of philanthropy, and Louison's swimming eyes, put the whole company into a quiet, tranquil, benevolent frame of mind, eminently in keeping with the weariness induced by the exertions of the feast. And this comfortable feeling rose yet a few degrees higher after the guests were settled in soft easy-chairs in the cool drawing-room.

There was no other light than the fire in the grate. Its red glimmer crept over the English carpet and up the gold borders in the tapestry; it shone upon a gilt picture-frame, on the piano that stood opposite, and, here and there, on a face further away in the gloom. Nothing else was visible except the red ends of cigars and cigarettes.

The conversation died away. The silence was broken only by an occasional whisper or the sound of a coffee-cup being put aside; each seemed disposed to enjoy, undisturbed, his genial mood and the quiet gladness of digestion. Even Monsieur Anatole forgot his truffles, as he reclined in a low chair close to the sofa, on which Mademoiselle Adèle had taken her seat.

'Is there no one who will give us a little music?' asked Senhor de Silvis from his chair. 'You are always so kind, Mademoiselle Adèle.'

'Oh no, no!' cried Mademoiselle; 'I am too tired.'

But the foreigner—the Irishman—rose from his corner and walked towards the instrument.

'Ah, you will play for us! A thousand thanks, Monsieur—.' Senhor de Silvis had forgotten the name—a thing that often happened to him with his guests.

'He is a musician,' said Mademoiselle Adèle to her friend. Anatole grunted admiringly.

Indeed, all were similarly impressed by the mere way in which he sat down and, without any preparation, struck a few chords here and there, as if to wake the instrument.

Then he began to play—lightly, sportively, frivolously, as befitted the situation. The melodies of the day were intermingled with fragments of waltzes and ballads; all the ephemeral trifles that Paris hums over for eight days he blended together with brilliantly fluent execution.

The ladies uttered exclamations of admiration, and sang a few bars, keeping time with their feet. The whole party followed the music with intense interest; the strange artist had hit their mood, and drawn them all with him from the beginning. 'Der liebe Doctor' alone listened with the Sedan smile on his face; the pieces were too easy for him.

But soon there came something for the German too; he nodded now and then with a sort of appreciation.

It was a strange situation: the piquant fragrance that filled the air, the pleasure-loving women—these people, so free and unconstrained, all strangers to one another, hidden in the elegant, half-dark salon, each following his most secret thoughts—thoughts born of the mysterious, muffled music; whilst the firelight rose and fell, and made everything that was golden glimmer in the darkness.

And there constantly came more for the doctor. From time to time he turned and signed to De Silvis, as he heard the loved notes of 'unser Schumann,' 'unser Beethoven,' or even of 'unser famoser Richard.'

Meanwhile the stranger played on, steadily and without apparent effort, slightly inclined to the left, so as to give power to the bass. It sounded as if he had twenty fingers, all of steel; he knew how to unite the multitudinous notes in a single powerful clang. Without any pause to mark the transition from one melody to another, he riveted the interest of the company by constant new surprises, graceful allusions, and genial combinations, so that even the least musical among them were constrained to listen with eager attention.

But the character of the music imperceptibly changed. The artist bent constantly over the instrument, inclining more to the left, and there was a strange unrest in the bass notes. The Baptists from 'The Prophet' came with heavy step; a rider from 'Damnation de Faust' dashed up from far below, in a desperate, hobbling hell-gallop.

The rumbling grew stronger and stronger down in the depths, and Monsieur Anatole again began to feel the effects of the truffles. Mademoiselle Adèle half rose; the music would not let her lie in peace.

Here and there the firelight shone on a pair of black eyes staring at the artist. He had lured them with him, and now they could not break loose; downward, ever downward, he led them—downward, where was a dull and muffled murmur as of threatenings and plaints.

'Er führt eine famose linke Hand,' said the doctor. But De Silvis did not hear him; he sat, like the others, in breathless expectancy.

A dark, sickening dread went out from the music and spread itself over them all. The artist's left hand seemed to be tying a knot that would never be loosened, while his right made light little runs, like flames, up and down in the treble. It sounded as if there was something uncanny brewing down in the cellar, whilst those above burnt torches and made merry.

A sigh was heard, a half-scream from one of the ladies, who felt ill; but no one heeded it. The artist had now got quite down into the bass, and his tireless fingers whirled the notes together, so that a cold shudder crept down the backs of all.

But into that threatening, growling sound far below there began to come an upward movement. The notes ran into, over, past each other—upward, always upward, but without making any way. There was a wild struggle to get up, as it were a multitude of small, dark figures scratching and tearing; a mad eagerness, a feverish haste; a scrambling, a seizing with hands and teeth; kicks, curses, shrieks, prayers—and all the while the artist's hands glided upward so slowly, so painfully slowly.

'Anatole,' whispered Adèle, pale as death, 'he is playing Poverty.'

'Oh, these truffles!' groaned Anatole, holding his stomach.

All at once the room was lit up. Two servants with lamps and candelabra appeared in the *portière*; and at the same moment the stranger finished by bringing down his fingers of steel with all his might in a dissonance, so startling, so unearthly, that the whole party sprang up.

'Out with the lamps!' shouted De Silvis.

'No, no!' shrieked Adèle; 'I dare not be in the dark. Oh, that dreadful man!'

Who was it? Yes, who was it? They involuntarily crowded round the host, and no one noticed the stranger slip out behind the servants.

De Silvis tried to laugh. 'I think it was the devil himself. Come, let us go to the opera.'

19

'To the opera! Not at any price!' exclaimed Louison. 'I will hear no music for a fortnight.'

'Oh, those truffles!' moaned Anatole.

The party broke up. They had all suddenly realized that they were strangers in a strange place, and each one wished to slip quietly home.

As the journalist conducted Mademoiselle Louison to her carriage, he said: 'Yes, this is the consequence of letting one's self be persuaded to dine with these semi-savages. One is never sure of the company he will meet.'

'Ah, how true! He quite spoiled my good spirits,' said Louison mournfully, turning her swimming eyes upon her companion. 'Will you accompany me to La Trinité? There is a low mass at twelve o'clock.'

The journalist bowed, and got into the carriage with her.

But as Mademoiselle Adèle and Monsieur Anatole drove past the English dispensary in the Rue de la Paix, he stopped the driver, and said pleadingly to his fair companion: 'I really think I must get out and get something for those truffles. You will excuse me, won't you? That music, you know.'

'Don't mind me, my friend. Speaking candidly, I don't think either of us is specially lively this evening. Good-night.'

She leant back in the carriage, relieved at finding herself alone; and this light, frivolous creature cried as if she had been whipped whilst she drove homeward.

Anatole was undoubtedly suffering from the truffles, but yet he thought he came to himself as the carriage rolled away. Never in their whole acquaintance had they been so well pleased with each other as at this moment of parting.

'Der liebe Doctor' had come best through the experience, because, being a German, he was hardened in music. All the same, he resolved to take a walk as far as Müller's *brasserie* in the Rue Richelieu to get a decent glass of German beer, and perhaps a little bacon, on the top of it all.

A MONKEY.

Yes, it was really a monkey that had nearly procured me 'Laudabilis'*
in my final law examination. As it was, I only got 'Haud';** but, after all,
this was pretty creditable.

But my friend the advocate, who had daily, with mingled feelings,
to read the drafts of my work, found my process-paper so good that
he hoped it might raise me into the 'Laud' list. And he did not wish
me to suffer the injury and annoyance of being plucked in the *vivâ voce*
examination, for he knew me and was my friend.

But the monkey was really a coffee-stain on the margin of page 496 of
Schweigaard's Process, which I had borrowed from my friend Cucumis.

Going up to a law examination in slush and semi-darkness in mid-
winter is one of the saddest experiences that a man can have. It may,
indeed, be even worse in summer; but this I have not tried.

One rushes through these eleven papers (or is it thirteen?—it is
certainly the most infamous number that the college authorities have
been able to devise)—like an unhappy *débutant* in a circus. He stands on
the back of a galloping horse, with his life in his hands and a silly circus
smile on his lips; and so he must leap eleven (or is it thirteen?) times
through one of these confounded paper-covered hoops.

The unhappy mortal who passes—or tries to pass—his law
examination, finds himself in precisely the same situation, only he does
not gallop round a ring, under brilliant gaslight, to the music of a full
band. He sits upon a hard chair in semi-darkness with his face to the wall,

---

*   A second-class pass.
**   A third-class pass.

and the only sound he hears is the creaking of the inspectors' boots. For in all the wide, wide world there are no such creaky boots as those of law examination inspectors.

And so comes the dreadful moment when the black-robed tormentor from the Collegium Juridicum brings in the examination-paper. He plants himself in the doorway, and reads. Coldly, impassively, with a cruel mockery of the horror of the situation, he raises aloft this fateful document—this wretched paper-covered hoop, through which we must all spring, or dismount and wend our way back—on foot!

The candidates settle themselves in the saddle. Some seem quite unable to get firmly seated; they rock uneasily hither and thither, and one rider dismounts. He is followed to the door by all eyes, and a sigh runs through the assembled students. 'You to-day; I to-morrow.'

Meanwhile one begins to hear a light trotting over the paper; they are leaping.

Some few individuals sit firmly and gracefully through it all, and come out on the other side 'standing for Laud.' Others think that leaping straight is too easy; therefore, they turn in the air and alight with backs first. These also get through, but backwards; and it is said that their agility does not win from the judges its deserved meed of appreciation.

Again, others leap, but miss the hoop. They spring underneath, to one side—some even high over the top, alighting safe and sound on the other side. These latter generally find the paper extremely simple, and continue the wild ride quite unconcernedly.

But if one is not fond of riding, and has had no practice in leaping, he is much to be pitied—unless, indeed, he has a monkey on page 496.

I do not know how many hoops I had passed when I found myself face to face with the process-paper.

It was an unhealthy life that we then led: leaping by day and reading by night. I sat at midnight half-way through Schweigaard's Process, alternately putting my head out of the window and into the washhand basin, and, between whiles, rushing like a whirlwind through the withered leaves of the musty volume.

However, even the most violent wind must eventually fall; and, indeed, this was my heartfelt wish. But the juridical momentum was strong within me. I sat stiffly, peering and reading for the eleventh time: 'One might thus certainly assume'—'One—might—thus—certainly,'—combine the useful with the agreeable—and lean back—a little in the chair. I can read just as well; the lamp doesn't bother me in the least. 'One—might—thus—'

But all manner of non-juridical images rose up from the book, entwined themselves about the lamp, and threatened to completely overshadow my clear legal brain. I could yet dimly see the white paper. 'One—might—thus—'. The rest disappeared in a myriad of small dark characters that flowed down the closely-printed pages; in dull despair my eyes followed the stream, and then I saw, towards the bottom of the right-hand page, a face.

It was a monkey that was drawn on the margin. It was excellently drawn, I thought, the brown colouring of the face being especially remarkable. I am ashamed to say that my interest in this work of art proved stronger than Schweigaard himself. I roused myself a little, and leant forward in order to see better.

By turning the leaf, I discovered that the remarkable brown colouring of the face was due to the fact that the whole monkey, after all, was only a coffee-stain. The artist had merely added a pair of eyes and a little hair; the genial expression of the picture was really to be credited to the individual who had spilt the coffee.

'Cucumis couldn't draw,' thought I; that I knew. 'But, by Jove! he *could* do his process!'

And now I came to think of Cucumis, of his handsome degree, of his triumphant home-coming, and of how much he must have read in order to become so learned. And, while I thought of all this, my consciousness awoke little by little, until my own ignorance suddenly stood clearly before me in all its horrible nakedness.

I pictured to myself the shame of having to 'dismount,' or, still worse, of being that one unfortunate of whom it is invariably said with sinister anonymity, 'One of the candidates received *non contemnendus*'. And as it sometimes happens that people lose their reason through much learning, so I grew half crazy with terror at my ignorance.

Up I jumped, and dipped my head in the wash-basin. Scarcely taking time to dry myself, I began to read with an energy that fixed every word in my memory.

Down the left page I hurried, with unabated vigour down the right; I reached the monkey, rushed past him, turned the leaf, and read bravely on.

I was not conscious of the fact that my strength was now completely exhausted. Although I caught a glimpse of a new section (usually so strong an incentive to increased effort), I could not help getting entangled in one of those artful propositions that one reads over and over again in illusory profundity.

I groped about for a way of escape, but there was none. Incoherent thoughts began to whirl through my brain. 'Where is the monkey?—a spot of coffee—one cannot be genial on both sides—everything in life has a right and a wrong side—for example, the university clock—but if I cannot swim, let me come out—I am going to the circus—I know very well that you are standing there grinning at me, Cucumis—but I can leap through the hoop, I can—and if that professor who is standing smoking at my paraffin lamp had only conscientiously referred to *corpus juris*, I should not now be lying here—in my night-shirt in the middle of Karl Johan's Gade*—but—' Then I sank into that deep, dreamless slumber which only falls to the lot of an evil conscience when one is very young.

I was in the saddle early next morning.

---

*   A principal street of Christiania.

I don't know if the devil ever had shoes on, but I must suppose he had, for his inspectors were in their boots, and they creaked past me, where I sat in my misery with my face to the wall.

A professor walked round the rooms and looked at the victims. Occasionally he nodded and smiled encouragingly, as his eye fell on one of those miserable lick-spittles who frequent the lectures; but when he discovered me, the smile vanished, and his ice-cold stare seemed to write upon the wall over my head: 'Mene, mene!* Wretch, I know thee not!'

A pair of inspectors walked creakily up to the professor and fawned upon him; I heard them whispering behind my chair. I ground my teeth in silent wrath at the thought that these contemptible creatures were paid for—yes, actually made their living by torturing me and some of my best friends.

The door opened; a glimmering yellow light fell upon the white faces; it called to mind 'The Victims of Terrorism' in Luxembourg. Then all again became dark, and the black-robed emissary of the College flitted through the room like a bat, with the famous white document in his claws.

He began to read.

Never in my life had I been less inclined for leaping; and yet I started violently at the first words. 'The monkey!' I had almost shouted; for he it was—it was evidently the coffee-stain on page 496. The paper bore precisely upon what I had read with so much energy the preceding night.

And I began to write. After a short, but superior and assured preamble, I introduced the high-sounding words of Schweigaard, 'One might thus certainly assume,' etc., and hurried down the left page, with unabated vigour down the right, reached the monkey, dashed past him, began to grope and fumble, and then I found I could not write a word more.

---

*   Dan. v. 25.

I felt that something was wanting, but I knew that it was useless to speculate; what a man can't do, he can't. I therefore made a full stop, and went away long before any of the others were half finished.

He has dismounted, thought my fellow-sufferers, or he may have leaped wide of the hoop. For it was a difficult paper.

* * * * *

'Why,' said the advocate, as he read, 'you are better than I thought. This is pure Schweigaard. You have left out the last point, but that doesn't matter very much; one can see that you are well up in these things. But why, then, were you so pitiably afraid of the process yesterday?'

'I didn't know a thing.'

He laughed. 'Was it last night, then, that you learned your process?'

'Yes.'

'Did anyone help you?'

'Yes.'

'He must be a devil of a crammer who could put so much law into your head in one night. May I ask what wizard it was?'

'A monkey!' I replied.

A TALE OF THE SEA.

Once there lay in a certain haven a large number of vessels. They had lain there very long, not exactly on account of storm, but rather because of a dead calm; and at last they had lain there until they no longer heeded the weather.

All the captains had gradually become good friends; they visited from ship to ship, and called one another 'Cousin.'

They were in no hurry to depart. Now and then a youthful steersman might chance to let fall a word about a good wind and a smooth sea. But such remarks were not tolerated; order had to be maintained on a ship. Those, therefore, who could not hold their tongues were set ashore.

Matters could not, however, go on thus for ever. Men are not so good as they ought to be, and all do not thrive under law and order.

The crews at length began to murmur a little; they were weary of painting and polishing the cabins, and of rowing the captains to and from the toddy suppers. It was rumoured that individual ships were getting ready for sailing. The sails of some were set one by one in all silence, the anchors were weighed without song, and the ships glided quietly out of the harbour; others sailed while their captains slept. Fighting and mutiny were also heard of; but then there came help from the neighbour captains, the malcontents were punished and put ashore, and all moorings were carefully examined and strengthened.

Nevertheless, all the ships, except one, at last left the harbour. They did not all sail with like fortune; one and another even came in again for a time, damaged. Others were little heard of. The captain of one ship, it was said, was thrown overboard by his men; another sailed with half the crew in irons, none knew where. But yet they were all in motion, each striving after its own fashion, now in storm, now in calm, towards its goal.

As stated, only one ship remained in the harbour, and it lay safe and sound, with two anchors at the bottom and three great cables attached to the quay.

It was a strange little craft. The hull was old, but it had been newly repaired, and they had given it a smart little modern figurehead, which contrasted strangely with the smooth sides and the heavy stern. One could see that the rigging had originally belonged to a large vessel, but had been very hastily adapted to the smaller hull, and this still further increased the want of proportion in the brig's whole appearance. Then it was painted with large portholes for guns, like a man-of-war, and always carried its flag at the main-mast.

The skipper was no common man. He himself had painted the sketch of the brig that hung in the cabin, and, besides, he could sing—both psalms and songs. Indeed, there were those who maintained that he composed the songs himself; but this was most probably a lie. And it was certainly a lie that they whispered in the forecastle: that the skipper had not quite got his sea-legs. Young men always tell such stories to cabin-boys, in order to appear manly. And, besides, there was a steersman on the brig, who could, on a pinch, easily round the headlands alone.

He had sailed as steersman for many years of our Lord, ever since the time of the skipper's late father. He had become as if glued to the tiller, and many could scarcely imagine the old brig with a new steersman.

He had certainly never voyaged in distant waters; but as his trade had always been the same, and as he had invariably been in the company of others, the brig had sailed pretty fortunately, without special damage and without special merit.

Therefore, both he and the skipper had arrived at the conviction that none could sail better than they, and hence they cared little what the others did. They looked up at the sky and shook their heads.

The men felt quite comfortable, for they were not used to better things. Most of them could not understand why the crews of the other ships were in such a hurry to be off; the month went round all the same, whether one lay in port or sailed, and then it was better to avoid work. So long as the skipper made no sign of preparation for sailing, the men might keep their minds easy, for he must surely have the most interest in getting away. And besides, they all knew what sort of fellow the steersman was, and if such a capable and experienced man lay still, they might be quite sure that he had good and powerful reasons.

But a little party among the crew—some quite youthful persons—thought it was a shame to let themselves be thus left astern by everybody. They had, indeed, no special advantage or profit to expect from the voyage, but at last the inaction became intolerable, and they conceived the daring resolve of sending a youth aft to beg the captain to fix a date for sailing.

The more judicious among the crew crossed themselves, and humbly entreated the young man to keep quiet; but the latter was a rash greenhorn, who had sailed in foreign service, and therefore imagined himself to be a 'regular devil of a fellow.' He went right aft and down into the cabin, where the skipper and the steersman sat with their whisky before them, playing cards.

'We would ask if the skipper would kindly set sail next week, for now we are all so weary of lying here,' said the young man, looking the skipper straight in the eyes without winking.

The latter's face first turned pale blue, and then assumed a deep violet tint; but he restrained himself, and said, as was his invariable custom:

'What think you, steersman?'

'H'm,' replied the steersman slowly. More he never used to say at first, when he was questioned, for he did not like to answer promptly. But when he got an opportunity of speaking alone, without being interrupted, he could utter the longest sentences and the very hardest words. And then the skipper was especially proud of him.

29

However short the steersman's reply might seem, the skipper at once understood its meaning. He turned towards the youth—gravely, but gracefully, for he was an exceedingly well-bred man.

'You cursed young fool! don't you think I understand these things better than you? I, who have thought of nothing but being a skipper since I was knee-high! But I know well enough what you and the like of you are thinking about. You don't care a d—about the craft, and if you could only get the power from us old ones, you would run her on the first islet you came to, so that you might plunder her of the whisky. But there will be none of that, my young whelp! Here we shall lie, as long as I choose.'

When this decision reached the forecastle, it awoke great indignation among the young and immature, which, indeed, was only to be expected. But even the skipper's friends and admirers shook their heads, and opined that it was a nasty answer; after all, it was only a civil question, which ought not to compromise anybody.

There now arose a growing ill-humour—something quite unheard-of among these peaceable fellows. Even the skipper, who was not usually quick to understand or remark anything, thought he saw many sullen faces, and he was no longer so well pleased with the bearing of the crew when he stepped out upon deck with his genial 'Good-morning, you rogues.'

But the steersman had long scented something, for he had a fine nose and long ears. Therefore, a couple of evenings after the young man's unfortunate visit, it was remarked that something extraordinary was brewing aft.

The cabin-boy had to make three journeys with the toddy-kettle, and the report he gave in the forecastle after his last trip was indeed disquieting.

The steersman seemed to have talked without intermission for two hours; before them on the table lay barometer, chronometer, sextant, journal, and half the ship's library. This consisted of Kingo's hymn-book and an old Dutch 'Kaart-Boikje';* for the skipper could do just as little with the new hymns as the steersman with the new charts.

The skipper now sat prodding the chart with a large pair of compasses, while the steersman talked, using all his longest and hardest words. There was one word in particular that was often repeated, and this the boy learned by heart. He said it over and over again to himself as he went up the cabin stairs and passed along the deck to the forecastle, and the moment he opened the door he shouted:

'Initiative! Mind that word, boys! Write it down—initiative!'

In-i-ti-a-tive was with much difficulty spelt out and written with chalk on the table. And during the boy's long statement all these men sat staring, uneasily and with anxious expectancy, at this long, mystic word.

'And then,' concluded the cabin-boy at last—'then says the steersman: "But we ourselves shall take the—" what is written on the table.'

All exclaimed simultaneously, 'Initiative.'

'Yes, that was it. And every time he said it, they both struck the table and looked at me as if they would eat me. I now think, therefore, that it is a new kind of revolver they intend to use upon us.'

But none of the others thought so; it was surely not so bad as that. But something was impending, that was clear. And the relieved watchman went to his berth with gloomy forebodings, and the middle watch did not get a wink of sleep that night.

At seven o'clock next morning both skipper and steersman were up on deck. No man could remember ever having seen them before so early in the day. But there was no time to stand in amazement, for now followed, in quick succession, orders for sailing.

'Heave up the anchors! Let two men go ashore and slip the cables!'

There was gladness and bustle among the crew, and the preparations proceeded so rapidly that in less than an hour the brig was under canvas.

---

*   Chart-book.

The skipper looked at the steersman and shook his head, muttering, 'This is the devil's own haste.'

After a few little turns in the spacious harbour, the brig passed the headland and stood out to sea. A fresh breeze was blowing, and the waves ran rather high.

The steersman, with a prodigious twist in his mouth, stood astride the tiller, for such a piece of devil's trumpery as a wheel should never come on board as long as *he* had anything to say in the matter.

The skipper stood on the cabin stairs, with his head above the companion. His face was of a somewhat greenish hue, and he frequently ran down into the cabin. The old boatswain believed that he went to look at the chart, the young man thought he drank whisky, but the cabin-boy swore that he went below to vomit.

The men were in excellent spirits; it was so refreshing to breathe the sea air, and to feel the ship once again moving under their feet. Indeed, the old brig herself seemed to be in a good humour; she dived as deep down between the seas as she could, and raised much more foam than was necessary.

The young sailors looked out for heavy seas. 'Here comes a whopper,' they shouted; 'if it would only hit us straight!' And it did.

It was a substantial sea, larger than the others. It approached deliberately, and seemed to lie down and take aim. It then rose suddenly, and gave the brig, which was chubby as a cherub, such a mighty slap on the port cheek that she quivered in every timber. And high over the railing, far in upon the deck, dashed the cold salt spray; the captain had scarcely time to duck his head below the companion.

Ah, how refreshing it was! It exhilarated both old and young; they had not had a taste of the cold sea-water for a long time, and with one voice the whole crew broke into a lusty 'Hurrah!'

But at this moment the steerman's stentorian voice rang out: 'Hard to leeward!' The brig luffed up close to the wind, the sails flapped so violently that the rigging shook, and now followed in rapid succession, even quicker than before, orders to anchor. 'Let fall the port anchor! Let go the starboard one too!'

Plump—fell the one; plump—went the other. The old chains rattled out, and a little red cloud of rust rose up on either side of the bowsprit.

The men, accustomed to obey, worked rapidly without thinking why, and the brig soon rode pretty quietly at her two anchors.

But now, after the work was finished, no one could conceal his astonishment at this sudden anchoring, just off the coast, among islets and skerries. And still more extraordinary seemed the behaviour of those in command. For they both stood right forward, with their backs to the weather, leaning over the railing and staring at the port bow. Some had even thought they had heard the captain cry, 'To the pumps, men,' but this point was never cleared up.

'What the devil can they be doing forward?' said the rash young man.

'They think she struck on a reef when we shipped the big sea,' whispered the cabin-boy.

'Hold your jaw, boy!' said the boatswain.

All the same, the cabin-boy's words passed from mouth to mouth; a little chuckle was heard here and there; the men's faces became more and more ludicrously uneasy, and their suppressed laughter was on the point of bursting forth. Then the steersman was seen to nudge the skipper in the side.

'Yes; but then you must whisper to me,' said the latter.

The steersman nodded, and then the skipper turned to the crew and solemnly spoke as follows:

'Yes, this time, fortunately, everything went well; but now I hope that each of you will have learnt how dangerous it is to lend an ear to these juvenile agitators, who can never be quiet and let evolution, as the steersman says, pursue its natural course. I yielded to your wishes this time, it is true, but not because I approved of your insane rashness; it was simply that I might convince you by—by the logic of events. And see—how did things go? Certainly we have, as by a miracle, been spared the worst; but now we lie here, outside our safe haven, our old anchorage, which we have forsaken to be tossed about on the turbulent waters of the unknown and the untried. But, believe me, henceforth you will find both our excellent steersman and your captain at our post, guarding against such crude, immature projects. And if things go badly with us in days to come, you must all remember that it is entirely your own fault; we wash our hands of the matter.'

Thereupon he strode through the men, who respectfully fell back to let him pass. The steersman, who had really whispered, dried his eyes and followed. They both disappeared in the cabin.

* * * * *

There was much strife in the forecastle that day, and it grew worse after.

The brig's happy days were all over. Dissension and discontent, suspicion and obstinacy, converted the narrow limits of the forecastle into a veritable hell.

Only skipper and steersman seemed to thrive well under all this. The general dissatisfaction did not affect them; for they, of course, were not to blame.

None thought of any change. The crew had done what they could, and the skipper, on his part, had also been accommodating.

Now they might keep their minds at rest. The brig lay in a dangerous place, but now she would have to lie—and there she lies to this day.

A DINNER.

There was a large dinner-party at the merchant's. The judge had made a speech in honour of the home-coming of the student, the eldest son of the house, and the merchant had replied with another in honour of the judge; so far all was well and good. And yet one could see that the host was disquieted about something. He answered inconsequentially, decanted Rhine wine into port, and betrayed absence of mind in all manner of ways.

He was meditating upon a speech—a speech beyond the scope of the regulation after-dinner orations. This was something very remarkable; for the merchant was no speaker, and—what was still more remarkable—he knew it himself.

When, therefore, well on in the dinner, he hammered upon the table for silence, and said that he must give expression to a sentiment that lay at his heart, everybody instantly felt that something unusual was impending.

There fell such a sudden stillness upon the table, that one could hear the lively chatter of the ladies, who, in accordance with Norse custom, were dining in the adjoining rooms.

At length the silence reached even them, and they crowded in the doorway to listen. Only the hostess held back, sending her husband an anxious look. 'Ah, dear me!' she sighed, half aloud, 'he is sure to make a muddle of it. He has already made all his speeches; what would he be at now?'

And he certainly did not begin well. He stammered, cleared his throat, got entangled among the usual toast expressions, such as 'I will not fail to—ahem—I am impelled to express my, my—that is, I would beg you, gentlemen, to assist me in—'

The gentlemen sat and stared down into their glasses, ready to empty them upon the least hint of a conclusion. But none came. On the contrary, the speaker recovered himself.

For something really lay at his heart. His joy and pride over his son, who had come home sound and well after having passed a respectable examination, the judge's flattering speech, the good cheer, the wine, the festive mood—all this put words into his mouth. And when he got over the fatal introductory phrases, the words came more and more fluently.

It was the toast of 'The Young.' The speaker dwelt upon our responsibility towards children, and the many sorrows—but also the many joys—that the parents have in them.

He was from time to time compelled to talk quickly to hide his emotion, for he felt what he said.

And when he came to the grown-up children, when he imagined his dear son a partner in his business, and spoke of grandchildren and so on, his words acquired a ring of eloquence which astonished all his hearers, and his peroration was greeted with hearty applause.

'For, gentlemen, it is in these children that we, as it were, continue our existence. We leave them not only our name, but also our work. And we leave them this, not that they may idly enjoy its fruits, but that they may continue it, extend it—yes, do it much better than their fathers were able to. For it is our hope that the rising generation may appropriate the fruits of the work of the age, that they may be freed from the prejudices that have darkened the past and partially darken the present; and, in drinking the health of the young, let us wish that, steadily progressing, they may become worthy of their sires—yes, let us say it—outgrow them.

'And only when we know that we leave the work of our generation in abler hands, can we calmly look forward to the time when we shall bid adieu to our daily task, and then we may confidently reckon upon a bright and glorious future for our dear Fatherland. A health to the Young!'

The hostess, who had ventured nearer when she heard that the speech was going on well, was proud of her husband; the whole company was in an exhilarated humour, but the gladdest of all was the student.

He had stood a little in awe of his father, whose severely patriarchal principles he well knew. He now heard that the old man was extremely liberal-minded towards youth, and he was very glad to be enabled to discourse with him upon serious matters.

But, for the moment, it was only a question of jesting; *à propos* of the toast, there ensued one of those interesting table-talks, about who was really young and who old. After the company had arrived at this witty result, that the eldest were in reality the youngest, they adjourned to the dessert-table, which was laid in the ladies' room.

But, no matter how gallant the gentlemen—especially those of the old school—may be towards the fair sex, neither feminine amiability nor the most *recherché* dessert has power to stop them for long on their way to the smoking-room. And soon the first faint aroma of cigars, so great a luxury to smokers, announced the beginning of that process which has obtained for our ladies the fame of being quite smoke-dried.

The student and a few other young gentlemen remained for a time with the young ladies—under the strict surveillance of the elder ones. But little by little they also were swallowed up in the gray cloud which indicated the way that their fathers had taken.

In the smoking-room they were carrying on a very animated conversation upon some matter of social politics. The host, who was speaking, supported his view with a number of 'historical facts,' which, however, were entirely unreliable.

His opponent, a solicitor of the High Court, was sitting chuckling inwardly at the prospect of refuting these inaccurate statements, when the student entered the room.

He came just in time to hear his father's blundering, and, in his jovial humour, in his delight over the new conception of his father that he had acquired after the toast, he said, with a cheery bluntness:

'Excuse me, father, you are mistaken there. The circumstances are not at all as you state. On the contrary—'

He got no further: the father laughingly slapped him on the shoulder, and said:

'There, there! are you, too, trifling with newspapers! But really, you must not disturb us; we are in the middle of a serious discussion.'

The son heard an irritating sniff from the gray cloud; he was provoked at the scorn implied in his interposition being regarded as disturbing a serious conversation.

He therefore replied somewhat sharply.

The father, who instantly remarked the tone, suddenly changed his own manner.

'Are you serious in coming here and saying that your father is talking nonsense?'

'I did not say that; I only said that you were mistaken.'

'The words are of little moment, but the meaning was there,' said the merchant, who was beginning to get angry. For he heard a gentleman say to his neighbour:

'If this had only happened in my father's time!'

One word now drew forth another, and the situation became extremely painful.

The hostess, who had always an attentive ear for the gentlemen's conversation, as she knew her husband's hasty temper, immediately came and looked in at the door.

'What is it, Adjunct* Hansen?'

'Ah,' replied Hansen, 'your son has forgotten himself a little.'

'To his own father! He must have had too much to drink. Dear Hansen, try and get him out.'

The Adjunct, who was more well-meaning than diplomatic, and who, besides (a rarer thing with old teachers than is generally supposed)

---

*   Assistant-teacher.

38

was esteemed by his former pupils, went and took the student without ceremony by the arm, saying: 'Come, shall we two take a turn in the garden?'

The young man turned round violently, but when he saw that it was the old teacher, and received, at the same time, a troubled, imploring glance from his mother, he passively allowed himself to be led away.

While in the doorway, he heard the lawyer, whom he had never been able to endure, say something about the egg that would teach the hen to lay, which witticism was received with uproarious laughter. A thrill passed through him; but the Adjunct held him firmly, and out they went.

It was long before the old teacher could get him sufficiently quieted to become susceptible to reason. The disappointment, the bitter sense of being at variance with his father, and, not least, the affront of being treated as a boy in the presence of so many—all this had to pour out for awhile.

But at last he became calm, and sat down with his old friend, who now pointed out to him that it must be very painful to an elderly man to be corrected by a mere youth.

'Yes, but I was right,' said the student, certainly for the twentieth time.

'Good, good! but yet you must not put on an air of wanting to be wiser than your own father.'

'Why, my father himself said that he would have it so.'

'What? When did your father say that?' The teacher almost began to believe that the wine had gone to the young gentleman's head.

'At the table—in his speech.'

'At the table—yes! In his speech—yes! But, don't you see, that is quite another matter. People allow themselves to say such things, especially in speeches; but it is by no means intended that these theories should be translated into practice. No, believe me, my dear boy, I am old, and I know humanity. The world must wag like this; we are not made otherwise. In youth one has his own peculiar view of life, but, young man, it is not the right one. Only when one has arrived at the calm restfulness of an advanced age does one see circumstances in the true light. And now I will tell you something, upon the truth of which you may confidently rely. When you come to your father's years and position, your opinions will be quite the same as his now are, and, like him, you will strive to maintain them and impress them upon your children.'

'No, never! I swear it,' cried the young man, springing to his feet. And now he spoke in glowing terms, to the effect that for him right would always be right, that he would respect the truth, no matter whence it came, that he would respect the young, and so on. In short, he talked as hopeful youths are wont to talk after a good dinner and violent mental disturbance.

He was beautiful, as he stood there with the evening sun shining upon his blonde hair, and his enthusiastic countenance turned upward.

There was in his whole personality and in his words something transporting and convincing, something that could not fail to work an impression—that is to say, if anybody but the teacher had seen and heard him.

For upon the teacher it made no impression whatever; he was old, of course.

The drama of which he had that day been a witness he had seen many times. He himself had successively played both the principal *rôles*; he had seen many *débutants* like the student and many old players like the merchant.

Therefore he shook his venerable head, and said to himself:

'Yes, yes; it is all well enough. But just see if I am not right; he will become precisely the same as the rest of us.'

And the teacher was right.

TROFAST.*

I.

Miss Thyra went and called into the speaking-tube:

'Will Trofast's cutlets be ready soon?'

The maid's voice came up from the kitchen: 'They are on the window-sill cooling; as soon as they are all right, Stine shall bring them up.'

Trofast, who had heard this, went and laid himself quietly down upon the hearthrug.

He understood much better than a human being, the merchant used to say.

Besides the people of the house, there sat at the breakfast-table an old enemy of Trofast's—the only one he had. But be it said that Cand. jur.** Viggo Hansen was the enemy of a great deal in this world, and his snappish tongue was well known all over Copenhagen. Having been a friend of the family for many years, he affected an especial frankness in this house, and when he was in a querulous mood (which was always the case) he wreaked his bitterness unsparingly upon anything or anybody.

In particular, he was always attacking Trofast.

'That big yellow beast,' he used to say, 'is being petted and pampered and stuffed with steak and cutlets, while many a human child must bite its fingers after a piece of dry bread.'

---

*   Faithful.
**   Graduate in law.

This, however, was a tender point, of which Dr. Hansen had to be rather careful.

Whenever anyone mentioned Trofast in words that were not full of admiration, he received a simultaneous look from the whole family, and the merchant had even said point-blank to Dr. Hansen that he might one day get seriously angry if the other would not refer to Trofast in a becoming manner.

But Miss Thyra positively hated Dr. Hansen for this; and although Waldemar was now grown up—a student, at any rate—he took a special pleasure in stealing the gloves out of the doctor's back pocket, and delivering them to Trofast to tear.

Yes, the good-wife herself, although as mild and sweet as tea, was sometimes compelled to take the doctor to task, and seriously remonstrate with him for daring to speak so ill of the dear animal.

All this Trofast understood very well; but he despised Dr. Hansen, and took no notice of him. He condescended to tear the gloves, because it pleased his friend Waldemar, but otherwise he did not seem to see the doctor.

When the cutlets came, Trofast ate them quietly and discreetly. He did not crunch the bones, but picked them quite clean, and licked the platter.

Thereupon he went up to the merchant, and laid his right fore-paw upon his knee.

'Welcome, welcome, old boy!' cried the merchant with emotion. He was moved in like manner every morning, when this little scene was re-enacted.

'Why, you can't call Trofast old, father,' said Waldemar, with a little tone of superiority.

'Indeed! Do you know that he will soon be eight?'

'Yes, my little man,' said the good wife gently; 'but a dog of eight is not an old dog.'

'No, mother,' exclaimed Waldemar eagerly. 'You side with me, don't you? A dog of eight is not an old dog.'

And in an instant the whole family was divided into two parties—two very ardent parties, who, with an unceasing flow of words, set to debating the momentous question:—whether one can call a dog of eight years an old dog or not. Both sides became warm, and, although each one kept on repeating his unalterable opinion into his opponent's face, it did not seem likely that they would ever arrive at unanimity—not even when old grandmother hurriedly rose from her chair, and positively insisted upon telling some story about the Queen-Dowager's lap-dog, which she had had the honour of knowing from the street.

But in the midst of the irresistible whirl of words there came a pause. Some one looked at his watch and said: 'The steamboat.' They all rose; the gentlemen, who had to go to town, rushed off; the whole company was scattered to the four winds, and the problem—whether one can call a dog of eight an old dog or not—floated away in the air, unsolved.

Trofast alone did not stir. He was accustomed to this domestic din, and these unsolved problems did not interest him. He ran his wise eyes over the deserted breakfast-table, dropped his black nose upon his powerful fore-paws, and closed his eyes for a little morning nap. As long as they were staying out in the country, there was nothing much for him to do, except eat and sleep.

Trofast was one of the pure Danish hounds from the Zoological Gardens. The King had even bought his brother, which fact was expressly communicated to all who came to the house.

All the same, he had had a pretty hard upbringing, for he was originally designated to be watch-dog at the merchant's large coalstore out at Kristianshavn.

Out there, Trofast's behaviour was exemplary. Savage and furious as a tiger at night, in the daytime he was so quiet, kindly, and even humble, that the merchant took notice of him, and promoted him to the position of house-dog.

And it was really from this moment that the noble animal began to develop all his excellent qualities.

From the very beginning he had a peculiar, modest way of standing at the drawing-room door, and looking so humbly at anybody who entered that it was quite impossible to avoid letting him into the room. And there he soon made himself at home—under the sofa at first, but afterwards upon the soft carpet in front of the fire.

And as the other members of the family learned to appreciate his rare gifts, Trofast gradually advanced in importance, until Dr. Hansen maintained that he was the real master of the house.

Certain it is that there came a something into Trofast's whole demeanour which distinctly indicated that he was well aware of the position he occupied. He no longer stood humbly at the door, but entered first himself as soon as it was opened. And if the door was not opened for him instantly when he scratched at it, the powerful animal would raise himself upon his hind-legs, lay his fore-paws upon the latch, and open it for himself.

The first time that he performed this feat the good-wife delightedly exclaimed:

'Isn't he charming? He's just like a human being, only so much better and more faithful!'

The rest of the family were also of opinion that Trofast was better than a human being. Each one seemed, as it were, to get quit of a few of his own sins and infirmities through this admiring worship of the noble animal; and whenever anybody was displeased with himself or others, Trofast received the most confidential communications, and solemn assurances that he was really the only friend upon whom one could rely.

When Miss Thyra came home disappointed from a ball, or when her best friend had faithlessly betrayed a frightfully great secret, she would throw herself, weeping, upon Trofast's neck, and say: 'Now, Trofast, I have only you left. There is nobody—nobody—nobody on the earth who likes me but you! Now we two are quite alone in the wide, wide world; but you will not betray your poor little Thyra—you must promise me that, Trofast.' And so she would weep on, until her tears trickled down Trofast's black nose.

No wonder, therefore, that Trofast comported himself with a certain dignity at home in the house. But in the street also it was evident that he felt self-confident, and that he was proud of being a dog in a town where dogs are in power.

When they were staying in the country in summer, Trofast went to town only once a week or so, to scent out old acquaintances. Out in the country, he lived exclusively for the sake of his health; he bathed, rolled in the flower-beds, and then went into the parlour to rub himself dry upon the furniture, the ladies, and finally upon the hearthrug.

But for the remainder of the year the whole of Copenhagen was at his disposal, and he availed himself of his privileges with much assurance.

What a treat it was, early in the spring, when the fine grass began to shoot upon the public lawns, which no human foot must tread, to run up and down and round in a ring with a few friends, scattering the tufts of grass in the air!

Or when the gardener's people had gone home to dinner, after having pottered and trimmed all the forenoon among the fine flowers and bushes, what fun it was to pretend to dig for moles; thrust his nose down into the earth in the centre of the flower-bed, snort and blow, then begin scraping up the earth with his fore-feet, stop for a little, thrust his muzzle down again, blow, and then fall to digging up earth with all his might, until the hole was so deep that a single vigorous kick from his hind-legs could throw a whole rose-bush, roots and all, high in the air!

When Trofast, after such an escapade, lay quietly in the middle of the lawn, in the warm spring sunshine, and saw the humans trudge wearily past outside, in dust or mud, he would silently and self-complacently wag his tail.

Then there were the great fights in Grönningen, or round the horse in Kongens Nytorv. * From thence, wet and bedraggled, he would dash up Östergade** among people's legs, rubbing against ladies' dresses and gentlemen's trousers, overthrowing old women and children, exercising an unlimited right-of-way on both sides of the pavement, now rushing into a backyard and up the kitchen stairs after a cat, now scattering terror and confusion by flying right at the throat of an old enemy. Or Trofast would sometimes amuse himself by stopping in front of a little girl who might be going an errand for her mother, thrusting his black nose up into her face, and growling, with gaping jaws, 'Bow, wow, wow!'

If you could see the little thing! She becomes blue in the face, her arms hang rigidly by her sides, her feet keep tripping up and down; she tries to scream, but cannot utter a sound.

But the grown ladies in the street cry shame upon her, and say:

'What a little fool! How *can* you be afraid of such a dear, nice dog? Why, he only wants to play with you! See what a great big, fine fellow he is. Won't you pat him?'

But this the little one will not do upon any account; and, when she goes home to her mother, the sobs are still rising in her throat. Neither her mother nor the doctor can understand, afterwards, why the healthy, lively child becomes rigid and blue in the face at the least fright, and loses the power to scream.

But all these diversions were colourless and tame in comparison with *les grands cavalcades d'amour*, in which Trofast was always one of the foremost. Six, eight, ten, or twelve large yellow, black, and red dogs, with a long following of smaller and quite small ones, so bitten and mud-bespattered that one could scarcely see what they were made of, but yet

---

*   King's Square.
**   East Street.

very courageous, tails in the air and panting with ardour, although they stood no chance at all, except of getting mauled again and rolled in the mud. And so off in a wild gallop through streets, squares, gardens, and flower-beds, fighting and howling, covered with blood and dirt, tongues lolling from mouths. Out of the way with humans and baby-carriages, room for canine warfare and love! And thus they would rush on like Aasgaard's demon riders* through the unhappy town.

Trofast heeded none of the people on the street except the policemen. For, with his keen understanding, he had long ago discerned that the police were there to protect him and his kind against the manifold encroachments of humanity. Therefore he obligingly stopped whenever he met a policeman, and allowed himself to be scratched behind the ear. In particular, he had a good, stout friend, whom he often met up in Aabenraa, where he (Trofast) had a *liaison* of many years' standing.

When Policeman Frode Hansen was seen coming upstairs from a cellar—a thing that often happened, for he was a jolly fellow, and it was a pleasure to offer him a half of lager-beer—his face bore a great likeness to the rising sun. It was round and red, warm and beaming.

But when he appeared in full view upon the pavement, casting a severe glance up and down the street, in order to ascertain whether any evil-disposed person had seen where he came from, there would arise a faint reminiscence of something that we, as young men, had read about in physics, and which, I believe, we called the co-efficient of expansion.

For, when we looked at the deep incision made by his strong belt, before, behind and at the sides, we involuntarily received the impression that such a co-efficient, with an extraordinarily strong tendency to expand, was present in Frode Hansen's stomach.

---

*   Aasgaard was the 'garth' or home of the gods. After the advent of Christianity, the Norse gods became demons, and it was the popular belief that they rode across the sky at night, foreboding evil.

And people who met him, especially when he heaved one of his deep, beery sighs, nervously stepped to one side. For if the co-efficient in there should ever happen to get the better of the strong belt, the pieces, and particularly the front buckle, would fly around with a force sufficient to break plate-glass windows.

In other respects, Frode Hansen was not very dangerous of approach. He was even looked upon as one of the most harmless of police-constables; he very rarely reported a case of any kind. All the same, he stood well with his superiors, for when anything was reported by others, no matter what, if they only asked Frode Hansen, he could always make some interesting disclosure or other about it.

In this way the world went well with him; he was almost esteemed in Aabenraa and down Vognmagergade. Yes, even Mam Hansen sometimes found means to stand him a half of lager beer.

And she had certainly little to give away. Poverty-stricken and besotted, she had enough to do to struggle along with her two children.

Not that Mam Hansen worked or tried to work herself forward or upward; if she could only manage to pay her rent and have a little left over for coffee and brandy, she was content. Beyond this she had no illusions.

In reality, the general opinion—even in Aabenraa—was that Mam Hansen was a beast; and, when she was asked if she were a widow, she would answer: 'Well, you see, that's not so easy to know.'

The daughter was about fifteen and the son a couple of years younger. About these, too, the public opinion of Aabenraa and district had it that a worse pair of youngsters had seldom grown up in those parts.

Waldemar was a little, pale, dark-eyed fellow, slippery as an eel, full of mischief and cunning, with a face of indiarubber, which in one second could change its expression from the boldest effrontery to the most sheepish innocence.

Nor was there anything good to say about Thyra, except that she gave promise of becoming a pretty girl. But all sorts of ugly stories were already told about her, and she gadded round the town upon very various errands.

Mam Hansen would never listen to these stories; she merely waved them off. She paid just as little attention to the advice of her female friends and neighbours, when they said:

'Let the children shift for themselves—really, they're quite brazen enough to do it—and take in a couple of paying lodgers.'

'No, no,' Mam Hansen would reply; 'as long as they have some kind of a home with me, the police will not get a firm grip of them, and they will not quite flow over.'

This idea, that the bairns should not quite 'flow over,' had grown and grown in her puny brain, until it had become the last point, around which gathered everything motherly that could be left, after a life like hers.

And therefore she slaved on, scolded and slapped the children when they came late home, made their bed, gave them a little food, and so held them to her, in some kind of fashion.

Mam Hansen had tried many things in the course of her life, and everything had brought her gradually downward, from servant-girl to waitress, down past washerwoman to what she now was.

Early in the mornings, before it was light, she would come over Knippelsbro* into the town, with a heavy basket upon each arm. Out of the baskets stuck cabbage-leaves and carrot-tops, so that one would suppose that she made a business of buying vegetables from the peasants out at Amager, in order to sell them in Aabenraa and the surrounding quarters.

All the same, it was not a greengrocery business that she carried on, but, on the contrary, a little coal business: she sold coals clandestinely and in small portions to poor folk like herself.

This evident incongruity was not noticed in Aabenraa; not even Policeman Frode Hansen seemed to find anything remarkable about

---

*   Bro, a bridge.

Mam Hansen's business. When he met her in the mornings, toiling along with the heavy baskets, he usually asked quite genially: 'Well, my little Mam Hansen, were the roots cheap to-day?'

And, if his greeting were less friendly than usual, he was treated to a half of lager later in the day.

This was a standing outlay of Madam Hansen's, and she had one besides. Every evening she bought a large piece of sugared Vienna bread. She did not eat it herself; neither was it for the children; no one knew what she did with it, nor did anybody particularly care.

* * * * *

When there was no prospect of halves of lager, Policeman Frode Hansen promenaded his co-efficient with dignity up and down the street.

If he then happened to meet Trofast or any other of his canine friends, he always made a long halt, for the purpose of scratching him behind the ear. And when he observed the great *nonchalance* with which the dogs comported themselves in the street, it was a real pleasure to him to sternly pounce upon some unhappy man and note down his full name and address, because he had taken the liberty of throwing an envelope into the gutter.

II.

It was late in the autumn. There was a dinner-party at the merchant's; the family had been back from the country for some time.

The conversation flowed on languidly and intermittently, until the flood-gates were suddenly lifted, and it became a wild *fos** For down at the hostess's end of the table this question had cropped up: 'Can one call a lady a fine lady—a real fine lady—if it be known that on a steam-

---

*　　Waterfall, cataract.

50

boat she has put her feet up on a stool, and disclosed small shoes and embroidered stockings?' And, strangely enough, as if each individual in the company had spent half his life in considering and weighing this question, all cast their matured, decided, unalterable opinions upon the table. The opposing parties were formed in an instant; the unalterable opinions collided with each other, fell down, were caught up again, and thrown with ever-increasing ardour.

Up at the other end of the table they took no part in this animated conversation. Near the host there sat mostly elderly gentlemen, and however ardently their wives might have desired to solve the problem once for all by expressing their unalterable opinion, they were compelled to give up the idea, as the focus of the animated conversation was among some young students right down beside the hostess, and the distance was too great.

'I don't think I see the big yellow beast to-day,' said Dr. Viggo Hansen in his querulous tone.

'Unfortunately not. Trofast is not here to-day. Poor fellow! I have been obliged to request him to do me a disagreeable service.'

The merchant always talked about Trofast as if he were an esteemed business friend.

'You make me quite curious. Where *is* the dear animal?'

'Ah, my dear madam, it is indeed a tiresome story. For, you know, there has been stealing going on out at our coal warehouse at Kristianshavn.'

'Oh, good gracious! Stealing?'

'The thefts have evidently been practised systematically for a long time.'

'Have you noticed the stock getting less, then?'

But now the merchant had to laugh, which he seldom did.

'No, no, my dear doctor, excuse my laughing, but you are really too naive. Why, there are now about ten thousand tons of coal out there, so you will see that it wants some—'

'They would have to steal from evening till morning with a pair of horses,' interjected a young business man, who was witty.

When the merchant had finished his laugh, he continued:

'No; the theft was discovered by means of a little snow that fell yesterday.'

'What! Snow yesterday? I don't know anything about that.'

'It was not at the time of day when we are awake, madam, it is true; but yet, very early yesterday morning there fell a little snow, and when my folks arrived at the coal store, they discovered the footprints of the thief or thieves. It was then found that a couple of boards in the wall were loose, but they had been so skilfully put in place that nobody would ever notice anything wrong. And the thief crawls through the opening night after night; is it not outrageous?'

'But don't you keep a watch-dog?'

'Certainly I do; but he is a young animal (of excellent breed, by the way, half a bloodhound), and, whatever way these wretches go about their work, it is evident that they must be on friendly terms with the beast, for the dog's footprints were found among those of the thieves.'

'That was indeed remarkable. And now Trofast is to try what he can do, I presume?'

'Yes, you are quite right. I have sent Trofast out there to-day; he will catch the villains for me.'

'Could you not nail the loose boards securely in position?'

'Of course we could, Dr. Hansen; but I must get hold of the fellows. They shall have their well-merited punishment. My sense of right is most deeply wounded.'

'It is really delightful to have such a faithful animal.'

'Yes, isn't it, madam? We men must confess to our shame that in many respects we are far behind the dumb animals.'

'Yes, Trofast is really a pearl, sir. He is, beyond comparison, the prettiest dog in all—'

'Constantinople,' interrupted Dr. Hansen.

'That is an old joke of Hansen's,' explained the merchant. 'He has re-christened the Northern Athens the Northern Constantinople, because he thinks there are too many dogs.'

'It is good for the dog-tax,' said some one.

'Yes, if the dog-tax were not so inequitably fixed,' snapped Dr. Hansen. 'There is really no sense in a respectable old lady, who keeps a dog in a hand-bag, having to pay as much as a man who takes pleasure in annoying his fellow-creatures by owning a half-wild animal as big as a little lion.'

'May I ask how you would have the dog-tax reckoned, Dr. Hansen?'

'According to weight, of course,' replied Dr. Viggo Hansen without hesitation.

The old merchants and councillors laughed so heartily at this idea of weighing the dogs, that the disputants at the lower end of the table, who were still vigorously bombarding each other with unalterable opinions, became attentive and dropped their opinions, in order to listen to the discussion on dogs. And the question, 'Can one call a lady a fine lady—a really fine lady—if it be known that on a steamboat she has put her feet up on a stool, and disclosed small shoes and embroidered stockings?' also floated away in the air, unsolved.

'You seem to be a downright hater of dogs, Dr. Hansen!' said the lady next to him, still laughing.

'I must tell you, madam,' cried a gentleman across the table, 'that he is terribly afraid of dogs.'

'But one thing,' continued the lady—'one thing you must admit, and that is, that the dog has always been the faithful companion of man.'

'Yes, that is true, madam, and I could tell you what the dog has learned from man, and man from the dog.'

'Tell us; do tell us!' was simultaneously exclaimed from several quarters.

'With pleasure. In the first place, man has taught the dog to fawn.'

'What a very queer thing to say!' cried old grandmother.

'Next, the dog has acquired all the qualities that make man base and unreliable: cringing flattery upward, and rudeness and contempt downward; the narrowest adhesion to his own, and distrust and hatred of all else. Indeed, the noble animal has proved such an apt pupil that he even understands the purely human art of judging people by their clothes. He lets well-dressed folks alone, but snaps at the legs of the ragged.'

Here the doctor was interrupted by a general chorus of disapproval, and Miss Thyra bitterly gripped the fruit-knife in her little hand.

But there were some who wanted to hear what mankind had learned from the dog, and Dr. Hansen proceeded, with steadily-growing passion and bitterness:

'Man has learned from the dog to set a high price upon this grovelling, unmerited worship. When neither injustice nor ill-treatment has ever met anything but this perpetually wagging tail, stomach upon earth, and licking tongue, the final result is that the master fancies himself a splendid fellow, to whom all this devotion belongs as a right. And, transferring his experience of the dog into his human intercourse, he puts little restraint upon himself, expecting to meet wagging tails and licking tongues. And if he be disappointed, then he despises mankind and turns, with loud-mouthed eulogies, to the dog.'

He was once more interrupted; some laughed, but the greater number were offended. By this time Viggo Hansen had warmed to his subject; his little, sharp voice pierced through the chorus of objections, and he proceeded as follows:

'And, while we are speaking of the dog, may I be allowed to present an extraordinarily profound hypothesis of my own? Is there not something highly characteristic of our national character in the fact that it is we who have produced this noble breed of dogs—the celebrated, pure Danish hounds? This strong, broad-chested animal with the heavy paws, the black throat, and the frightful teeth, but so good-natured, harmless, and amiable withal—does he not remind you of the renowned, indestructible Danish loyalty, which has never met injustice or ill-treatment with anything but perpetually wagging tail, stomach upon earth, and licking tongue? And when we admire this animal, formed in our own image, is it not with a kind of melancholy self-praise that we pat him upon the head, and say: "You are indeed a great, good, faithful creature!"'

'Do you hear, Dr. Hansen? I must point out to you that in my house there are certain matters which—'

The host was angry, but a good-natured relation of the family hastened to interrupt him, saying: 'I am a countryman, and you will surely admit, Dr. Hansen, that a good farm watch-dog is an absolute necessity for *us*. Eh?'

'Oh yes, a little cur that can yelp, so as to awake the master.'

'No, thank you. We must have a decent dog, that can lay the rascals by the heels. I have now a magnificent bloodhound.'

'And if an honest fellow comes running up to tell you that your outbuildings are burning, and your magnificent bloodhound flies at his throat—what then?'

'Why, that would be awkward,' laughed the countryman. And the others laughed too.

Dr. Hansen was now so busily engaged in replying to all sides, employing the most extravagant paradoxes, that the young folks in particular were extremely amused, without specially noting the increasing bitterness of his tone.

'But our watch-dogs, our watch-dogs! You will surely let us keep them, doctor?' exclaimed a coal-merchant laughingly.

'Not at all. Nothing is more unreasonable than that a poor man, who comes to fill his bag from a coal mountain, should be torn to pieces by wild beasts. There is absolutely no reasonable relation between such a trifling misdemeanour and so dreadful a punishment.'

'May we ask how you would protect your coal mountain, if you had one?'

'I should erect a substantial fence of boards, and if I were very anxious, I should keep a watchman, who would say politely, but firmly, to those who came with bags: "Excuse me, but my master is very particular about that. You must not fill your bag; you must take yourself off at once."'

Through the general laughter which followed this last paradox, a clerical gentleman spoke from the ladies' end of the table:

'It appears to me that there is something lacking in this discussion—something that I would call the ethical aspect of the question. Is it not a fact that in the hearts of all who sit here there is a clear, definite sense of the revolting nature of the crime we call theft?'

These words were received with general and hearty applause.

'And I think it does very great violence to our feelings to hear Dr. Hansen minimising a crime that is distinctly mentioned in Divine and human law as one of the worst—to hear him reduce it to the size of a trifling and insignificant misdemeanour. Is not this highly demoralizing and dangerous to Society?'

'Permit me, too,' promptly replied the indefatigable Hansen, 'to present an ethical aspect of the question. Is it not a fact that in the hearts of innumerable persons who do not sit here there is a clear, definite sense of the revolting nature of the crime they call wealth? And must it not greatly outrage the feelings of those who do not themselves possess any coal except an empty bag, to see a man who permits himself to own two or three hundred thousand sacks letting wild beasts loose to guard his coal mountain, and then going to bed after having written on the gate: "Watch-dogs unfastened at dusk"? Is not that very provoking and very dangerous to Society?'

'Oh, good God and Father! He is a regular *sans-culotte*!' cried old grandmother.

The majority gave vent to mutterings of displeasure; he was going too far; it was no longer amusing. Only a few still laughingly exclaimed: 'He does not mean a word of what he says; it is only his way. Good health, Hansen!'

But the host took the matter more seriously. He thought of himself, and he thought of Trofast. With ominous politeness, he began:

'May I venture to ask what you understand by a reasonable relation between a crime and its punishment?'

'For example,' replied Dr. Viggo Hansen, who was now thoroughly roused, 'if I heard that a merchant possessing two or three hundred thousand sacks of coal had refused to allow a poor creature to fill his bag, and that this same merchant, as a punishment, had been torn to pieces by wild beasts, then that would be something that I could very easily understand, for between such heartlessness and so horrible a punishment there is a reasonable relation.'

'Ladies and gentlemen, my wife and I beg you to make yourselves at home, and welcome.'

There was a secret whispering and muttering, and a depressed feeling among the guests, as they dispersed themselves through the salons.

The host walked about with a forced smile on his lips, and, as soon as he had welcomed every one individually, he went in search of Hansen, in order to definitely show him the door once for all.

But this was not necessary. Dr. Viggo Hansen had already found it.

III.

There had really been some snow, as the merchant had stated. Although it was so early in the winter, a little wet snow fell towards morning for several days in succession, but it turned into fine rain when the sun rose.

This was almost the only sign that the sun had risen, for it did not get much lighter or warmer all day. The air was thick with fog—not the whitish-gray sea mist, but brown-gray, close, dead Russian fog, which had not become lighter in passing over Sweden; and the east wind came with it and packed it well and securely down among the houses of Copenhagen.

Under the trees along Kastelgraven and in Gronningen the ground was quite black after the dripping from the branches. But along the middle of the streets and on the roofs there was a thin white layer of snow.

All was yet quite still over at Burmeister and Wain's; the black morning smoke curled up from the chimneys, and the east wind dashed it down upon the white roofs. Then it became still blacker, and spread over the harbour among the rigging of the ships, which lay sad and dark in the gray morning light, with white streaks of snow along their sides. At the Custom House the bloodhounds would soon be shut in, and the iron gates opened.

The east wind was strong, rolling the waves in upon Langelinie, and breaking them in grayish-green foam among the slimy stones, whilst long swelling billows dashed into the harbour, broke under the Custom House, and rolled great names and gloomy memories over the stocks round the fleet's anchorage, where lay the old dismantled wooden frigates in all their imposing uselessness.

The harbour was still full of ships, and goods were piled high in the warehouses and upon the quays.

Nobody could know what kind of winter they were to have—whether they would be cut off for months from the world, or if it would go by with fogs and snow-slush.

Therefore there lay row upon row of petroleum casks, which, together with the enormous coal mountains, awaited a severe winter, and there lay pipes and hogsheads of wine and cognac, patiently waiting for new adulterations; oil and tallow and cork and iron—all lay and waited, each its own destiny.

Everywhere lay work waiting—heavy work, coarse work, and fine work, from the holds of the massive English coal-steamers, right up to the three gilded cupolas on the Emperor of Russia's new church in Bredgade.

But as yet there was no one to put a hand to all this work. The town slept heavily, the air was thick, winter hung over the city, and it was so still in the streets that one could hear the water from the melting snow on the roofs fall down into the spouts with a deep gurgling, as if even the great stone houses yet sobbed in semi-slumber.

A little sleepy morning clock chimed over upon Holmen; here and there a door was opened, and a dog came out to howl; curtains were rolled up and windows were opened; the servant-girls went about in the houses, and did their cleaning by a naked light which stood and flickered; at a window in the palace sat a gilded lacquey and rubbed his nose in that early morning hour.

The fog lay thick over the harbour, and hung in the rigging of the great ships as if in a forest; rain and flakes of wet snow made it still thicker, but the east wind pressed it down between the houses, and completely filled Amalieplads, so that Frederick V. sat as if in the clouds, and turned his proud nose unconcernedly towards his half-finished church.

Some more sleepy clocks now began to chime; a steam-whistle joined in with a diabolical shriek. In the taverns which 'open before the clock strikes' they were already serving early refections of hot coffee and schnapps; girls with hair hanging down their backs, after a wild night, came out of the sailors' houses by Nyhavn, and sleepily began to clean windows.

It was bitterly cold and raw, and those who had to cross Kongens Nytorv hurried past Öhlenschläger, whom they had set outside the theatre, bare-headed, with his collar full of snow, which melted and ran down into his open shirt-front.

Now came the long, relentless blasts of steam-whistles from the factories all round the town, and the little steamers in the harbour whistled for no reason at all.

The work, which everywhere lay waiting, began to swallow up the many small dark figures, who, sleepy and freezingly cold, appeared and disappeared all round the town. And there was almost a quiet bustle in the streets; some ran, others walked—both those who had to go down into the coal steamers, and those who must up and gild the Emperor of

Russia's cupolas, and thousands of others who were being swallowed by all kinds of work.

And waggons began to rumble, criers to shout, engines raised their polished, oily shoulders, and turned their buzzing wheels; and little by little the heavy, thick atmosphere was filled with a muffled murmur from the collective work of thousands. The day was begun; joyous Copenhagen was awake.

Policeman Frode Hansen froze even to his innermost co-efficient. It had been an unusually bitter watch, and he walked impatiently up and down in Aabenraa, and waited for Mam Hansen. She was in the habit of coming at this time, or even earlier, and to-day he had almost resolved to carry matters as far as a half lager or a cup of warm coffee.

But Mam Hansen came not, and he began to wonder whether it was not really his duty to report her. She was carrying the thing too far; it would not do at all any longer, this humbug with these cabbage-leaves and that coal business.

Thyra and Waldemar had also several times peeped out into the little kitchen, to see if their mother had come and had put the coffee-pot on the fire. But it was black under the kettle, and the air was so dark and the room so cold that they jumped into bed again.

* * * * *

When they opened the great gates of merchant Hansen's coalstore at Kristianshavn, Trofast sat there and shamefacedly looked askance; it was really a loathsome piece of work that they had set him to do.

In a corner, between two empty baskets, they found a bundle of rags, from which there came a faint moaning. There were a few drops of blood upon the snow, and close by there lay, untouched, a piece of sugared Vienna bread.

When the foreman understood the situation, he turned to Trofast to praise him. But Trofast had already gone home; the position was quite too uncomfortable for *him*.

They gathered her up, such as she was, wet and loathsome, and the foreman decided that she should be placed upon the first coal-cart going into town, and that they could stop at the hospital, so that the professor himself might see whether she was worth repairing.

* * * * *

About ten o'clock the merchant's family began to assemble at the breakfast-table. Thyra came first. She hurried up to Trofast, patted and kissed him, and overwhelmed him with words of endearment.

But Trofast did not move his tail, and scarcely raised his eyes. He kept on licking his fore-paws, which were a little black after the coal.

'Good gracious, my dear mother!' cried Miss Thyra; 'Trofast is undoubtedly ill. Of course he has caught cold in the night; it was really horrid of father.'

But when Waldemar came in, he declared, with a knowing air, that Trofast was affronted.

All three now fell upon him with entreaties and excuses and kind words, but Trofast coldly looked from one to the other. It was clear that Waldemar was right.

Thyra then ran out for her father, and the merchant came in serious—somewhat solemn. They had just told him by telephone from the office how well Trofast had acquitted himself of his task, and, kneeling down on the hearthrug before Trofast, he thanked him warmly for the great service.

This mollified Trofast a good deal.

Still kneeling, with Trofast's paw in his hand, the merchant now told his family what had occurred during the night. That the thief was a hardened old woman, one of the very worst kind, who had even—just imagine it!—driven a pretty considerable trade in the stolen coal. She had been cunning enough to bribe the young watch-dog with a dainty piece of bread; but, of course, that was no use with Trofast.

'And that brings me to think how often a certain person, whom I do not wish to name, would rant about it being a shame that a beast should refuse bread, for which many a human being would be thankful. Do we not now see the good of that? Through that—ahem!—that peculiarity, Trofast was enabled to reveal an abominable crime; to contribute to the just punishment of evildoers, and thus benefit both us and society.'

'But, father,' exclaimed Miss Thyra, 'will you not promise me one thing?'

'What is that, my child?'

'That you will never again require such a service of Trofast. Rather let them steal a little.'

'That I promise you, Thyra; and you, too, my brave Trofast,' said the merchant, rising with dignity.

'Trofast is hungry,' said Waldemar, with his knowing air.

'Goodness, Thyra! fetch his cutlets!'

Thyra was about to rush down into the kitchen, but at that moment Stine came puffing upstairs with them.

* * * * *

Presumably, the professor did not find Mam Hansen worth repairing. At any rate, she was never seen again, and the children 'flowed quite over.' I do not know what became of them.

KAREN.*

There was once in Krarup Kro** a girl named Karen. She had to wait upon all the guests, for the innkeeper's wife almost always went about looking for her keys. And there came many to Krarup Kro—folk from the surrounding district, who gathered in the autumn gloamings, and sat in the inn parlour drinking coffee-punches, usually without any definite object; and also travellers and wayfarers, who tramped in, blue and weather-beaten, to get something hot to carry them on to the next inn.

But Karen could manage everything all the same, although she walked about so quietly, and never seemed in a hurry.

She was small and slim, quite young, grave and silent, so that with her there was no amusement for the commercial travellers. But decent folks who went into the tavern in earnest, and who set store on their coffee being served promptly and scalding hot, thought a great deal of Karen. And when she slipped quietly forward among the guests with her tray, the unwieldy frieze-clad figures fell back with unaccustomed celerity to make way for her, and the conversation stopped for a moment. All had to look after her, she was so charming.

Karen's eyes were of that large gray sort which seem at once to look at one and to look far, far beyond, and her eyebrows were loftily arched, as if in wonder.

Therefore strangers thought she did not rightly understand what they asked for. But she understood very well, and made no mistakes. There was

---

* The scene of this tale is laid in Denmark.
** Kro, a country inn.

only something strange about her, as if she were looking for something far away, or listening, or waiting, or dreaming.

The wind came from the west over the low plains. It had rolled long, heavy billows across the Western Sea;* salt and wet with spray and foam, it had dashed in upon the coast. But on the high downs with the tall wrack-grass it had become dry and full of sand and somewhat tired, so that when it came to Krarup Kro it had quite enough to do to open the stable-doors.

But open they flew, and the wind filled the spacious building, and forced its way in at the kitchen-door, which stood ajar. And at last there was such a pressure of air that the doors in the other end of the stable also burst open; and now the west wind rushed triumphantly right through the building, swinging the lantern that hung from the roof, whisking the ostler's cap out into the darkness, blowing the rugs over the horses' heads, and sweeping a white hen off the roost into the watering-trough. And the cock raised a frightful screech, and the ostler swore, and the hens cackled, and in the kitchen they were nearly smothered with smoke, and the horses grew restless, and struck sparks from the stones. Even the ducks, which had huddled themselves together near the mangers, so as to be first at the spilt corn, began quacking; and the wind howled through the stable with a hellish din, until a couple of men came out from the inn parlour, set their broad backs against the doors and pressed them to again, while the sparks from their great tobacco-pipes flew about their beards.

After these achievements the wind plunged down into the heather, ran along the deep ditches, and took a substantial grip of the mail-coach, which it met half a mile from the town.

'He is always in a devil of a hurry to get to Krarup Kro!' growled Anders, the postboy, cracking his whip over the perspiring horses.

---

*   German Ocean.

For this was certainly the twentieth time that the guard had lowered the window to shout something or other up to Anders. First it was a friendly invitation to a coffee-punch in the inn; but each time the friendliness became scantier, until at last the window was let down with a bang, and out sped some brief but expressive remarks about both driver and horses, which Anders, at all events, could not have cared to hear.

Meanwhile the wind swept low along the ground, and sighed long and strangely in the dry clusters of heather. The moon was full, but so densely beclouded that only a pale hazy shimmer hovered over the night.

Behind Krarup Kro lay a peat moss, dark with black turf-stacks and dangerous deep pits. And among the heathery mounds there wound a strip of grass that looked like a path; but it was no path, for it stopped on the very brink of a turf-pit that was larger than the others, and deeper also.

In this grassy strip the fox lay and lurked, quite flat, and the hare bounded lightly over the heather.

It was easy for the fox to calculate that the hare would not describe a wide circle so late in the evening. It cautiously raised its pointed nose and made an estimate; and as it sneaked back before the wind, to find a good place from which it could see where the hare would finish its circuit and lie down, it self-complacently thought that the foxes were always getting wiser and wiser, and the hares more foolish than ever.

In the inn they were unusually busy, for a couple of commercial travellers had ordered roast hare; besides, the landlord was at an auction in Thisted, and Madame had never been in the habit of seeing to anything but the kitchen. But now it unfortunately chanced that the lawyer wanted to get hold of the landlord, and, as he was not at home, Madame had to receive a lengthy message and an extremely important letter, which utterly bewildered her.

By the stove stood a strange man in oilskins, waiting for a bottle of soda-water; two fish-buyers had three times demanded cognac for their coffee; the stableman stood with an empty lantern waiting for a light, and a tall, hard-featured countryman followed Karen anxiously with his eyes; he had to get sixty-three öre change out of a krone.*

But Karen went to and fro without hurrying herself, and without getting confused. One could scarcely understand how she kept account of all this. The large eyes and the wondering eyebrows were strained as if in expectation. She held her fine little head erect and steady, as if not to be distracted from all she had to think of. Her simple dress of blue serge had become too tight for her, so that the collar cut slightly into her neck, forming a little fold in the skin below the hair.

'These country girls are very white-skinned,' said one of the fish-buyers to the other. They were young men, and talked about Karen as connoisseurs.

At the window was a man who looked at the clock and said: 'The post comes early to-night.'

There was a rumbling of wheels on the paving-stones without, the stable-door was flung open, and the wind again rattled all the doors and drove smoke out of the stove.

Karen slipped out into the kitchen the moment the door of the parlour was opened. The mail-guard entered, and said 'good-evening' to the company.

He was a tall, handsome man, with dark eyes, black curly hair and beard, and a small, well-shaped head. The long rich cloak of King of Denmark's magnificent red cloth was adorned with a broad collar of curled dogskin that drooped over his shoulders.

All the dim, sickly light from the two paraffin lamps that hung over the table seemed to fall affectionately upon the red colour, which contrasted so strikingly with the sober black and gray tints of all else in the room. And the tall figure with the small curly head, the broad collar, and the

---

*   A krone contains 100 öre, and is equal to 1 S. 1-1/2 d.

66

long purple folds, became, as he walked through the low-roofed, smoky room, a marvel of beauty and magnificence.

Karen came hurriedly in from the kitchen with her tray. She bent her head, so that one could not see her face, as she hastened from guest to guest.

She placed the roast hare right in front of the two fish-buyers, whereupon she took a bottle of soda-water to the two commercial travellers, who sat in the inner room. Then she gave the anxious countryman a tallow candle, and, as she slipped out again, she put sixty-three öre into the hand of the stranger by the stove.

The innkeeper's wife was in utter despair. She had, indeed, quite unexpectedly found her keys, but lost the lawyer's letter immediately after, and now the whole inn was in the most frightful commotion. None had got what they wanted—all were shouting together. The commercial men kept continuously ringing the table bell; the fish-buyers went into fits of laughter over the roast hare, which lay straddling on the dish before them. But the anxious countryman tapped Madame on the shoulder with his tallow candle; he trembled for his sixty-three öre. And, amid all this hopeless confusion, Karen had disappeared without leaving a trace.

Anders the post-boy sat on the box; the innkeeper's boy stood ready to open the gates; the two passengers inside the coach became impatient, as did also the horses—although they had nothing to look forward to—and the wind rustled and whistled through the stable.

At length came the guard, whom they awaited. He carried his large cloak over his arm, as he walked up to the coach and made a little excuse for having kept the party waiting. The light of the lantern shone upon his face; he looked very warm, and smilingly said as much, as he drew on his cloak and climbed up beside the driver.

The gates were opened, and the coach rumbled away. Anders let the horses go gently, for now there was no hurry. Now and then he stole a glance at the guard by his side; he was still sitting smiling to himself, and letting the wind ruffle his hair.

Anders the post-boy also smiled in his peculiar way. He began to understand.

The wind followed the coach until the road turned; thereupon it again swept over the plain, and whistled and sighed long and strangely among the dry clusters of heather. The fox lay at his post; everything was calculated to a nicety; the hare must soon be there.

In the inn Karen had at last reappeared, and the confusion had gradually subsided. The anxious countryman had got quit of his candle and received his sixty-three öre, and the commercial gentlemen had set to work upon the roast hare.

Madame whined a little, but she never scolded Karen; there was not a person in the world who could scold Karen.

Quietly and without haste Karen again walked to and fro, and the air of peaceful comfort that always followed her once more overspread the snug, half-dark parlour. But the two fish-buyers, who had had both one and two cognacs with their coffee, were quite taken up with her. She had got some colour in her cheeks, and wore a little half-hidden gleam of a smile, and when she once happened to raise her eyes, a thrill shot through their whole frames.

But when she felt their eyes following her, she went into the room where the commercial men sat dining, and began to polish some teaspoons at the sideboard.

'Did you notice the mail-guard?' asked one of the travellers.

'No, not particularly; I only got a glimpse of him. I think he went out again directly,' replied the other, with his mouth full of food.

'He's a devilish fine fellow! Why, I danced at his wedding.'

'Indeed. So he is married?'

'Yes; his wife lives in Lemvig; they have at least two children. She was a daughter of the innkeeper of Ulstrop, and I arrived there on the very evening of the wedding. It was a jolly night, you may be sure.'

Karen dropped the teaspoons and went out. She did not hear them calling to her from the parlour. She walked across the courtyard to her chamber, closed the door, and began half-unconsciously to arrange the bedclothes. Her eyes stood rigid in the darkness; she pressed her hands to her head, to her breast; she moaned; she did not understand—she did not understand—

But when she heard Madame calling so piteously, 'Karen, Karen!' she sprang up, rushed out of the yard, round the back of the house, out—out upon the heath.

In the twilight the little grassy strip wound in and out among the heather, as if it were a path; but it was no path—no one must believe it to be a path—for it led to the very brink of the great turf-pit.

The hare started up; it had heard a splash. It dashed off with long leaps, as if mad; now contracted, with legs under body and back arched, now drawn out to an incredible length, like a flying accordion, it bounded away over the heather.

The fox put up its pointed nose, and stared in amazement after the hare. It had not heard any splash. For, according to all the rules of art, it had come creeping along the bottom of a deep ditch; and, as it was not conscious of having made any mistake, it could not understand the strange conduct of the hare.

Long it stood, with its head up, its hindquarters lowered, and its great bushy tail hidden in the heather; and it began to wonder whether the hares were getting wiser or the foxes getting more foolish.

But when the west wind had travelled a long way it became a north wind, then an east wind, then a south wind, and at last it again came over the sea as a west wind, dashed in upon the downs, and sighed long and strangely among the dry clusters of heather. But then a pair of wondering gray eyes were lacking in Krarup Kro, and a blue serge dress that had grown too tight. And the innkeeper's wife whined and whimpered more than ever. She could not understand it—nobody could understand it—except Anders the post-boy—and one beside.

But when old folks wished to give the young a really serious admonition, they used to begin thus: 'There was once in Krarup Kro a girl named Karen—

MY SISTER'S JOURNEY TO MODUM.

My sister was going to Modum. It was before the opening of the Drammen Railway, and it was a dreadfully long carriole drive from Christiania to Drammen.

But everything depended upon getting off—hyp—getting to Drammen—hyp, hyp—in time to catch the train which left for Modum at two o'clock. Hyp—oh, dear, if the train should be gone—to wait until next day—alone—in Drammen!

My sister stimulated the post-boys with drink-money, and the horses with small pokes of her umbrella; but both horses and post-boys were numerous upon this route, and much time was lost at the stopping-places.

First, the luggage had to be transferred to the new carriole. There were the big trunk and the little one, and the plaids with loosened strap, the umbrella, the *en-tout-cas*, the bouquet, and the book.

Then there was paying, and reckoning, and changing; and the purse was crammed so extraordinarily full that it would shower three-skilling pieces,* or a shining half-dollar would swing itself over the side, make a graceful curve, like a skater, round the floor, and disappear behind the stove. It had to be got out before it could be changed, and that nobody could do.

As soon as the fresh horses appeared in the yard, my sister would spring resolutely out, and swing herself into the carriole.

'Thanks; I am ready now. Let us be off. Good-bye.'

---

*   Skilling, a halfpenny.

70

Yes, then they would all come running after her—the umbrella, the *en-tout-cas*, the plaids with loosened strap, the bouquet, and the book, everything would be thrown into her lap, and she would hold on to them until the next station was reached, while the station-master's honest wife stood and feebly waved the young lady's pocket-handkerchief, in a manner which could not possibly attract her attention.

Although she thus lost no time, the drive was, nevertheless, extremely trying, and it was a great relief to my sister when she at length rattled down the hill from Gjelleboek, and saw Drammen extended below her. There were not many minutes left.

At last she was down in the town. 'In Drammen, in Drammen!' muttered my sister, beginning to triumph. Like a fire-engine she dashed along the streets to the station. Everything was paid. She had only to jump out of the carriole; but when she looked up at the station clock, the minute-hand was just passing the number twelve.

Undismayed, my sister collected her knick-knacks and rushed into the waiting-room, which was quite empty. But the young man who had sold the tickets, and who was in the act of drawing down the panel, caught a glimpse of this belated lady, and was good-natured enough to wait.

'A ticket—for Heaven's sake! A ticket for Drammen! What does it cost?'

'Where are you going, miss?' asked the good-natured young man.

'To Drammen—do you hear? But do make haste. I am sure the train will be gone.'

'But, miss,' said the young man, with a modest smile, 'you *are* in Drammen.'

'Ah! I beg your pardon. Yes, so I am; it is to Modum, to Modum that I want to go.'

She received her ticket, filled her lap with her things, and, purse in mouth, hurried out upon the platform.

She was instantly seized by powerful hands, lifted off the ground, and tenderly deposited in a *coupé*.

'Puff,' said the locomotive impatiently, beginning to strain at the carriages.

My sister leant back on the velvet sofa, happy and triumphant; she had been in time. Before her, upon the other sofa, she had all her dear little things, which seemed to lie and smile at her—the bouquet and the book, the *en-tout-cas* and the umbrella, and the very plaids, with the strap completely unfastened.

Then, as the train slowly began to glide out of the station, she heard the footstep of a man—rap, rap—of a man running—rap, rap, rap—running on the platform alongside the train; and although, of course, it did not concern her, still she would see what he was running for.

But no sooner did my sister's head become visible than the running man waved his arms and cried:

'There she is, there she is—the young lady who came last! Where shall we send your luggage?'

Then my sister cried in a loud and firm voice:

'To Drammen!'

And with these words she was whirled away.

LETTERS FROM MASTER-PILOT SEEHUS.

KRYDSVIG FARM,
January 1, 1889.
MR. EDITOR,

Referring to our talk of last December, when I said I was not unwilling to send you occasional letters, if anything important should happen, I do not know of anything that I could think worthy of being published or made public in your paper except the weather, which always and ever gives cause for alternate praise and blame, when one is living, so to speak, out among the sea's breakers, where there is no quietness to expect on a winter's day, but storms and rough weather as we had in the last Yule-nights, with a violent storm from the east and with such tremendous gusts of wind that the pots and pans flew about like birds. And there is much damage done by the east wind and nothing gained, because it only drives wreckage out to sea. But it was not quite so bad as it was in the great storms in the last days of November, which culminated or reached their highest point on Monday, the 26th November, when it was rougher than old folk can remember it to have ever been, with such a tremendous sea that it seemed as if it would reach the fields that we here at Krydsvig have owned from old times; it almost touched the cowhouses. After that time we had light frosts with changeable weather and a smoother sea, which was not covered, but richly sown, with many sad relics of the storm, mostly deck cargo, which is not so great a loss, as it is always lying, so to speak, upon expectancy or adventure; and when it goes, it is a relief to the ship and a great and especial blessing to these treeless coasts, particularly when it comes ashore well split up and distributed, a few planks at each place, so that the Lensmand* cannot see any greater accumulation at any one place than that he can, with a good conscience, abandon an auction and let the folk keep what they have been lucky enough to find or diligent enough to garner in from the sea in their boats; but this time it did not repay the trouble, because of frost and an easterly land-wind, which kept the wreck from land for some time. But now the most of it has come in that is to come at this time, and it may be long to another time, as we must hope, for the seaman's sake, although I, for my part, have never been able to join with any particular devotion in prayers and supplications that we may be free from storms and foul weather; for our Lord has made the sea thus and not otherwise, so that there must come storms and tumults in the atmosphere of the air, and, as a consequence, towering billows. And it seems to me, further, that we cannot decently turn to the Lord and ask Him to do something over again or in a different way; but we can well wish each other God's help and all good luck in danger, and especially good gear for our own ones, who sail with wit and canniness, while the Englishman is mostly a demon to sail and go with full steam on in fogs and driving rain-storms, of which we can expect enough in Januarius month at the beginning of the new year, which I hope may be a good year for these coasts, with decent weather, as it may fall out, and something respectable in the way of wreckage.

Yours very truly,
LAURITZ BOLDEMANN SEEHUS,
Late Master-Pilot.

* * * * *

---

*   Sheriff's officer.

KRYDSVIG,
January 22, 1889.
MR. EDITOR,

I take up my pen to-day to inform you that I, the undersigned, address you for the last time, as I will not write more because of my sore eyes, which are not to be wondered at, after all that they have seen in bitter weather and in a long life of trouble and hardship from my youth up, mostly at sea in spray and driving snow-storms at the fishing, which is all over and past, as everything old is past. But things new are coming to the front, and here I sit alone like Job, though he, to be sure, had some friends, but loneliness is a sore thing for old folk, and idleness which they are not used to, so that the Sheriff might as well have given me back my post as master-pilot on my return from America. But he would not do it, because I was not cunning enough to agree with him, when he did not understand anybody, but it is given out officially that I am too old, and thus I sit here without having shaved for a week, because I am angry and my hand trembles, but not owing to old age. And I don't think, either, that anybody is much to be envied for having friends like Job's, and I am not stricken with boils and sitting among potsherds, but am quite hale and strong, if I am rather dried-up and stiff, but I would undertake to dance a reel and a Hamburg schottische if I could only get a girl with a fairly round waist to take hold of, but it seems to me that they are shrinking in and becoming flatter than they were in my young days; but then I think that it is surely the sore eyes that are cheating me, for I have always held this belief, that girls are girls in all times, but old folks should be quiet and mind what they understand, which is nothing that relates to the young. But a man should not get sour *in finem*, for all that, and I have found that it is a dangerous thing to grow old, for this reason, that one becomes so surly before one's time, and that is against my inner construction, and I have now sat here awhile and gazed out on the sea through rain and mist, and then I straightened my old back and spat out my quid, which in all truth smacked more of the brass box than of tobacco, because it had been chewed several times, but I have cut myself a new one with my knife, as I can no longer bite it off, for the reason that there are hardly any teeth, but I have still a few front ones, and I have one good tooth, which is hidden and is no ornament, but it is useful when I eat tough things like dried ham. And I take up the pen again because I want to let you know that I am not so ill but that I may hold out for a while yet; and, if I keep my health, you shall hear from me soon, but I have nothing to say about the weather, because we have not had any weather for a long time, and I am wondering whether this winter will come to anything, or if it will pass over in damp and wet and loose wind.

Yours very truly,
LAURITZ BOLDEMANN SEEHUS,
Late Master-Pilot.

* * * * *

KRYDSVIG,
April 13, 1889.
MR. EDITOR,

About the rotten feet on the sheep, which animal I by nature despise, on account of its cowardice and a tremendous silliness, the one running after the other, but if a man *will* plague himself with farming who has been a sailor from his mother's apron-string, he must keep these beasts and others like his neighbours, although he understands nothing, or very little, about the whole tribe. So I have upon my small patch of ground two good ewes, with little wit, but wool, and I sent them long before Yule to a ram at Börevig, one of the fine kind from Scotland, as folk bothered me that I must do it, because of the breed and the wool and many things, but not a rotten foot did I hear of until after much jangling among folk and a great to-do among the learned and such like, which is nothing new to me in that kind of folk, who always and always stand behind each other's backs, crying with a loud cry, 'It was not my fault,' but, faith, it was. So I say to myself, 'What shall I do with these rotten feet from Scotland, if I get the disease ingrafted, and likewise upon the innocent offspring,' who are already toddling about all three, because there were two in the one ewe. But foreign sickness is not a thing to be afflicted with, at a time when we have scab among our sheep and much else, and more than I know of, and thus I turned my look again and again to that Government, to see if it will ever gather sense. But yet the Government had not so very rotten feet in that other important matter of a Sheriff, whom we got with unexpected smartness and promptness, much to our gain and the reverse, when we think of what the man now is, but there must be a skipper all the same. And now it is growing light all over the world; that is, in our hemisphere, for spring has come upon us with extraordinary quickness, and the ice, it went with Peder-Varmestol,* and the lapwing, she came one morning with her back shining as if she had been polished out of bronze, with her crest erect, and throwing herself about in the air like a dolphin in the sea, with her head down and her tail up, crying and screaming. But the lark is really the silliest creature, to sing on without ceasing the livelong day, and the sea-pie has come, and stands bobbing upon the same stone as last year, and the wild-goose and the water-wagtail. So we are all cheered up again, all the men of Jæderen, and the cod bites, too, for those who have time, but folk are mostly carting sea-weed, and ploughing and sowing, not without grumbling in some places, but the work must be done.

Yours very truly,
L.B. SEEHUS.

---

*   February 22nd.

* * * * *

KRYDSVIG,
July 1, 1889.
MR. EDITOR,

Your letter of the 20th ult. received, and contents noted, and I now beg to reply that it is not very convenient, for the reason that old folk's talk is mostly about winter storms and seldom about summer, when the sun shines, and the lambs frisk and throw their tails high in the air. But, you see, they were tups all three, which was not unlooked-for after such a ram, and consequently no letter can be expected from me before autumn, when the sea gets some life in it and a grown man's voice, so to speak, for now it lies—God bless me—like a basin of milk, to the inward vexation of folk who know what the sea should be in Nature's household with ships and storms and wreckage, and a decent number of wrecks at those places where the structure of the coast permits the rescue of men and a distribution of the wreck if it be of wood, but some trash are now of iron. And I am now as parched in the hide as I was that time in Naples when the helmsman sailed the brig on to the pier-head because a hurricane had risen, and Skipper Worse and I stood on the quay and cried, though he swore mostly, and I had a basket on my arm with something that they called bananas, which they fry in butter. And it is not very nice nowadays, when the sun rises and sets in nothing but blue sky, and not a cloud to be seen, as if it were the Mediterranean of my young days, and I smell the bananas, but we here have no other stinking stuff, that I know, than ware and cods' heads. But, Mr. Editor, the young are dull and heavy with the sunshine; I myself went about singing, and wanted to show the flabby wenches of Varhaug how one once danced a real *molinask*, as it was Sunday and the young folk hung round the walls like half-dead flies in the heat. But there had been grease burnt, which made it more slippery than soft soap on the deck, and there lay the whole master-pilot in the middle of the *molinask*, and bit off the stalk of his clay pipe, but he kept his tooth, which has already been spoken about, and to his shame had to be lifted by four firm-handed fellows with much laughing, wherefore I have sat myself down in my chair to wait for the autumn, because I cannot speak or write about the drought, but only get angry and unreasonable.

Yours very truly,
LAURITZ BOLDEMANN SEEHUS.

* * * * *

KRYDSVIG,
October 20, 1889.
MR. EDITOR,

I could have continued my silence a very long time yet, for it has not been a great autumn either on land or sea, but little summer storms, as if for frolic, with small seas and loose wreckage, but unusually far out, about three miles from land. But the long, dark lamp-lit evenings are come, and this shoal of fish which I must write to you about and ask what the end is going to be; for now we almost think that the sea up north Stavanger way must be choke-full, as it was of herrings in the good old days that are no more, but it is now big with coal-fish, mostly north by the Reef, they say, but the undersigned and old Velas, who is a still older man, got about four boxes of right nice coal-fish yesterday, a little to the south-east. But half Jæren* was on the sea, boat upon boat, for the double reason of the coal-fish and that they had not an earthly thing to do upon the land, for this year the earth has yielded us everything well and very early, but the straw is short, which, if the truth must be told, is the only thing to complain of. But the farmers are making wry faces, like the merchants

---

*   Jæderen, the coast district near Stavanger.

in Östersöen when they complain of the herrings, for they must always complain, except about the sheep, which are going off very well to the Englishman, and I can't conceive what there will be left of this kind of beast in Jæren, but it is all the same to me, seeing that I have never liked the sheep at all until last year, when he paid taxes for all Jæren, which was more than was expected of him. And it would be well if any one were able to put bounds upon this burning of sea-ware, which the devil or somebody has invented for use as a medicine in Bergen—they say, but I do not believe it, because it has a stink that goes into the innermost part of your nostrils and into your tobacco besides. But then the east wind is good for something, at least, for it sends the heaps of ware out to sea, and I can imagine how it will surprise the Queen of England when she knows how we stink. And I have a grievance of my own, viz., boys shooting with blunderbusses and powder, and with so little wit that my eyes flash with anger every time I see them creeping on their stomachs towards a starling or a couple of lean ring-plovers, and I shout and cast stones to warn the innocent creatures, since the farmer of Jæren is, as it were, his thrall's thrall, and lets the servant-boys make a fool of him and play the concertina all night, which might be put up with, but no powder and shooting should be allowed, so that Jæren may not become a desert for bird-life, and only concertinas left and rascals of boys on their stomachs as above.

Yours very truly,
LAURITZ BOLDEMANN SEEHUS.

* * * * *

KRYDSVIG,
December 25, 1889.
MR. EDITOR,

After having, in the course of a long and very stormy life, given heed to the clouds of the sky and the various aspects of the sea, which can change before your eyes as you look, like a woman who discovers another whom she likes better, and you stand forsaken and rejected, because a girl's mind is like the ocean above-mentioned, and full of storms as the Spanish Sea, and I early received my shock of that kind for life, of which I do not intend to speak, but the weather is of a nature that I have never before observed in this country, with small seas, rare and moderate storms, and on this first Yule-day a peace on the earth and such a complacent calm on the sea that you might row out in a trough. The wreckage that came in on the 8th and 9th December last was the only extravagance, so to speak, of the sea this year, for there was too much in some places, and this will probably give the Lensmand a pretext for holding an auction, to the great ruination of the people, for the planks were rare ones, both long and good-hearted timber. But at an auction half the pleasure is lost, besides more that is very various in kind—for instance, brandy: and the town gentlemen who sell such liquor to the farmer must answer to their consciences what substances and ingredients such a drink is cooked out of, as it brings on mental weakness and bodily torment, proof of which I have seen numberless times in strong and well-fabricated persons, especially during the Yule-days. But this is not my friendship's time, for they say at the farm that the Oldermand* is haughty, and will not swallow their devil's drink at any price. But I sit alone before a bottle of old Jamaica, which is part of what Jacob Worse brought home from the West Indies in 1825, and I think of him and Randulf and the old ones, and the smell of the liquor seems to call up living conversations, which

---

*   Master-pilot

you can hear, and you must laugh, although you are alone, and you have such a desire to write everything down as it happened; but no more to the newspapers for this reason, that they have been after me with false teeth and a nice, neat widow, of whom nothing more will be said. And this extraordinarily mild winter has in some way kept the rheumatism out of my limbs; besides, I am strong by nature and no age to speak of; but, of course, it must be admitted that youth is better and more lively, of which, as above, nothing more will be said.

As the years go on, Mr. Editor, disappointments bite fast into us, like barnacles and mussels under ships; but we ourselves do not feel that our speed is decreasing, and that we are dropping astern, and, as already hinted, old age does not protect us against folly.

Yours very truly,
LAURITZ BOLDEMANN SEEHUS.

OLD DANCES.

We really strove honestly, swung ourselves and swung our ladies, although many were stiff enough to get round. We were not invited to a ball; this dance was merely a surprise frolic.

We had dined in all good faith—at least, the stranger cousin had; and while I stood thinking of coffee, and dreading no danger, the house began to swarm with young folks who had dined upstairs or downstairs, or at home, or not at all, or God knows where. The dining-room doors were thrown open again, the floor was cleared as if by magic, partners caught hold of each other, two rushed to the piano, and—one, two, three, they were in the middle of a galop before I could recover my wits.

They immediately forsook me again, when I received a frightful blow in the region of the heart. It was Uncle Ivar himself, who shouted:

'Come, boy; inside with you, and move your legs. Don't stand there like a snivelling chamberlain, but show what kind of fellow you are with those long pipe-stalks that our Lord has sent you out upon.'

Thus the dance began; and although I did not at all like uncle's way of arranging matters, I good-naturedly set to work, and we strove honestly, that I can say, with the cousins as well as the lighter of the aunts.

By degrees we even became lively; and everything might have passed off in peace and joy if uncle had not taken it into his head that we were not doing our utmost in the dance, especially we gentlemen.

'What kind of dancing is that to show to people?' he exclaimed contemptuously. 'There they go, mincing and tripping, as spindle-shanked as pencils and parasols. No, there was another kind of legs in my time! Pooh, boys, that was dancing, that was!'

We held up our heads and footed it until our ears tingled. But every time that Uncle Ivar passed the ball-room door, his jeers became more aggravating, until we were almost exhausted, each one trying to be nimbler than another.

But what was the use? Every time uncle came back from his round through the smoking-room, where he cooled his head in an enormous ale-bowl, he was bolder and bolder, and at last he had aled so long in the cooling bowl that his boldness was not to be repressed.

'Out of the way with these long-shanked flamingoes!' he cried. 'Now, boys, you are going to see a real national dance. Come, Aunt Knoph, we two old ones will make these miserable youngsters of nowadays think shame.'

'Oh, no, my dear, do let me alone,' begged respectable Mrs. Knoph; 'remember, we are both old.'

'The devil is old,' laughed uncle merrily; 'you were the smartest of the lasses, and I was not the greatest lout among the boys, that I know. So come along, old girl!'

'Oh no, my dear Ivaren; won't you excuse me?' pleaded Mrs. Knoph. But what was the use? The hall was cleared, room had to be made, and we miserable flamingoes were squeezed up against the walls, so that we might be out of the way, at all events.

All the young ladies were annoyed at the interruption, and we gentlemen were more or less sulky over all the affronts that we had endured. But the lady who had to play was quite in despair. She had merely received orders to play something purely national; and no matter how often she asked what dance it was to be, uncle would only stare politely at her over his spectacles, and swear that this would be another kind of dance.

As far as Uncle Ivar was concerned, 'Sons of Norway' was no doubt good enough for any or every dance; and as to the dance itself, the music was really not so very important; for, you see, it happened in this way:

Uncle Ivar came swinging in with one arm by his side, and tall, respectable Mrs. Knoph on the other. He placed her with a chivalrous sweep in the middle of the floor, bowed in the fashion of elderly gallants, with head down between his legs and arms hanging in front, but quickly straightened himself up again and looked about with a provoking smile.

Uncle Ivar, without a coat and with vest unbuttoned, was a sight to see in a ball-room. A flaming red poll, one of the points of his collar up and one down, his false shirtfront thrust under a pair of home-made braces, which were green, two white bands of tape hanging down, a tuft of woollen shirt visible here and there.

But one began to respect the braces when one saw what they carried—a trousers-button as big as a square-sail, and another behind—I am sure that one could have written 'Constantinople' in full across it in a large hand.

'Tush, boys!' cried uncle, clapping his hands, 'now, by Jove, you shall see a dance worth looking at!' And then it began—at least, I *think* that it began here, but, as will presently appear, this is not quite certain. It happened in this way:

The pianist struck up some national tune or other; uncle swung his arms and shuffled a little with his feet, amorously ogling old Mrs. Knoph over his spectacles.

All attention was now concentrated upon Uncle Ivar's legs; it was clear that after the little preliminary steps he would let himself go! I stood and wondered whether he would spring into the air clear over Mrs. Knoph, or only kick the cap off her head.

That would have been quite like him, and it is not at all certain whether he himself did not think of performing some such feat, for, as will presently appear, we cannot know; it happened, you see, in this way:

As Uncle Ivar, after some little pattering, collected his energies for the decisive *coup*, he violently stamped his feet upon the floor.

But, as if he had trodden upon soft soap, like lightning his heels glided forward from under him. The whole of Uncle Ivar fell backward upon Constantinople, his legs beat the air, and the crown of his head struck the floor with a boom that resounded through the whole house.

Yes, there he lay stretched in all his *rondeur*, with the square-sail just in front of the feet of respectable Mrs. Knoph, who resembled a deserted tower in the desert.

I was irreverent enough to let the others gather him up. Of course he would not fall to pieces; I knew the Constantinople architecture. I slipped out into the corridor and laughed until I was quite exhausted.

But since then I have often wondered what kind of dance it could have been.

AUTUMN.

AARRE,
October 7, 1890.

I had intended to send a few observations upon the wild-goose to *Nature*, but since they have extended to quite a long letter, they go to *Dagbladet*. It is not because I believe that they represent anything new that no one has observed before; but I know how thoughtlessly most of us let the sun shine, and the birds fly, without any idea of what a refreshment it is for a man's soul to understand what he sees in Nature, and how interesting animal life becomes when we have once learned that there is a method and a thought in every single thing that the animal undertakes, and what a pleasure it is to discover this thought, and trace the beautiful reasoning power which is Nature's essence.

And thus most of us go through life, and down into a hole in the ground like moles, without having taken any notice of the bird that flew or the bill that sang. We believe that the small birds are sparrows, the larger probably crows; barndoor fowls are the only ones we know definitely.

I met a lady the other day who was extremely indignant about this. She had asked the man at whose house she was staying—a very intelligent peasant—what kind of bird it was that she had seen in the fields. It was evident that it was a thrush—merely a common thrush—and she described the bird to him: it was about half as large as a pigeon, gray and speckled with yellow; it hopped in the fields, and so on.

'Would it be the bird they call a swallow?' suggested the man.

'Not at all,' replied the lady angrily. 'I rather think it was a kind of thrush.'

'Oh! then you had better ask my wife.'

'So she understands birds, does she?' exclaimed the lady, much mollified.

'Yes, she is mad with them, they do so much mischief among the cherries.'

With this my lady had to go. But the story is not yet finished; the worst is to come.

For when, indignant at the countryman's ignorance of the bird-world, she told all this in town, there was one very solemn gentleman who said:

'Are you sure that it was not a gull?'

This went beyond all bounds, thought my lady, and she came and complained bitterly to me.

When wild-geese fly in good order, as they do when in the air for days and nights together, the lines generally form the well-known plough, with one bird at the point, and the two next ones on either side of him a little way behind.

Hitherto I have always been content with the explanation that we received and gave one another as boys, viz., that the birds chose this formation in order to cleave the air, like a snow-plough clearing a way.

But it suddenly occurred to me the other day that this was pure nonsense—an association of ideas called forth by the resemblance to a plough, which moves in earth or snow, but which has no meaning up in the air.

What *is* cloven air? And who gets any benefit by it?

Yes, if the geese flew as they walk—one directly behind the other—there might perhaps, in a contrary wind, be some little shelter and relief for the very last ones. But they fly nearly side by side in such a manner that each one, from first to last, receives completely 'uncloven' air right in the breast; there can be no suggestion that it is easier for the last than for the first bird to cut a way.

The peculiar order of flight has quite another meaning, viz., to keep the flock together on the long and fatiguing journey; and if we start from this basis, the reasoning thought becomes also evident in the arrangement itself.

Out here by the broad Aarre Water there pass great flights of wild-geese; and in bad weather it may happen that they sit in thousands on the water, resting and waiting.

But even if the flock flies past, there is always uneasiness and noise when they come over Aarre Water. The ranks break, for a time the whole becomes a confused mass, while they all scream and quack at the same time.

Only slowly do they form again and fly southward in long lines, until they shrink to thinner and thinner threads in the gray autumn sky, and their last sound follows them upon the north wind.

Then I always believe that there has been a debate as to whether they should take a little rest down on Aarre Water. There are certainly many old ones who know the place again, and plenty of the young are tender-winged, and would fain sit on the water and dawdle away a half-day's time.

But when it is eventually resolved to fly on without stopping, and the lines again begin to arrange themselves, it has become clear to me that each seeks his own place in the ranks slanting outwards behind the leaders, so that by this means he may be conducted along with the train without being under the necessity of troubling about the way.

If these large, heavy birds were to fly in a cluster for weeks, day and night, separation and confusion would be inevitable. They would get in each other's way every minute with their heavy wings, there would be such a noise that the leader's voice could not be distinguished, and it would be impossible to keep an eye upon him after dark. Besides, over half the number are young birds, who are undertaking this tremendous journey for the first time, and who naturally, at Aarre Water, begin to ask if it be the Nile that they see. Time would be lost, the flock would be broken up, and all the young would perish on the journey, if there were not, in the very disposition of the ranks, something of the beautiful reasoning thought binding them together.

Let us now consider the first bird, who leads the flock—presumably an old experienced gander. He feels an impulse towards the south, but he undoubtedly bends his neck and looks down for known marks in the landscape. That is why the great flocks of geese follow our coast-line southward until the land is lost to view.

But the birds do not look straight forward in the direction of their bills: they look to both sides. Therefore, the bird next to the leader does not follow right behind him in the 'cloven' air, but flies nearly alongside, so that it has the leader in a direct line with its right or left eye at a distance of about two wing-flaps.

And the next bird does the same, and the next; each keeps at the same distance from its fore-bird.

And what each bird sees of its fore-bird are the very whitest feathers of the whole goose, under the wings and towards the tail, and this, in dark nights, is of great assistance to the tired, half-sleeping creatures.

Thus each, except the pilot himself, has a fore-bird's white body in a line with one eye, and more they do not need to trouble about. They can put all their strength into the monotonous work of wing-flapping, as long as they merely keep the one eye half open and see that they have the fore-bird in his place. Thus they know that all is in order, that they are in connection with the train, and with him at the head who knows the way.

If from any cause a disturbance arises, it is soon arranged upon this principle; and when the geese have flown a day or two from the starting-point, such rearrangement is doubtless effected more rapidly and more easily. For I am convinced that they soon come to know one another personally so well that each at once finds his comrade in flight, whom he is accustomed to have before his eye, and therefore they are able to take their fixed places in the ranks as surely and accurately as trained soldiers.

We can all the more readily imagine such a personal acquaintance among animals, as we know that even men learn with comparative ease to distinguish individuals in flocks of the same species of beasts. If we townspeople see a flock of sheep, it presents to us the same ovine face— only with some difference between old and young. But a peasant-woman can at once take out her two or three ewes from the big flock that stands staring by the door—indeed, she can even recognise very young lambs by their faces.

Thus I believe I understand the reason for the wild-goose's order of flight better than when I thought of a plough that 'clove' the air; and, as already stated, it may well be that many have been just as wise long ago. But I venture to wager that the great majority of people have never thought of the matter at all, and I fear that multitudes will think of it somewhat in this fashion: 'What is it to me how those silly geese fly?'

I often revert to the strangely thoughtless manner in which knowledge of animal life is skipped over in the teaching of the young. The rude and wild conception of animals which the clergy teach from the Old Testament seems to cause only deep indifference on the part of the girls, and, in the boys, an unholy desire to ramble about and blaze away with a gun.

Here there has been a shooting as on a drill-ground all the summer, until now only the necessary domestic animals are left. Among the cows, the starlings were shot into tatters, so that they crawled wingless, legless, maimed, into holes in the stone fences to die. If a respectable curlew sat by the water's edge mirroring his long bill, a rascal of a hunter lay behind a stone and sighted; and was there a water-puddle with rushes that could conceal a young duck, there immediately came a fully-armed hero with raised gun. Even English have been here! They had some new kind of guns—people said—that shot as far as you pleased, and round corners and behind knolls. They murdered, I assure you; they laid the district bare as pest and pox! I must stop, for I am growing so angry.

I have had thoughts of applying for a post as inspector of birds in the Westland. I should travel round and teach people about the birds, exhibit the common ones, so that all might have the pleasure of recognising them in Nature; accustom people to listen to their song and cry, and to take an interest in their life, their nests, eggs, and young.

Then I should inflame the peasants against the armed farm-boys, day-labourers, and poachers, and against the sportsmen from town, who stroll around without permission and crack away where they please. It only wants a beginning and a little combination, for the peasant, in his heart, is furious at this senseless shooting.

Perhaps some day, when not a single bird is left, my idea of an inspector may come to be honoured and valued. Would that a godly Storthing* may then succeed in finding a pious and well-recommended man, who can instruct the people in a moral manner as to where the humid Noah accommodated the ostriches in the ark, or what he managed to teach the parrots during the prolonged rainy weather.

We, too, have recently had a deluge. The lakes and the river have risen to the highest winter-marks. But the soil of this blessed place is so sandy that roads and fields remain firm and dry, the water running off and disappearing in a moment.

It has also blown from all quarters, with varying force, for three weeks. We press onward over the plain, and stagger about among the houses, where the gusts of wind rush in quite unexpectedly with loud claps. The fishing-rod has had to be carried against the wind, and the water of the river has risen in the air like smoke.

And the sea, white with wrath, begins to form great heavy breakers far out in many fathoms of water, rolls them in upon the strand, inundates large tracts, and carries away the young wrack-grass and what we call

---

*   Parliament.

'strandkaal'*—all that has grown in summer and gathered a little flying sand around it as tiny fortifications; the sea has washed the beach quite bare again, and fixed its old limits high up among the sand-heaps, where they are strong enough to hold out for the winter.

I have now been here four months to a day, and have seen the corn since it was light-green shoots until now, when it is well secured in the barns,—where there was room. For the crop has been so heavy—not in the memory of man has there been such a year on this coast—that rich stacks of corn are standing on many farms, and the lofts are crammed to the roof-trees.

Inland there is corn yet standing out; it is yellowing on the fields, which are here green and fresh as in the middle of spring.

We have had many fine days; but autumn is the time when Jæderen is seen at its best.

As the landscape nowhere rises to any great height, we always see much sky; and, although we do not really know it, we look quite as much at the magnificent, changeful clouds as at the fine scenery, which recedes far into the distance and is never strikingly prominent.

And all day long, in storm and violent showers, the autumn sky changes, as if in a passionate uproar of wrath and threatenings, alternating with reconciliation and promise, with dark brewing storm-clouds, gleams of sunshine and rainbows, until the evening, when all is gathered together out on the sea to the west.

Then cloud chases cloud, with deep openings between, which shine with a lurid yellow. The great bubbling storm-clouds form a framework around the western sky, while everywhere shoot yellow streaks and red beams, which die away and disappear and are pressed down into the sea, until we see only one sickly yellow stripe of light, far out upon the wave.

---

*   Sea-kale.

Then darkness rolls up from the sea in the west and glides down from the fjelds in the east, lays itself to rest upon the black wastes of heather, and spreads an uncanny covering over the troubled Aarre Waters, which groan and sob and sigh among rushes and stones. A stupendous melancholy rises up from the sea and overflows all things, while the wakeful breakers, ever faithful, murmur their watchman-song the livelong night.

TALES OF TWO COUNTRIES

TRANSLATED FROM THE NORWEGIAN BY
WILLIAM ARCHER

WITH AN INTRODUCTION BY
H. H. BOYESEN

INTRODUCTION.

In June, 1867, about a hundred enthusiastic youths were vociferously celebrating the attainment of the baccalaureate degree at the University of Norway. The orator on this occasion was a tall, handsome, distinguished-looking young man named Alexander Kielland, from the little coast-town of Stavanger. There was none of the crudity of a provincial dither in his manners or his appearance. He spoke with a quiet self-possession and a pithy incisiveness which were altogether phenomenal.

"That young man will be heard from one of these days," was the unanimous verdict of those who listened to his clear-cut and finished sentences, and noted the maturity of his opinions.

But ten years passed, and outside of Stavanger no one ever heard of Alexander Kielland. His friends were aware that he had studied law, spent some winters in France, married, and settled himself as a dignitary in his native town. It was understood that he had bought a large brick and tile factory, and that, as a manufacturer of these useful articles, he bid fair to become a provincial magnate, as his fathers had been before him. People had almost forgotten that great things had been expected of him; and some fancied, perhaps, that he had been spoiled by prosperity. Remembering him, as I did, as the most brilliant and notable personality among my university friends, I began to apply to him Malloch's epigrammatic damnation of the man of whom it was said at twenty that he would do great things, at thirty that he might do great things, and at forty that he might have done great things.

This was the frame of mind of those who remembered Alexander Kielland (and he was an extremely difficult man to forget), when in the year 1879 a modest volume of "novelettes" appeared, bearing his name. It was, to all appearances, a light performance, but it revealed a sense of style which made it, nevertheless, notable. No man had ever written the Norwegian language as this man wrote it. There was a lightness of touch, a perspicacity, an epigrammatic sparkle and occasional flashes of wit, which seemed altogether un-Norwegian. It was obvious that this author was familiar with the best French writers, and had acquired through them that clear and crisp incisiveness of utterance which was supposed, hitherto, to be untransferable to any other tongue.

As regards the themes of these "novelettes" (from which the present collection is chiefly made up), it was remarked at the time of their first appearance that they hinted at a more serious purpose than their style seemed to imply. Who can read, for instance, "Pharaoh" (which in the original is entitled "A Hall Mood") without detecting the revolutionary note which trembles quite audibly through the calm and unimpassioned language? There is, by-the-way, a little touch of melodrama in this tale which is very unusual with Kielland. "Romance and Reality," too, is glaringly at variance with the conventional romanticism in its satirical contributing of the pre-matrimonial and the pos-tmatrimonial view of love and marriage. The same persistent tendency to present the wrong side as well as the right side—and not, as literary good-manners are supposed to prescribe, ignore the former—is obvious in the charming tale "At the Fair," where a little spice of wholesome truth spoils the thoughtlessly festive mood; and the squalor, the want, the envy, hate, and greed which prudence and a regard for business compel the performers to disguise to the public, become the more cruelly visible to the visitors of the little alley-way at the rear of the tents. In "A Good Conscience" the satirical note has a still more serious ring; but the same admirable self-restraint which, next to the power of thought and expression, is the happiest gift an author's fairy godmother can bestow upon him, saves Kielland from saying too much—from enforcing his lesson by marginal comments, *à la*

George Eliot. But he must be obtuse, indeed, to whom this reticence is not more eloquent and effective than a page of philosophical moralizing.

"Hope's Clad in April Green" and "The Battle of Waterloo" (the first and the last tale in the Norwegian edition), are more untinged with a moral tendency than any of the foregoing. The former is a mere *jeu d'esprit*, full of good-natured satire on the calf-love of very young people, and the amusing over-estimate of our importance to which we are all, at that age, peculiarly liable.

As an organist with vaguely-melodious hints foreshadows in his prelude the musical *motifs* which he means to vary and elaborate in his fugue, so Kielland lightly touched in these "novelettes" the themes which in his later works he has struck with a fuller volume and power. What he gave in this little book was it light sketch of his mental physiognomy, from which, perhaps, his horoscope might be cast and his literary future predicted.

Though an aristocrat by birth and training, he revealed a strong sympathy with the toiling masses. But it was a democracy of the brain, I should fancy, rather than of the heart. As I read the book, twelve years ago, its tendency puzzled me considerably, remembering, as I did, with the greatest vividness, the fastidious and elegant personality of the author. I found it difficult to believe that he was in earnest. The book seemed to me to betray the whimsical *sans-culottism* of a man of pleasure who, when the ball is at an end, sits down with his gloves on and philosophizes on the artificiality of civilization and the wholesomeness of honest toil. An indigestion makes him a temporary communist; but a bottle of seltzer presently reconciles him to his lot, and restores the equilibrium of the universe. He loves the people at a distance, can talk prettily about the sturdy son of the soil, who is the core and marrow of the nation, etc.; but he avoids contact with him, and, if chance brings them into contact, he loves him with his handkerchief to his nose.

I may be pardoned for having identified Alexander Kielland with this type with which I am very familiar; and he convinced me, presently, that

I had done him injustice. In his next book, the admirable novel *Garman and Worse*, he showed that his democratic proclivities were something more than a mood. He showed that he took himself seriously, and he compelled the public to take him seriously. The tendency which had only flashed forth here and there in the "novelettes" now revealed its whole countenance. The author's theme was the life of the prosperous bourgeoisie in the western coast-towns; he drew their types with a hand that gave evidence of intimate knowledge. He had himself sprung from one of these rich ship-owning, patrician families, had been given every opportunity to study life both at home and abroad, and had accumulated a fund of knowledge of the world, which he had allowed quietly to grow before making literary drafts upon it. The same Gallic perspicacity of style which had charmed in his first book was here in a heightened degree; and there was, besides, the same underlying sympathy with progress and what is called the ideas of the age. What mastery of description, what rich and vigorous colors Kielland had at his disposal was demonstrated in such scenes as the funeral of Consul Garman and the burning of the ship. There was, moreover, a delightful autobiographical note in the book, particularly in boyish experiences of Gabriel Garman. Such things no man invents, however clever; such material no imagination supplies, however fertile. Except Fritz Reuter's Stavenhagen, I know no small town in fiction which is so vividly and completely individualized, and populated with such living and credible characters. Take, for instance, the two clergymen, Archdeacon Sparre and the Rev. Mr. Martens, and it is not necessary to have lived in Norway in order to recognize and enjoy the faithfulness and the artistic subtlety of these portraits. If they have a dash of satire (which I will not undertake to deny), it is such delicate and well-bred satire that no one, except the originals, would think of taking offence. People are willing, for the sake of the entertainment which it affords, to forgive a little quiet malice at their neighbors' expense. The members of the provincial bureaucracy are drawn with the same firm but delicate touch, and everything has that beautiful air of reality which proves the world akin.

It was by no means a departure from his previous style and tendency which Kielland signalized in his next novel, *Laboring People* (1881). He only emphasizes, as it were, the heavy, serious bass chords in the composite theme which expresses his complex personality, and allows the lighter treble notes to be momentarily drowned. Superficially speaking, there is perhaps a reminiscence of Zola in this book, not in the manner of treatment, but in the subject, which is the corrupting influence of the higher classes upon the lower. There is no denying that in spite of the ability, which it betrays in every line, *Laboring People* is unpleasant reading. It frightened away a host of the author's early admirers by the uncompromising vigor and the glaring realism with which it depicted the consequences of vicious indulgence. It showed no consideration for delicate nerves, but was for all that a clean and wholesome book.

Kielland's third novel, *Skipper Worse*, marked a distinct step in his development. It was less of a social satire and more of a social study. It was not merely a series of brilliant, exquisitely-finished scenes, loosely strung together on a slender thread of narrative, but it was a concise, and well constructed story, full of beautiful scenes and admirable portraits. The theme is akin to that of Daudet's *L'Evangéliste*; but Kielland, as it appears to me, has in this instance outdone his French *confrère* as regards insight into the peculiar character and poetry of the pietistic movement. He has dealt with it as a psychological and not primarily as a pathological phenomenon. A comparison with Daudet suggests itself constantly in reading Kielland. Their methods of workmanship and their attitude towards life have many points in common. The charm of style, the delicacy of touch and felicity of phrase, is in both cases pre-eminent. Daudet has, however, the advantage (or, as he himself asserts, the disadvantage) of working in a flexible and highly-finished language, which bears the impress of the labors of a hundred masters; while Kielland has to produce his effects of style in a poorer and less pliable language, which often pants and groans in its efforts to render a subtle thought. To have polished this tongue and sharpened its capacity for refined and incisive utterance is one—and not the least—of his merits.

Though he has by nature no more sympathy with the pietistic movement than Daudet, Kielland yet manages to get, psychologically, closer to his problem. His pietists are more humanly interesting than those of Daudet, and the little drama which they set in motion is more genuinely pathetic. Two superb figures—the lay preacher, Hans Nilsen, and Skipper Worse—surpass all that the author had hitherto produced, in depth of conception and brilliancy of execution. The marriage of that delightful, profane old sea-dog Jacob Worse, with the pious Sara Torvested, and the attempts of his mother-in-law to convert him, are described, not with the merely superficial drollery to which the subject invites, but with a sweet and delicate humor, which trembles on the verge of pathos.

The beautiful story *Elsie*, which, though published separately, is scarcely a full-grown novel, is intended to impress society with a sense of responsibility for its outcasts. While Björnstjerne Björnson is fond of emphasizing the responsibility of the individual to society, Kielland chooses by preference to reverse the relation. The former (in his remarkable novel *Flags are Flying in City and Harbor*) selects a hero with vicious inherited tendencies, redeemed by wise education and favorable environment; the latter portrays in Elsie a heroine with no corrupt predisposition, destroyed by the corrupting environment which society forces upon those who are born in her circumstances. Elsie could not be good, because the world is so constituted that girls of her kind are not expected to be good. Temptations, perpetually thronging in her way, break down the moral bulwarks of her nature. Resistance seems in vain. In the end there is scarcely one who, having read her story, will have the heart to condemn her.

Incomparably clever is the satire on the benevolent societies, which appear to exist as a sort of moral poultice to tender consciences, and to furnish an officious sense of virtue to its prosperous members. "The Society for the Redemption of the Abandoned Women of St. Peter's Parish" is presided over by a gentleman who privately furnishes subjects for his public benevolence. However, as his private activity is not bounded by the precincts of St. Peter's Parish, within which the society confines its remedial labors, the miserable creatures who might need its aid are sent away uncomforted. The delicious joke of the thing is that "St. Peter's" is a rich and exclusive parish, consisting of what is called "the better classes," and has no "abandoned women." Whatever wickedness there may be in St. Peter's is discreetly veiled, and makes no claim upon public charity. The virtuous horror of the secretary when she hears that the "abandoned woman" who calls upon her for aid has a child, though she is unmarried, is both comic and pathetic. It is the clean, "deserving poor," who understand the art of hypocritical humility—it is these whom the society seeks in vain in St. Peter's Parish.

Still another problem of the most vital consequence Kielland has attacked in his two novels, *Poison* and *Fortuna* (1884). It is, broadly stated, the problem of education. The hero in both books is Abraham Lövdahl, a well-endowed, healthy, and altogether promising boy who, by the approved modern educational process, is mentally and morally crippled, and the germs of what is great and good in him are systematically smothered by that disrespect for individuality and insistence upon uniformity, which are the curses of a small society. The revolutionary discontent which vibrates in the deepest depth of Kielland's nature; the profound and uncompromising radicalism which smoulders under his polished exterior; the philosophical pessimism which relentlessly condemns all the flimsy and superficial reformatory movements of the day, have found expression in the history of the childhood, youth, and manhood of Abraham Lvdahl. In the first place, it is worthy of note that to Kielland the knowledge which is offered in the guise of intellectual nourishment is poison. It is the dry and dusty accumulation of antiquarian lore, which has little or no application to modern life—it is this which the young man of the higher classes is required to assimilate. Apropos of this, let me quote Dr. G. Brandes, who has summed up the tendency of these two novels with great felicity:

"The author has surveyed the generation to which he himself belongs, and after having scanned these wide domains of emasculation, these prairies of spiritual sterility, these vast plains of servility and irresolution, he has addressed to himself the questions: How does a whole generation become such? How was it possible to nip in the bud all that was fertile and eminent? And he has painted a picture of the history of the development of the present generation in the home-life and school-life of Abraham Lövdahl, in order to show from what kind of parentage those most fortunately situated and best endowed have sprung, and what kind of education they received at home and in the school. This is, indeed, a simple and an excellent theme.

"We first see the child led about upon the wide and withered common of knowledge, with the same sort of meagre fodder for all; we see it trained in mechanical memorizing, in barren knowledge concerning things and forms that are dead and gone; in ignorance concerning the life that is, in contempt for it, and in the consciousness of its privileged position, by dint of its possession of this doubtful culture. We see pride strengthened; the healthy curiosity, the desire to ask questions, killed."

We are apt to console ourselves on this side of the ocean with the idea that these social problems appertain only to the effete monarchies of Europe, and have no application with us. But, though I readily admit that the keenest point of this satire is directed against the small States which, by the tyranny of the dominant mediocrity, cripple much that is good and great by denying it the conditions of growth and development, there is yet a deep and abiding lesson in these two novels which applies to modern civilization in general, exposing glaring defects which are no less prevalent here than in the Old World.

Besides being the author of some minor comedies and a full-grown drama ("The Professor"), Kielland has published two more novels, *St.*

John's Eve (1887) and *Snow*. The latter is particularly directed against the orthodox Lutheran clergy, of which the Rev. Daniel Jürges is an excellent specimen. He is, in my opinion, not in the least caricatured; but portrayed with a conscientious desire to do justice to his sincerity. Mr. Jürges is a worthy type of the Norwegian country pope, proud and secure in the feeling of his divine authority, passionately hostile to "the age," because he believes it to be hostile to Christ; intolerant of dissent; a guide and ruler of men, a shepherd of the people. The only trouble in Norway, as elsewhere, is that the people will no longer consent to be shepherded. They refuse to be guided and ruled. They rebel against spiritual and secular authority, and follow no longer the bell-wether with the timid gregariousness of servility and irresolution. To bring the new age into the parsonage of the reverend obscurantist in the shape of a young girl—the *fiancée* of the pastor's son—was an interesting experiment which gives occasion for strong scenes and, at last, for a drawn battle between the old and the new. The new, though not acknowledging itself to be beaten, takes to its heels, and flees in the stormy night through wind and snow. But the snow is moist and heavy; it is beginning to thaw. There is a vague presentiment of spring in the air.

This note of promise and suspense with which the book ends is meant to be symbolic. From Kielland's point of view, Norway is yet wrapped in the wintry winding-sheet of a tyrannical orthodoxy; and all that he dares assert is that the chains of frost and snow seem to be loosening. There is a spring feeling in the air.

This spring feeling is, however, scarcely perceptible in his last book, *Jacob*, which is written in anything but a hopeful mood. It is, rather, a protest against that optimism which in fiction we call poetic justice. The harsh and unsentimental logic of reality is emphasized with a ruthless disregard of rose-colored traditions. The peasant lad Wold, who, like all Norse peasants, has been brought up on the Bible, has become deeply impressed with the story of Jacob, and God's persistent partisanship for him, in spite of his dishonesty and tricky behavior. The story becomes, half unconsciously, the basis of his philosophy of life, and he undertakes to model his career on that of the Biblical hero. He accordingly cheats and steals with a clever moderation, and in a cautious and circumspect manner which defies detection. Step by step he rises in the regard of his fellow-citizens; crushes, with long-headed calculation or with brutal promptness (as it may suit his purpose) all those who stand in his way, and arrives at last at the goal of his desires. He becomes a local magnate, a member of parliament, where he poses as a defender of the simple, old-fashioned orthodoxy, is decorated by the King, and is an object of the envious admiration of his fellow townsmen.

From the pedagogic point of view, I have no doubt that *Jacob* would be classed as an immoral book. But the question of its morality is of less consequence than the question as to its truth. The most modern literature, which is interpenetrated with the spirit of the age, has a way of asking dangerous questions—questions before which the reader, when he perceives their full scope, stands aghast. Our old idyllic faith in the goodness and wisdom of all mundane arrangements has undoubtedly received a shock from which it will never recover. Our attitude towards the universe is changing with the change of its attitude towards us. What the thinking part of humanity is now largely engaged in doing is to readjust itself towards the world and the world towards it. Success is but a complete adaptation to environment; and success is the supreme aim of the modern man. The authors who, by their fearless thinking and speaking, help us towards this readjustment should, in my opinion, whether we choose to accept their conclusions or not, be hailed as benefactors. It is in the ranks of these that Alexander Kielland has taken his place, and now occupies a conspicuous position.

HJALMAR HJORTH BOYESEN.
NEW YORK, May 15, 1891.

PHARAOH.

She had mounted the shining marble steps with without mishap, without labor, sustained by her great beauty and her fine nature alone. She had taken her place in the salons of the rich and great without laying for her admittance with her honor or her good name. Yet no one could say whence she came, though people whispered that it was from the depths.

As a waif of a Parisian faubourg, she had starved through her childhood among surroundings of vice and poverty, such as those only can conceive who know them by experience. Those of us who get our knowledge from books and from hearsay have to strain our imagination in order to form an idea of the hereditary misery of a great city, and yet our most terrible imaginings are apt to pale before the reality.

It had been only a question of time when vice should get its clutches upon her, as a cog-wheel seizes whoever comes too near the machine. After whirling her around through a short life of shame and degradation, it would, with mechanical punctuality, have cast her off into some corner, there to drag out to the end, in sordid obscurity, her caricature of an existence.

But it happened, as it does sometimes happen, that she was "discovered" by a man of wealth and position, one day when, a child of fourteen, she happened to cross one of the better streets. She was on her way to a dark back room in the Rue des Quatre Vents, where she worked with a woman who made artificial flowers.

It was not only her extraordinary beauty that attracted her patron; her movements, her whole bearing, and the expression of her half-formed features, all seemed to him to show that here was an originally fine nature struggling against incipient corruption. Moved by one of the incalculable whims of the very wealthy, he determined to try to rescue the unhappy child.

It was not difficult to obtain control of her, as she belonged to no one. He gave her a name, and placed her in one of the best convent schools. Before long her benefactor had the satisfaction of observing that the seeds of evil died away and disappeared. She developed an amiable, rather indolent character, correct and quiet manners, and a rare beauty.

When she grew up he married her. Their married life was peaceful and pleasant; in spite of the great difference in their ages, he had unbounded confidence in her, and she deserved it.

Married people do not live in such close communion in France as they do with us; so that their claims upon each other are not so great, and their disappointments are less bitter.

She was not happy, but contented. Her character lent itself to gratitude. She did not feel the tedium of wealth; on the contrary, she often took an almost childish pleasure in it. But no one could guess that, for her bearing was always full of dignity and repose. People suspected that there was something questionable about her origin, but as no one could answer questions they left off asking them. One has so much else to think of in Paris.

She had forgotten her past. She had forgotten it just as we have forgotten the roses, the ribbons, and faded letters of our youth—because we never think about them. They lie locked up in a drawer which we never open. And yet, if we happen now and again to cast a glance into this secret drawer, we at once notice if a single one of the roses, or the least bit of ribbon, is wanting. For we remember them all to a nicety; the memories are ran fresh as ever—as sweet as ever, and as bitter.

It was thus she had forgotten her past—locked it up and thrown away the key.

But at night she sometimes dreamed frightful things. She could once more feel the old witch with whom she lived shaking her by the shoulder, and driving her out in the cold mornings to work at her artificial flowers.

Then she would jump up in her bed, and stare out into the darkness in the most deadly fear. But presently she would touch the silk coverlet and the soft pillows; her fingers would follow the rich carvings of her luxurious bed; and while sleepy little child-angels slowly drew aside the heavy dream-curtain, she tasted in deep draughts the peculiar, indescribable well-being we feel when we discover that an evil and horrible dream was a dream and nothing more.

* * * * *

Leaning back among the soft cushions, she drove to the great ball at the Russian ambassador's. The nearer they got to their destination the slower became the pace, until the carriage reached the regular queue, where it dragged on at a foot-pace.

In the wide square in front of the hôtel, brilliantly lighted with torches and with gas, a great crowd of people had gathered. Not only passers-by who had stopped to look on, but more especially workmen, loafers, poor women, and ladies of questionable appearance, stood in serried ranks on both sides of the row of carriages. Humorous remarks and coarse witticisms in the vulgarest Parisian dialect hailed down upon the passing carriages and their occupants.

She heard words which she had not heard for many years, and she blushed at the thought that she was perhaps the only one in this whole long line of carriages who understood these low expressions of the dregs of Paris.

She began to look at the faces around her: it seemed to her as if she knew them all. She knew what they thought, what was passing in each of these tightly-packed heads; and little by little a host of memories streamed in upon her. She fought against them as well as she could, but she was not herself this evening.

She had not, then, lost the key to the secret drawer; reluctantly she drew it out, and the memories overpowered her.

She remembered how often she herself, still almost a child, had devoured with greedy eyes the fine ladies who drove in splendor to balls or theatres; how often she had cried in bitter envy over the flowers she laboriously pieced together to make others beautiful. Here she saw the same greedy eyes, the same inextinguishable, savage envy.

And the dark, earnest men who scanned the equipages with half-contemptuous, half-threatening looks—she knew them all.

Had not she herself, as a little girl, lain in a corner and listened, wide-eyed, to their talk about the injustice of life, the tyranny of the rich, and the rights of the laborer, which he had only to reach out his hand to seize?

She knew that they hated everything—the sleek horses, the dignified coachmen, the shining carriages, and, most of all, the people who sat within them—these insatiable vampires, these ladies, whose ornaments for the night cost more gold than any one of them could earn by the work of a whole lifetime.

And as she looked along the line of carriages, as it dragged on slowly through the crowd, another memory flashed into her mind—a half-forgotten picture from her school-life in the convent.

She suddenly came to think of the story of Pharaoh and his war-chariots following the children of Israel through the Red Sea. She saw the waves, which she had always imagined red as blood, piled up like a wall on both sides of the Egyptians.

Then the voice of Moses sounded. He stretched out his staff over the waters, and the Red Sea waves hurtled together and swallowed up Pharaoh and all his chariots.

She knew that the wall which stood on each side of her was wilder and more rapacious than the waves of the sea; she knew that it needed only a voice, a Moses, to set all this human sea in motion, hurling it irresistibly onward until it should sweep away all the glory of wealth and greatness in its blood-red waves.

Her heart throbbed, and she crouched trembling into the corner of the carriage. But it was not with fear; it was so that those without should not see her—for she was ashamed to meet their eyes.

For the first time in her life, her good-fortune appeared to her in the light of an injustice, a thing to blush for.

Was she in her right place, in this soft-cushioned carriage, among these tyrants and blood-suckers? Should she not rather be out there in the billowing mass, among the children of hate?

Half-forgotten thoughts and feelings thrust up their heads like beasts of prey which have long lain bound. She felt strange and homeless in her glittering life, and thought with a sort of demoniac longing of the horrible places from which she had risen.

She seized her rich lace shawl; there came over her a wild desire to destroy, to tear something to pieces; but at this moment the carriage turned into the gate-way of the hôtel.

The footman tore open the door, and with her gracious smile, her air of quiet, aristocratic distinction, she alighted.

A young attaché rushed forward, and was happy when she took his arm, still more enraptured when he thought he noticed an unusual gleam in her eyes, and in the seventh heaven when he felt her arm tremble.

Full of pride and hope, he led her with sedulous politeness up the shining marble steps.

* * * * *

"'Tell me, *belle dame*, what good fairy endowed you in your cradle with the marvellous gift of transforming everything you touch into something new and strange. The very flower in your hair has a charm, as though it were wet with the fresh morning dew. And when you dance it seems as though the floor swayed and undulated to the rhythm of your footsteps."

The Count was himself quite astonished at this long and felicitous compliment, for as a rule he did not find it easy to express himself coherently. He expected, too, that his beautiful partner would show her appreciation of his effort.

But he was disappointed. She leaned over the balcony, where they were enjoying the cool evening air after the dance, and gazed out over the crowd and the still-advancing carriages. She seemed not to have understood the Count's great achievement; at least he could only hear her whisper the inexplicable word, "Pharaoh."

He was on the point of remonstrating with her, when she turned round, made a step towards the salon, stopped right in front of him, and looked him in the face with great, wonderful eyes, such as the Count had never seen before.

"I scarcely think, Monsieur le Comte, that any good fairy—perhaps not even a cradle—was present at my birth. But in what you say of my flowers and my dancing your penetration has led you to a great discovery. I will tell you the secret of the fresh morning dew which lies on the flowers. It is the tears, Monsieur le Comte, which envy and shame, disappointment and remorse, have wept over them. And if you seem to feel the floor swaying as we dance, that is because it trembles under the hatred of millions."

She had spoken with her customary repose, and with a friendly bow she disappeared into the salon.

* * * * *

The Count remained rooted to the spot. He cast a glance over the crowd outside. It was a right he had often seen, and he had made sundry snore or less trivial witticisms about the "many-headed monster." But to-night it struck him for the first time that this monster was, after all, the most unpleasant neighbor for a palace one could possibly imagine.

Strange and disturbing thoughts whirled in the brain of Monsieur le Comte, where they found plenty of space to gyrate. He was entirely thrown off his balance, and it was not till after the next polka that his placidity returned.

THE PARSONAGE.

It seemed as though the spring would never come. All through April the north wind blew and the nights were frosty. In the middle of the day the sun shone so warmly that a few big flies began to buzz around, and the lark proclaimed, on its word of honor, that it was the height of summer.

But the lark is the most untrustworthy creature under heaven. However much it might freeze at night, the frost was forgotten at the first sunbeam; and the lark soared, singing, high over the heath, until it bethought itself that it was hungry.

Then it sank slowly down in wide circles, singing, and beating time to its song with the flickering of its wings. But a little way from the earth it folded its wings and dropped like a stone down into the heather.

The lapwing tripped with short steps among the hillocks, and nodded its head discreetly. It had no great faith in the lark, and repeated its wary "Bi litt! Bi litt!" [Note: "Wait a bit! Wait a bit!" Pronounced *Bee leet*] A couple of mallards lay snuggling in a marsh-hole, and the elder one was of opinion that spring would not come until we had rain.

Far on into May the meadows were still yellow; only here and there on the sunny leas was there any appearance of green. But if you lay down upon the earth you could see a multitude of little shoots—some thick, others as thin as green darning-needles—which thrust their heads cautiously up through the mould. But the north wind swept so coldly over them that they turned yellow at the tips, and looked as if they would like to creep back again.

But that they could not do; so they stood still and waited, only sprouting ever so little in the midday sun.

The mallard was right; it was rain they wanted. And at last it came—cold in the beginning, but gradually warmer; and when it was over the sun came out in earnest. And now you would scarcely have known it again; it shone warmly, right from the early morning till the late evening, so that the nights were mild and moist.

Then an immense activity set in; everything was behindhand, and had to make up for lost time. The petals burst from the full buds with a little crack, and all the big and little shoots made a sudden rush. They darted out stalks, now to the one side, now to the other, as quickly as though they lay kicking with green legs. The meadows were spangled with flowers and weeds, and the heather slopes towards the sea began to light up.

Only the yellow sand along the shore remained as it was; it has no flowers to deck itself with, and lyme-grass is all its finery. Therefore it piles itself up into great mounds, seen far and wide along the shore, on which the long soft stems sway like a green banner.

There the sand-pipers ran about so fast that their legs looked like a piece of a tooth comb. The sea-gulls walked on the beach, where the waves could sweep over their legs. They held themselves sedately, their heads depressed and their crops protruded, like old ladies in muddy weather.

The sea-pie stood with his heels together, in his tight trousers, his black swallow-tail, and his white waistcoat.

"Til By'n! Til By'n!" he cried [Note: "To Town! To Town!"], and at each cry ho made a quick little bow, so that his coat tails whisked up behind him.

Up in the heather the lapwing flew about flapping her wings. The spring had overtaken her so suddenly that she had not had time to find a proper place for her nest. She had laid her eggs right in the middle of a flat-topped mound. It was all wrong, she knew that quite well; but it could not be helped now.

The lark laughed at it all; but the sparrows were all in a hurry-scurry. They were not nearly ready. Some had not even a nest; others had laid an egg or two; but the majority had sat on the cow-house roof, week out, week in, chattering about the almanac.

Now they were in such a fidget they did not know where to begin. They held a meeting in a great rose-bush, beside the Pastor's garden-fence, all cackling and screaming together. The cock-sparrows ruffled themselves up, so that all their feathers stood straight on end; and then they perked their tails up slanting in the air, so that they looked like little gray balls with a pin stuck in them. So they trundled down the branches and ricochetted away over the meadow.

All of a sudden, two dashed against each other. The rest rushed up, and all the little balls wound themselves into one big one. It rolled forward from under the bush, rose with a great hubbub a little way into the air, then fell in one mass to the earth and went to pieces. And then, without uttering a sound, each of the little balls suddenly went his way, and a moment afterwards there was not a sparrow to be seen about the whole Parsonage.

Little Ansgarius had watched the battle of the sparrows with lively interest. For, in his eyes, it was a great engagement, with charges and cavalry skirmishes. He was reading *Universal History* and the *History of Norway* with his father, and therefore everything that happened about the house assumed a martial aspect in one way or another. When the cows came home in the evening, they ware great columns of infantry advancing; the hens were the volunteer forces, and the cock was Burgomaster Nansen.

Ansgarius was a clever boy, who had all his dates at his fingers' ends; but he had no idea of the meaning of time. Accordingly, he jumbled together Napoleon and Eric Blood-Axe and Tiberius; and on the ships which he saw sailing by in the offing he imagined Tordenskiold doing battle, now with Vikings, and now with the Spanish Armada.

In a secret den behind the summer-house he kept a red broom-stick, which was called Bucephalus. It was his delight to prance about the garden with his steed between his legs, and a flowerstick in his hand.

A little way from the garden there was a hillock with a few small trees upon it. Here he could lie in ambush and keep watch far and wide over the heathery levels and the open sea.

He never failed to descry one danger or another drawing near; either suspicious-looking boats on the beach, or great squadrons of cavalry advancing so cunningly that they looked like nothing but a single horse. But Ansgarius saw through their stealthy tactics; he wheeled Bucephalus about, tore down from the mound and through the garden, and dashed at a gallop into the farm-yard. The hens shrieked as if their last hour had come, and Burgomaster Nansen flew right against the Pastor's study window.

The Pastor hurried to the window, and just caught sight of Bucephalus's tail as the hero dashed round the corner of the cow-house, where he proposed to place himself in a posture of defence.

"That boy is deplorably wild," thought the Pastor. He did not at all like all these martial proclivities. Ansgarius was to be a man of peace, like the Pastor himself; and it was a positive pain to him to see how easily the boy learned and assimilated everything that had to do with war and fighting.

The Pastor would try now and then to depict the peaceful life of the ancients or of foreign nations. But he made little impression. Ansgarius pinned his faith to what he found in his book; and there it was nothing but war after war. The people were all soldiers, the heroes waded in blood; and it was fruitless labor for the Pastor to try to awaken the boy to any sympathy with those whose blood they waded in.

It would occur to the Pastor now and again that it might, perhaps, have been better to have filled the young head from the first with more peaceful ideas and images than the wars of rapacious monarchs or the murders and massacres of our forefathers. But then he remembered that

117

he himself had gone through the same course in his boyhood, so that it must be all right. Ansgarius would be a man of peace none the less—and if not! "Well, everything is in the hand of Providence," said the Pastor confidingly, and set to work again at his sermon.

"You're quite forgetting your lunch to-day, father," said a blond head in the door-way.

"Why, so I am, Rebecca; I'm a whole hour too late," answered the father, and went at once into the dining-room.

The father and daughter sat down at the luncheon-table. Ansgarius was always his own master on Saturdays, when the Pastor was taken up with his sermon.

You would not easily have found two people who suited each other better, or who lived on terms of more intimate friendship, than the Pastor and his eighteen-year-old daughter. She had been motherless from childhood; but there was so much that was womanly in her gentle, even-tempered father, that the young girl, who remembered her mother only as a pale face that smiled on her, felt the loss rather as a peaceful sorrow than as a bitter pain.

And for him she came to fill up more and more, as she ripened, the void that had been left in his soul; and all the tenderness, which at his wife's death had been se clouded in sorrow and longing, now gathered around the young woman who grew up under his eyes; so that his sorrow was assuaged and peace descended upon his mind.

Therefore he was able to be almost like a mother to her. He taught her to look upon the world with his own pure, untroubled eyes. It became the better part of his aim in life to hedge her around and protect her fragile and delicate nature from all the soilures and perturbations which make the world so perplexing, so difficult, and so dangerous an abiding-place.

When they stood together on the hill beside the Parsonage, gazing forth over the surging sea, he would say: "Look, Rebecca! yonder is an image of life—of that life in which the children of this world are tossed to and fro; in which impure passions rock the frail skiff about, to litter the shore at last with its shattered fragments. He only can defy the storm who builds strong bulwarks around a pure heart—at his feet the waves break powerlessly."

Rebecca clung to her father; she felt so safe by his side. There was such a radiance over all he said, that when she thought of the future she seemed to see the path before her bathed in light. For all her questions he had an answer; nothing was too lofty for him, nothing too lowly. They exchanged ideas without the least constraint, almost like brother and sister.

And yet one point remained dark between them. On all other matters she would question her father directly; here she had to go indirectly to work, to get round something which she could never get over.

She knew her father's great sorrow; she knew what happiness he had enjoyed and lost. She followed with the warmest sympathy the varying fortunes of the lovers in the books she read aloud during the winter evenings; her heart understood that love, which brings the highest joy, may also cause the deepest sorrow. But apart from the sorrows of ill-starred love, she caught glimpses of something else—a terrible something which she did not understand. Dark forms would now and then appear to her, gliding through the paradise of love, disgraced and abject. The sacred name of love was linked with the direst shame and the deepest misery. Among people whom she knew, things happened from time to time which she dared not think about; and when, in stern but guarded words, her father chanced to speak of moral corruption, she would shrink, for hours afterwards, from meeting his eye.

He remarked this and was glad. In such sensitive purity had she grown up, so completely had he succeeded in holding aloof from her whatever could disturb her childlike innocence, that her soul was like a shining pearl to which no mire could cling.

He prayed that he might ever keep her thus!

So long as he himself was there to keep watch, no harm should approach her. And if he was called away, he had at least provided her with armor of proof for life, which would stand her in good stead on the day of battle. And a day of battle no doubt would come. He gazed at her with a look which she did not understand, and said with his strong faith, "Well, well, everything is in the hand of Providence!"

"Haven't you time to go for a walk with me to-day, father?" asked Rebecca, when they had finished dinner.

"Why, yes; do you know, I believe it would do me good. The weather is delightful, and I've been so industrious that my sermon is as good as finished."

They stepped out upon the threshold before the main entrance, which faced the other buildings of the farm. There was this peculiarity about the Parsonage, that the high-road, leading to the town, passed right through the farm-yard. The Pastor did not at all like this, for before everything he loved peace and quietness; and although the district was sufficiently out-of-the-way, there was always a certain amount of life on the road which led to the town.

But for Ansgarius the little traffic that came their way was an inexhaustible source of excitement. While the father and daughter stood on the threshold discussing whether they should follow the road or go through the heather down to the beach, the young warrior suddenly came rushing up the hill and into the yard. He was flushed and out of breath, and Bucephalus was going at a hand gallop. Right before the door he reined in his horse with a sudden jerk, so that he made a deep gash in the sand; and swinging his sword, he shouted, "They're coming, they're coming!"

"Who are coming?" asked Rebecca.

"Snorting black chargers and three war chariots full of men-at-arms."

"Rubbish, my boy!" said his father, sternly.

"Three phaetons are coming with townspeople in them," said Ansgarius, and dismounted with an abashed air.

"Let us go in, Rebecca," said the Pastor, turning.

But at the same moment the foremost horses came at a quick pace over the brow of the hill. They were not exactly snorting chargers; yet it was a pretty sight as carriage after carriage came into view in the sunshine, full of merry faces and lively colors. Rebecca could not help stopping.

On the back seat of the foremost carriage sat an elderly gentleman and a buxom lady. On the front seat she saw a young lady; and just as they entered the yard, a gentleman who sat at her side stood up, and, with a word of apology to the lady on the back seat, turned and looked forward past the driver. Rebecca gazed at him without knowing what she was doing.

"How lovely it is here!" cried the young man.

For the Parsonage lay on the outermost slope towards the sea, so that the vast blue horizon suddenly burst upon you as you entered the yard.

The gentleman on the back seat leaned a little forward. "Yes, it's very pretty here," he said; "I'm glad that you appreciate our peculiar scenery, Mr. Lintzow."

At the same moment the young man's glance met Rebecca's, and she instantly lowered her eyes. But he stopped the driver, and cried, "Let us remain here!"

"Hush!" said the older lady, with a low laugh. "This won't do, Mr. Lintzow; this is the Parsonage."

"It doesn't matter," cried the young man, merrily, as he jumped out of the carriage. "I say," he shouted backward towards the other carriages, "sha'n't we rest here?"

"Yes, yes," came the answer in chorus; and the merry party began at once to alight.

But now the gentleman on the back seat rose, and said, seriously: "No, no, my friends! this really won't do! It's out of the question for us to descend upon the clergyman, whom we don't know at all. It's only ten minutes' drive to the district judge's, and there they are in the habit of receiving strangers."

He was on the point of giving orders to drive on, when the Pastor appeared in the door-way, with a friendly bow. He knew Consul Hartvig by sight—the leading man of the town.

"If your party will make the best of things here, it will be a great pleasure to me; and I think I may say that, so far as the view goes—"

"Oh no, my dear Pastor, you're altogether too kind; it's out of the question for us to accept your kind invitation, and I must really beg you to excuse these young madcaps," said Mrs. Hartvig, half in despair when she saw her youngest son, who had been seated in the last carriage, already deep in a confidential chat with Ansgarius.

"But I assure you, Mrs. Hartvig," answered the Pastor, smiling, "that so pleasant an interruption of our solitude would be most welcome both to my daughter and myself."

Mr. Lintzow opened the carriage-door with a formal bow, Consul Hartvig looked at his wife and she at him, the Pastor advanced and renewed his invitation, and the end was that, with half-laughing reluctance, they alighted and suffered the Pastor to usher them into the spacious garden-room.

Then came renewed excuses and introductions. The party consisted of Consul Hartvig's children and some young friends of theirs, the picnic having been arranged in honor of Max Lintzow, a friend of the eldest son of the house, who was spending some days as the Consul's guest.

"My daughter Rebecca," said the Pastor, presenting her, "who will do the best our humble house-keeping permits."

"No, no, I protest, my dear Pastor," the lively Mrs. Hartvig interrupted him eagerly, "this is going too far! Even if this incorrigible Mr. Lintzow and my crazy sons have succeeded in storming your house and home, I won't resign the last remnants of my authority. The entertainment shall most certainly be my affair. Off you go, young men," she said, turning to her sons, "and unpack the carriages. And you, my dear child, must by all means go and amuse yourself with the young people; just leave the catering to me; I know all about that."

And the kind-hearted woman looked with her honest gray eyes at her host's pretty daughter, and patted her on the cheek.

How nice that felt! There was a peculiar coziness in the touch of the comfortable old lady's soft hand. The tears almost rose to Rebecca's eyes; she stood as if she expected that the strange lady would put her arms round her neck and whisper to her something she had long waited to hear.

But the conversation glided on. The young people, with ever-increasing glee, brought all sorts of strange parcels out of the carriages. Mrs. Hartvig threw her cloak upon a chair and set about arranging things as best she could. But the young people, always with Mr. Lintzow at their head, seemed determined to make as much confusion as possible. Even the Pastor was infected by their merriment, and to Rebecca's unspeakable astonishment she saw her own father, in complicity with Mr. Lintzow, biding a big paper parcel under Mrs. Hartvig's cloak.

At last the racket became too much for the old lady. "My dear Miss Rebecca," she exclaimed, "have you not any show-place to exhibit in the neighborhood—the farther off the better—so that I might get these crazy beings off my hands for a little while?"

"There's a lovely view from the King's Knoll; and then there's the beach and the sea."

"Yes, let's go down to the sea!" cried Max Lintzow.

"That's just what I want," said the old lady. "If you can relieve me of *him* I shall be all right, for he is the worst of them all."

"If Miss Rebecca will lead the way, I will follow wherever she pleases," said the young man, with a bow.

Rebecca blushed. Nothing of that sort had ever been said to her before. The handsome young man made her a low bow, and his words had such a ring of sincerity. But there was no time to dwell upon this impression; the whole merry troop were soon out of the house, through the garden, and, with Rebecca and Lintzow at their head, making their way up to the little height which was called the King's Knoll.

Many years ago a number of antiquities had been dug up on the top of the Knoll, and one of the Pastor's predecessors in the parish had planted some hardy trees upon the slopes. With the exception of a rowan-tree, and a walnut-avenue in the Parsonage garden, these were the only trees to be found for miles round on the windy slopes facing the open sea. In spite of storms and sand-drifts, they had, in the course of time, reached something like the height of a man, and, turning their bare and gnarled stems to the north wind, like a bent back, they stretched forth their long, yearning arms towards the south. Rebecca's mother had planted some violets among them.

"Oh, how fortunate!" cried the eldest Miss Hartvig; "here are violets! Oh, Mr. Lintzow, do pick me a bouquet of them for this evening!"

The young man, who had been exerting himself to hit upon the right tone in which to converse with Rebecca, fancied that the girl started at Miss Frederica's words.

"You are very fond of the violets?" he said, softly.

She looked up at him in surprise; how could he possibly know that?

"Don't you think, Miss Hartvig, that it would be better to pick the flowers just as we are starting, so that they may keep fresher?"

"As you please," she answered, shortly.

"Let's hope she'll forget all about it by that time," said Max Lintzow to himself, under his breath.

But Rebecca heard, and wondered what pleasure he could find in protecting her violets, instead of picking them for that handsome girl.

After they had spent some time in admiring the limitless prospect, the party left the Knoll and took a foot-path downward towards the beach.

On the smooth, firm sand, at the very verge of the sea, the young people strolled along, conversing gayly. Rebecca was at first quite confused. It seemed as though these merry towns-people spoke a language she did not understand. Sometimes she thought they laughed at nothing; and, on the other hand, she herself often could not help laughing at their cries of astonishment and their questions about everything they saw.

124

But gradually she began to feel at her ease among these good-natured, kindly people; the youngest Miss Hartvig even put her arm around her waist as they walked. And then Rebecca, too, thawed; she joined in their laughter, and said what she had to say as easily and freely as any of the others. It never occurred to her to notice that the young men, and especially Mr. Lintzow, were chiefly taken up with her; and the little pointed speeches which this circumstance called forth from time to time were as meaningless for her as much of the rest of the conversation.

They amused themselves for some time with running down the shelving beach every time the wave receded, and then rushing up again when the next wave came. And great was the glee when one of the young men was overtaken, or when a larger wave than usual sent its fringe of foam right over the slope, and forced the merry party to beat a precipitate retreat.

"Look! Mamma's afraid that we shall be too late for the ball," cried Miss Hartvig, suddenly; and they now discovered that the Consul and Mrs. Hartvig and the Pastor were standing like three windmills on the Parsonage hill, waving with pocket handkerchiefs and napkins.

They turned their faces homeward. Rebecca took them by a short cut over the morass, not reflecting that the ladies from the town could not jump from tuft to tuft as she could. Miss Frederica, in her tight skirt, jumped short, and stumbled into a muddy hole. She shrieked and cried piteously for help, with her eyes fixed upon Lintzow.

"Look alive, Henrik!" cried Max to Hartvig junior, who was nearer at hand; "why don't you help your sister?"

Miss Frederica extricated herself without help, and the party proceeded.

The table was laid in the garden, along the wall of the house; and although the spring was so young, it was warm enough in the sunshine. When they had all found seats, Mrs. Hartvig cast a searching glance over the table.

"Why—why—surely there's something wanting! I'm convinced I saw the house-keeper wrapping up a black grouse this morning. Frederica, my dear, don't you remember it?"

"Excuse me, mother, you know that housekeeping is not at all in my department."

Rebecca looked at her father, and so did Lintzow; the worthy Pastor pulled a face upon which even Ansgarius could read a confession of crime.

"I can't possibly believe," began Mrs. Hartvig, "that you, Pastor, have been conspiring with—" And then he could not help laughing and making a clean breast of it, amid great merriment, while the boys in triumph produced the parcel with the game. Every one was in the best possible humor. Consul Hartvig was delighted to find that their clerical host could join in a joke, and the Pastor himself was in higher spirits than he had been in for many a year.

In the course of the conversation some one happened to remark that although the arrangements might be countrified enough, the viands were too town-like; "No country meal is complete without thick milk." [Note: Milk allowed to stand until it has thickened to the consistency of curds, and then eaten, commonly with sugar.]

Rebecca at once rose and demanded leave to bring a basin of milk; and, paying no attention to Mrs. Hartvig's protests, she left the table.

"Let me help you, Miss Rebecca," cried Max, and ran after her.

"That is a lively young man," said the Pastor.

"Yes, isn't he?" answered the Consul, "and a deuced good business man into the bargain. He has spent several years abroad, and now his father has taken him into partnership."

"He's perhaps a little unstable," said Mrs. Hartvig, doubtfully.

"Yes, he is indeed," sighed Miss Frederica.

The young man followed Rebecca through the suite of rooms that led to the dairy. At bottom, she did not like this, although the dairy was her pride; but he joked and laughed so merrily that she could not help joining in the laughter.

She chose a basin of milk upon the upper shelf, and stretched out her arms to reach it.

"No, no, Miss Rebecca, it's too high for you!" cried Max; "let me hand it down to you." And as he said so he laid his hand upon hers.

Rebecca hastily drew back her hand. She knew that her face had flushed, and she almost felt as if she must burst into tears.

Then he said, softly and earnestly, lowering his eyes, "Pray, pardon me, Miss Rebecca. I feel that my behavior must seem far too light and frivolous to such a woman as you; but I should be sorry that you should think of me as nothing but the empty coxcomb I appear to be. Merriment, to many people, is merely a cloak for their sufferings, and there are some who laugh only that they may not weep."

At the last words he looked up. There was something so mournful, and at the same time so reverential, in his glance, that Rebecca all of a sudden felt as if she had been unkind to him. She was accustomed to reach things down from the upper shelf, but when she again stretched out her hands for the basin of milk, she let her arms drop, and said, "No, perhaps it *is* too high for me, after all."

A faint smile passed over his face as he took the basin and carried it carefully out; she accompanied him and opened the doors for him. Every time he passed her she looked closely at him. His collar, his necktie, his coat—everything was different from her father's, and he carried with him a peculiar perfume which she did not know.

When they came to the garden door, he stopped for an instant, and looked up with a melancholy smile: "I must take a moment to recover my expression of gayety, so that no one out there may notice anything."

Then he passed out upon the steps with a joking speech to the company at the table, and she heard their laughing answers; but she herself remained behind in the garden-room.

Poor young man! how sorry she was for him; and how strange that she of all people should be the only one in whom he confided. What secret sorrow could it be that depressed him? Perhaps he, too, had lost his mother. Or could it be something still mote terrible? How glad she would be if only she could help him.

When Rebecca presently came out he was once more the blithest of them all. Only once in a while, when he looked at her, his eyes seemed again to assume that melancholy, half-beseeching expression; and it cut her to the heart when he laughed at the same moment.

At last came the time for departure; there was hearty leave-taking on both sides. But as the last of the packing was going on, and in the general confusion, while every one was finding his place in the carriages, or seeking a new place for the homeward journey, Rebecca slipped into the house, through the rooms, out into the garden, and away to the King's Knoll. Here she seated herself in the shadow of the trees, where the violets grew, and tried to collect her thoughts.

—"What about the violets, Mr. Lintzow?" cried Miss Frederica, who had already taken her seat in the carriage.

The young man had for some time been eagerly searching for the daughter of the house. He answered absently, "I'm afraid it's too late."

But a thought seemed suddenly to strike him. "Oh, Mrs. Hartvig," he cried, "will you excuse me for a couple of minutes while I fetch a bouquet for Miss Frederica?"

—Rebecca heard rapid steps approaching; she thought it could be no one but he.

"Ah, are you here, Miss Rebecca? I have come to gather some violets."

She turned half away from him and began to pluck the flowers.

"Are these flowers for me?" he asked, hesitatingly.

"Are they not for Miss Frederica?"

"Oh no, let them be for me!" he besought, kneeling at her side.

128

Again his voice had such a plaintive ring in it—almost like that of a begging child.

She handed him the violets without looking up. Then he clasped her round the waist and held her close to him. She did not resist, but closed her eyes and breathed heavily. Then she felt that he kissed her—over and over again—on the eyes, on the mouth, meanwhile calling her by her name, with incoherent words, and then kissing her again. They called to him from the garden; he let her go and ran down the mound. The horses stamped, the young man sprang quickly into the carriage, and it rolled away. But as he was closing the carriage door he was so maladroit as to drop the bouquet; only a single violet remained in his hand.

"I suppose it's no use offering you this one, Miss Frederica?" he said.

"No, thanks; you may keep that as a memento of your remarkable dexterity," answered Miss Hartvig; he was in her black books.

"Yes—you are right—I shall do so," answered Max Lintzow, with perfect composure.

—Next day, after the ball, when he put on his morning-coat, he found a withered violet in the button-hole. He nipped off the flower with his fingers, and drew out the stalk from beneath.

"By-the-bye," he said, smiling to himself in the mirror, "I had almost forgotten *her!*"

In the afternoon he went away, and then he *quite* forgot her.

The summer came with warm days and long, luminous nights. The smoke of the passing steamships lay in long black streaks over the peaceful sea. The sailing-ships drifted by with flapping sails and took nearly a whole day to pass out of sight.

It was some time before the Pastor noticed any change in his daughter. But little by little he became aware that Rebecca was not flourishing that summer. She had grown pale, and kept much to her own room. She scarcely ever came into the study, and at last he fancied that she avoided him.

Then he spoke seriously to her, and begged her to tell him if she was ill, or if mental troubles of any sort had affected her spirits.

But she only wept, and answered scarcely a word.

After this conversation, however, things went rather better. She did not keep so much by herself, and was oftener with her father. But the old ring was gone from her voice, and her eyes were not so frank as of old.

The Doctor came, and began to cross-question her. She blushed as red as fire, and at last burst into such a paroxysm of weeping, that the old gentleman left her room and went down to the Pastor in his study.

"Well, Doctor, what do you think of Rebecca?"

"Tell me now, Pastor," began the Doctor, diplomatically, "has your daughter gone through any violent mental crisis—hm—any—"

"Temptation, do you mean?"

"No, not exactly. Has she not had any sort of heartache? Or, to put it plainly, any love-sorrow?"

The Pastor was very near feeling a little hurt. How could the Doctor suppose that his own Rebecca, whose heart was as an open book to him, could or would conceal from her father any sorrow of such a nature! And, besides—! Rebecca was really not one of the girls whose heads were full of romantic dreams of love. And as she was never away from his side, how could she—? "No, no, my dear Doctor! That diagnosis does you little credit!" the Pastor concluded, with a tranquil smile.

"Well, well, there's no harm done!" said the old Doctor, and wrote a prescription which was at least innocuous. He knew of no simples to cure love-sorrows; but in his heart of hearts he held to his diagnosis.

The visit of the Doctor had frightened Rebecca. She now kept still stricter watch upon herself, and redoubled her exertions to seem as before. For no one must suspect what had happened: that a young man, an utter stranger, had held her in his arms and kissed her—over and over again!

As often as she realized this the blood rushed to her cheeks. She washed herself ten times in the day, yet it seemed she could never be clean.

For what was it that had happened? Was it of the last extremity of shame? Was she now any better than the many wretched girls whose errors she had shuddered to think of, and had never been able to understand? Ah, if there were only any one she could question! If she could only unburden her mind of all the doubt and uncertainty that tortured her; learn clearly what she had done; find out if she had still the right to look her father in the face—or if she were the most miserable of all sinners.

Her father often asked her if she could not confide to him what was weighing on her mind; for he felt that she was keeping something from him. But when she looked into his clear eyes, into his pure open face, it seemed impossible, literally impossible, to approach that terrible impure point and she only wept. She thought sometimes of that good Mrs. Hartvig's soft hand; but she was a stranger, and far away. So she must e'en fight out her fight in utter solitude, and so quietly that no one should be aware of it.

And he, who was pursuing his path through life with so bright a countenance and so heavy a heart! Should she ever see him again? And if she were ever to meet him, where should she hide herself? He was an inseparable part of all her doubt and pain; but she felt no bitterness, no resentment towards him. All that she suffered bound her closer to him, and he was never out of her thoughts.

In the daily duties of the household Rebecca was as punctual and careful as ever. But in everything she did he was present to her memory. Innumnerable spots in the house and garden recalled him to her thoughts; she met him in the door-ways; she remembered where he stood when first he spoke to her. She had never been at the King's Knoll since that day; it was there that he had clasped her round the waist, and—kissed her.

The Pastor was full of solicitude about his daughter; but whenever the Doctor's hint occurred to him he shook his head, half angrily. How could he dream that a practised hand, with a well-worn trick of the fence, could pierce the armor of proof with which he had provided her?

If the spring had been late, the autumn was early.

One fine warm summer evening it suddenly began to rain. The next day it was still raining; and it poured incessantly, growing ever colder and colder, for eleven days and nights on end. At last it cleared up; but the next night there were four degrees of frost. [Note: Réaumur.]

On the bushes and trees the leaves hung glued together after the long rain; and when the frost had dried them after its fashion, they fell to the ground in multitudes at every little puff of wind.

The Pastor's tenant was one of the few that had got their corn in; and now it had to be threshed while there was water for the machine. The little brook in the valley rushed foaming along, as brown as coffee, and all the men on the farm were taken up with tending the machine and carting corn and straw up and down the Parsonage hill.

The farm-yard was bestrewn with straw, and when the wind swirled in between the houses it seized the oat-straws by the head, raised them on end, and set them dancing along like yellow spectres. It was the juvenile autumn wind trying its strength; not until well on in the winter, when it has full-grown lungs, does it take to playing with tiles and chimney-pots.

A sparrow sat crouched together upon the dog-kennel; it drew its head down among its feathers, blinked its eyes, and betrayed no interest in anything. But in reality it noted carefully where the corn was deposited. In the great sparrow-battle of the spring it had been in the very centre of the ball, and had pecked and screamed with the best of them. But it had sobered down since then; it thought of its wife and children, and reflected how good it was to have something in reserve against the winter.

—Ansgarius looked forward to the winter—to perilous expeditions through the snow-drifts and pitch-dark evenings with thundering breakers. He already turned to account the ice which lay on the puddles after the frosty nights, by making all his tin soldiers, with two brass cannons, march out upon it. Stationed upon an overturned bucket, he watched the ice giving way, little by little, until the whole army was immersed, and only the wheels of the cannons remained visible. Then he shouted, "Hurrah!" and swung his cap.

132

"What are you shouting about?" asked the Pastor, who happened to pass through the farm-yard.

"I'm playing at Austerlitz!" answered Ansgarius, beaming.

The father passed on, sighing mournfully; he could not understand his children.

—Down in the garden sat Rebecca on a bench in the sun. She looked out over the heather, which was in purple flower, while the meadows were putting on their autumn pallor.

The lapwings were gathering in silence, and holding flying drills in preparation for their journey; wad all the strand birds were assembling, in order to take flight together. Even the lark had lost its courage and was seeking convoy voiceless and unknown among the other gray autumn birds. But the sea-gull stalked peaceably about, protruding its crop; it was not under notice to quit.

The air was so still and languid and hazy. All sounds and colors were toning down against the winter, and that vas very pleasant to her.

She was weary, and the long dead winter would suit her well. She knew that her winter would be longer than all the others, and she began to shrink from the spring.

Then everything would awaken that the winter had laid to sleep. The birds would come back and sing the old songs with new voices; and upon the King's Knoll her mother's violets would peer forth afresh in azure clusters; it was there that he had clasped her round the waist and kissed her—over and over again.

THE PEAT MOOR.

High over the heathery wastes flew a wise old raven.

He was bound many miles westward, right out to the sea-coast, to unearth a sow's ear which he had buried in the good times.

It was now late autumn, and food was scarce.

When you see one raven, says Father Brehm, you need only look round to discover a second.

But you might have looked long enough where this wise old raven came flying; he was, and remained, alone. And without troubling about anything or uttering a sound, he sped on his strong coal-black wings through the dense rain-mist, steering due west.

But as he flew, evenly and meditatively, his sharp eyes searched the landscape beneath, and the old bird was full of chagrin.

Year by year the little green and yellow patches down there increased in number and size; rood after rood was cut out of the heathery waste, little houses sprang up with red-tiled roofs and low chimneys breathing oily peat-reek. Men and their meddling everywhere!

He remembered how, in the days of his youth—several winters ago, of course—this was the very place for a wide-awake raven with a family: long, interminable stretches of heather, swarms of leverets and little birds, eider-ducks on the shore with delicious big eggs, and tidbits of all sorts abundant as heart could desire.

Now he saw house upon house, patches of yellow corn-land and green meadows; and food was so scarce that a gentlemanly old raven had to fly miles and miles for a paltry sow's ear.

Oh, those men! those men! The old bird knew them.

He had grown up among men, and, what was more, among the aristocracy. He had passed his childhood and youth at the great house close to the town.

But now, whenever he passed over the house, he soared high into the air, so as not to be recognized. For when he saw a female figure down in the garden, he thought it was the young lady of the house, wearing powdered hair and a white head-dress; whereas it was in reality her daughter, with snow-white curls and a widow's cap.

Had he enjoyed his life among the aristocracy? Oh, that's as you please to look at it. There was plenty to eat and plenty to learn; but, after all, it was captivity. During the first years his left wing was clipped, and afterwards, as his old master used to say, he was upon *parole d'honneur*.

This parole he had broken one spring when a glossy-black young she-raven happened to fly over the garden.

Some time afterwards—a few winters had slipped away—he came back to the house. But some strange boys threw stones at him; the old master and the young lady were not at home.

"No doubt they are in town," thought the old raven; and he came again some time later. But he met with just the same reception.

Then the gentlemanly old bird—for in the meantime he had grown old—felt hurt, and now he flew high over the house. He would have nothing more to do with men, and the old master and the young lady might look for him as long as they pleased. That they did so he never doubted.

And he forgot all that he had learned, both the difficult French words which the young lady taught him in the drawing-room, and the incomparably easier expletives which he had picked up on his own account in the servants' hall.

Only two human sounds clung to his memory, the last relics of his vanished learning. When he was in a thoroughly good humor, he would often say, "Bonjour, madame!" But when he was angry, he shrieked, "Go to the devil!"

Through the dense rain-mist he sped swiftly and unswervingly; already he saw the white wreath of surf along the coast. Then he descried a great black waste stretching out beneath him. It was a peat moor.

It was encircled with farms on the heights around; but on the low plain—it must have been over a mile [Note: One Norwegian mile is equal to seven English miles.] long—there was no trace of human meddling; only a few stacks of peat on the outskirts, with black hummocks and gleaming water-holes between them.

"Bonjour, madame!" cried the old raven, and began to wheel in great circles over the moor. It looked so inviting that he settled downward, slowly and warily, and alighted upon a tree-root in the midst of it.

Here it was just as in the old days-a silent wilderness. On some scattered patches of drier soil there grew a little short heather and a few clumps of rushes. They were withered; but on their stiff stems there still hung one or two tufts—black, and sodden by the autumn rain. For the most part the soil was fine, black, and crumbling—wet and full of water-holes. Gray and twisted tree-roots stuck up above the surface, interlaced like a gnarled net-work.

The old raven well understood all that he saw. There had been trees here in the old times, before even his day.

The wood had disappeared; branches, leaves, everything was gone. Only the tangled roots remained, deep down in the soft mass of black fibres and water.

But further than this, change could not possibly go; so it must endure, and here, at any rate, men would have to stint their meddling.

The old bird held himself erect. The farms lay so far away that he felt securely at home, here in the middle of the bottomless morass. One relic, at least, of antiquity must remain undisturbed. He smoothed his glossy black feathers, and said several times, "Bonjour, madame!"

But down from the nearest farm came a couple of men with a horse and cart; two small boys ran behind. They took a crooked course among the hummocks, but made as though to cross the morass.

"They must soon stop," thought the raven.

But they drew nearer and nearer; the old bird turned his head uneasily from side to side; it was strange that they should venture so far out.

At last they stopped, and the men set to work with spades and axes. The raven could see that they were struggling with a huge root which they wanted to loosen.

"They will soon tire of that," thought the raven.

But they did not tire, they hacked with their axes—the sharpest the raven had ever seen—they dug and hauled, and at last they actually got the huge stem turned over on its side, so that the whole tough net-work of roots stood straight up in the air.

The small boys wearied of digging canals between the water-holes. "Look at that great big crow over there," said one of them.

They armed themselves with a stone in each hand, and came sneaking forward behind the hummocks.

The raven saw them quite well. But that was not the worst thing it saw.

Not even out on the morass was antiquity to be left in peace. He had now seen that even the gray tree-roots, older than the oldest raven, and firmly inwoven into the deep, bottomless morass—that even they had to yield before the sharp axes.

And when the boys had got so near that they were on the point of opening fire, he raised his heavy wings and soared aloft.

But as he rose into the air and looked down upon the toiling men and the stupid boys, who stood gaping at him with a stone in each hand, a great wrath seized the old bird.

He swooped down upon the boys like an eagle, and while his great wings flounced about their ears, he shrieked in a terrible voice, "Go to the devil!"

The boys gave a yell and threw themselves down upon the ground. When they presently ventured to look up again, all was still and deserted as before. Far away, a solitary blackbird winged to the westward.

But till they grew to be men—aye, even to their dying day—they were firmly convinced that the Evil One himself had appeared to them out on the black morass, in the form of a monstrous black bird with eyes of fire.

But it was only an old raven, flying westward to unearth a sow's ear which it had buried.

"HOPE'S CLAD IN APRIL GREEN."

"You're kicking up the dust!" cried Cousin Hans.

Ola did not hear.

"He's quite as deaf as Aunt Maren," thought Hans. "You're kicking up the dust!" he shouted, louder.

"Oh, I beg your pardon!" said Cousin Ola, and lifted his feet high in air at every step. Not for all the world would he do anything to annoy his brother; he had too much on his conscience already.

Was he not at this very moment thinking of her whom he knew that his brother loved? And was it not sinful of him to be unable to conquer a passion which, besides being a wrong towards his own brother, was so utterly hopeless?

Cousin Ola took himself sternly to task, and while he kept to the other side of the way, so as not to make a dust, he tried with all his might to think of the most indifferent things. But however far away his thoughts might start, they always returned by the strangest short-cuts to the forbidden point, and began once more to flutter around it, like moths around a candle.

The brothers, who were paying a holiday visit to their uncle, the Pastor, were now on their way to the Sheriff's house, where there was to be a dancing-party for young people. There were many students paying visits in the neighborhood, so that these parties passed like an epidemic from house to house.

Cousin Hans was thus in his very element; he sang, he danced, he was entertaining from morning to night; and if his tone had been a little sharp when he declared that Ola was kicking up the dust, it was really because of his annoyance at being unable, by any means, to screw his brother up to the same pitch of hilarity.

We already know what was oppressing Ola. But even under ordinary circumstances he was more quiet and retiring than his brother. He danced "like a pair of nut-crackers," said Hans; he could not sing at all (Cousin Hans even declared that his speaking voice was monotonous and unsympathetic); and, in addition to all this, he was rather absent and ill-at-ease in the society of ladies.

As they approached the Sheriff's house, they heard a carriage behind them.

"That's the Doctor's people," said Hans, placing himself in position for bowing; for the beloved one was the daughter of the district physician.

"Oh, how lovely she is—in light pink!" said Cousin Hans.

Cousin Ola saw at once that the beloved one was in light green; but he dared not say a word lest he should betray himself by his voice, for his heart was in his throat.

The carriage passed at full speed; the young men bowed, and the old Doctor cried out, "Come along!"

"Why, I declare, that was she in light green!" said Cousin Hans; he had barely had time to transfer his burning glance from the light-pink frock to the light-green. "But wasn't she lovely, Ola?"

"Oh yes," answered Ola with an effort.

"What a cross-grained being you are!" exclaimed Hans, indignantly. "But even if you're devoid of all sense for female beauty, I think you might at least show more interest in—in your brother's future wife."

"If you only knew how she interests me," thought the nefarious Ola, hanging his head.

But meanwhile this delightful meeting had thrown Hans into an ecstatic mood of amorous bliss; he swung his stick, snapped his fingers, and sang at the pitch of his voice.

140

As he thought of the fair one in the light-green frock—fresh as spring, airy as a butterfly, he called it—the refrain of an old ditty rose to his lips, and he sang it with great enjoyment:

"Hope's clad in April green—
　　Trommelommelom, trommelommelom,
Tender it's vernal sheen—
　　Trommelommelom, trommelommelom."

This verse seemed to him eminently suited to the situation, and he repeated it over and over again—now in the waltz-time of the old melody, now as a march, and again as a serenade—now in loud, jubilant tones, and then half whispering, as if he were confiding his love and his hope to the moon and the silent groves.

Cousin Ola was almost sick; for, great as was his respect for his brother's singing, he became at last so dog-tired of this April-green hope and this eternal "Trommelommelom" that it was a great relief to him when they at last arrived at the Sheriff's.

The afternoon passed as it always does on such occasions; they all enjoyed themselves mightily. For most of them were in love, and those who were not found almost a greater pleasure in keeping an eye upon those who were.

Some one proposed a game of "La Grace" in the garden. Cousin Hans rushed nimbly about and played a thousand pranks, threw the game into confusion, and paid his partner all sorts of attentions.

Cousin Ola stood at his post and gave his whole mind to his task; he caught the ring and sent it off again with never failing precision. Ola would have enjoyed himself, too, if only his conscience had not so bitterly upbraided him for his nefarious love for his brother's "future wife."

When the evening began to grow cool the party went in-doors, and the dancing began.

Ola did not dance much at any time, but to-day he was not at all in the humor. He occupied himself in observing Hans, who spent the whole evening in worshipping his lady-love. A spasm shot through Ola's heart when he saw the light-green frock whirl away in his brother's arms, and it seemed to him that they danced every dance together.

At last came the time for breaking up. Most of the older folks had already taken their departure in their respective carriages, the young people having resolved to see each other home in the delicious moonlight.

But when the last galop was over, the hostess would not hear of the young ladies going right out into the evening air, while they were still warm with dancing. She therefore decreed half an hour for cooling down, and, to occupy this time in the pleasantest manner, she begged Cousin Hans to sing a little song.

He was ready at once, he was not one of those foolish people who require pressing; he knew quite well the value of his talent.

There was, however, this peculiarity about Hans's singing, or rather about its reception, that opinion was more than usually divided as to its merits. By three persons in the world his execution was admired as something incomparable. These three persons were, first, Cousin Ola, then Aunt Maren, and lastly Cousin Hans himself. Then there was a large party which thought it great fun to hear Cousin Hans sing. "He always makes something out of it." But lastly there came a few evil-disposed people who asserted that he could neither sing nor play.

It was with respect to the latter point, the accompaniment, that Cousin Ola always cherished a secret reproach against his brother—the only shadow upon his admiration for him.

He knew how much labor it had cost both Hans himself and his sisters to get him drilled in these accompaniments, especially in the three minor chords with which he always finished up, and which he practised beforehand every time he went to a party.

So, when he saw his brother seated at the piano, letting his fingers run lightly and carelessly over the key-board, and then looking up to the ceiling and muttering, "What key is it in again?" as if he were searching for the right one, a shiver always ran through Cousin Ola. For he knew that Hans had mastered three accompaniments, and no more—one minor and two major.

And when the singer, before rising from the piano, threw in these three carefully-practised minor chords so lightly, and with such an impromptu air, as if his fingers had instinctively chanced upon them, then Ola shook his head and said to himself, "This is not quite straightforward of Hans."

In the mean time his brother sang away at his rich repertory. Schumann and Kierulf were his favorites, so he performed *"Du bist die Ruh," "My loved one, I am prison'd" "Ich grolle nicht," "Die alten bösen Lieder," "I lay my all, love, at thy feet," "Aus meiren grossen Schmerzen mach' ich die kleinen Lieder"*—all with the same calm superiority, and that light, half-sportive accompaniment. The only thing that gave him a little trouble was that fatal point, *'Ich legt' auch meine Liebe, Und meinen Schmerz hinein;"* but even of this he made something.

Then Ola, who knew to a nicety the limits of his brother's musical accomplishment, noticed that he was leaving the beaten track, and beginning to wander among the keys; and presently he was horrified to find that Hans was groping after that unhappy "Hope's clad in April green." But fortunately he could not hit upon it, so he confined himself to humming the song half aloud, while he threw in the three famous minor chords.

"Now we're quite cool again," cried the fair one in light green, hastily.

There was a general burst of laughter at her eagerness to get away, and she was quite crimson when she said good-night.

Cousin Ola, who was standing near the hostess, also took his leave. Cousin Hans, on the other hand, was detained by the Sheriff, who was anxious to learn under what teachers he had studied music; and that took time.

Thus it happened that Ola and the fair one in the light green passed out into the passage at the same time. There the young folks were crowding round the hat-pegs, some to find their own wraps, some to take down other people's.

"I suppose it's no good trying to push our way forward," said the fair one.

Ola's windpipe contracted in such a vexatious way that he only succeeded in uttering a meaningless sound. They stood close to each other in the crush, and Ola would gladly have given a finger to be able to say something pleasant to her, or at least something rational; but he found it quite impossible.

"Of course you've enjoyed the evening?" said she, in a friendly tone.

Cousin Ola thought of the pitiful part he had been playing all evening; his unsociableness weighed so much upon his mind that he answered— the very stupidest thing he could have answered, he thought, the moment the words were out of his lips—"I'm so sorry that I can't sing."

"I suppose it's a family failing," answered the fair one, with a rapid glance.

"N-n-no," said Ola, exceedingly put out, "my brother sings capitally."

"Do you think so?" she said, drily.

This was the most astounding thing that had ever happened to Ola: that there could be more than one opinion about his brother's singing, and that she, his "future wife," did not seem to admire it! And yet it was not quite unpleasant to him to hear it.

Again there was a silence, which Ola sought in vain to break.

"Don't you care for dancing?" she asked.

"Not with every one," he blurted out.

She laughed: "No, no; but gentlemen have the right to choose."

Now Ola began to lose his footing. He felt like a man who is walking, lost in thought, through the streets on a winter evening, and who suddenly discovers that he has got upon a patch of slippery ice. There was nothing for it but to keep up and go ahead; so, with the courage of despair, he said "If I knew—or dared to hope—that one of the ladies—no—that the lady I wanted to dance with—that she would care to—hm—that she would dance with me, then—then—" he could get no further, and after saying "then" two or three times over, he came to a stand-still.

"You could ask her," said the fair one.

Her bracelet had come unfastened, and its clasp was so stiff that she had to bend right forward and pinch it so hard that she became quite red in the face, in order to fasten it again.

"Would you, for example, dance with me?" Ola's brain was swimming.

"Why not?" she answered. She stood pressing the point of her shoe into a crack in the floor.

"We're to have a party at the Parsonage on Friday—would you give me a dance then?"

"With pleasure; which would you like?" she answered, trying her best to assume a "society" manner.

"A quadrille?" said Ola; thinking: "Quadrilles are so long."

"The second quadrille is disengaged," answered the lady.

"And a galop?"

"Yes, thank you; the first galop," she replied, with a little hesitation.

"And a polka?"

"No, no! no more," cried the fair one, looking at Ola with alarm.

At the same moment, Hans came rushing along at full speed. "Oh, how lucky I am to find you!—but in what company!"

Thereupon he took possession of the fair one in his amiable fashion, and drew her away with him to find her wraps and join the others.

"A quadrille and a galop; but no more—so so! so so!" repeated Cousin Ola. He stood as though rooted to the spot. At last he became aware that he was alone. He hastily seized a hat, slunk out by the back way, sneaked through the garden, and clambered with great difficulty over the garden fence, not far from the gate which stood ajar.

He struck into the first foot-path through the fields, fixing his eyes upon the Parsonage chimneys. He was vaguely conscious that he was getting wet up to the knees in the long grass; but on the other hand, he was not in the least aware that the Sheriff's old uniform cap, which he had had the luck to snatch up in his haste, was waggling about upon his head, until at last it came to rest when the long peak slipped down over his ear.

"A quadrille and a galop; but no more—so so! so so!—"

—It was pretty well on in the night when Hans approached the Parsonage. He had seen the ladies of the Doctor's party home, and was now making up the accounts of the day as he went along.

"She's a little shy; but on the whole I don't dislike that."

When he left the road at the Parsonage garden, he said, "She's dreadfully shy—almost more than I care for."

But as he crossed the farm-yard, he vowed that coy and capricious girls were the most intolerable creatures he knew. The thing was that he did not feel at all satisfied with the upshot of the day. Not that he for a moment doubted that she loved him; but, just on that account, he thought her coldness and reserve doubly annoying. She had never once thrown the ring to him; she had never once singled him out in the cotillion; and on the way home she had talked to every one but him. But he would adopt a different policy the next time; she should soon come to repent that day.

He slipped quietly into the house, so that his uncle might not hear how late he was. In order to reach his own and his brother's bedroom he had to pass through a long attic. A window in this attic was used by the young men as a door through which to reach a sort of balcony, formed by the canopy over the steps leading into the garden.

Cousin Hans noticed that this window was standing open; and out upon the balcony, in the clear moonlight, he saw his brother's figure.

Ola still wore his white dancing-gloves; he held on to the railing with both hands, and stared the moon straight in the face.

Cousin Hans could not understand what his brother was doing out there at that time of night; and least of all could he understand what had induced him to put a flower-pot on his head.

"He must be drunk," thought Hans, approaching him warily.

Then he heard his brother muttering something about a quadrille and a galop; after which he began to make some strange motions with his hands.

Cousin Hans received the impression that he was trying to snap his fingers; and presently Ola said, slowly, and clearly, in his monotonous and unsympathetic speaking voice: "Hope's clad in April green— trommelommelom, trommelommelom;" you see, poor fellow, he could not sing.

AT THE FAIR.

It was by the merest chance that Monsieur and Madame Tousseau came to Saint-Germain-en-Laye in the early days of September.

Four weeks ago they had been married in Lyons, which was their home; but where they had passed these four weeks they really could not have told you. The time had gone hop skip-and-jump; a couple of days had entirely slipped out of their reckoning, and, on the other hand, they remembered a little summer-house at Fontainebleau, where they had rested one evening, as clearly as if they had passed half their lives there.

Paris was, strictly speaking, the goal of their wedding journey, and there they established themselves in a comfortable little *hôtel garni*. But the city was sultry and they could not rest; so they rambled about among the small towns in the neighborhood, and found themselves, one Sunday at noon, in Saint-Germain.

"Monsieur and Madame have doubtless come to take part in the fête?" said the plump little landlady of the Hôtel Henri Quatre, as she ushered her guests up the steps.

The fête? They knew of no fête in the world except their own wedded happiness; but they did not say so to the landlady.

They soon learned that they had been lucky enough to drop into the very midst of the great and celebrated fair which is held every year, on the first Sunday of September, in the Forest of Saint-Germain.

The young couple were highly delighted with their good hap. It seemed as though Fortune followed at their heels, or rather ran ahead of them, to arrange surprises. After a delicious tête-à-tête dinner behind one of

148

the clipped yew trees in the quaint garden, they took a carriage and drove off to the forest.

In the hotel garden, beside the little fountain in the middle of the lawn, sat a ragged condor which the landlord had bought to amuse his guests. It was attached to its perch by a good strong rope. But when the sun shone upon it with real warmth, it fell a-thinking of the snow-peaks of Peru, of mighty wing-strokes over the deep valleys—and then it forgot the rope.

Two vigorous strokes with its pinions would bring the rope up taut, and it would fall back upon the sward. There it would lie by the hour, then shake itself and clamber up to its little perch again.

When it turned its head to watch the happy pair, Madame Tousseau burst into a fit of laughter at its melancholy mien.

The afternoon sun glimmered through the dense foliage of the interminable straight-ruled avenue that skirts the terrace. The young wife's veil fluttered aloft as they sped through the air, and wound itself right round Monsieur's head. It took a long time to put it in order again, and Madame's hat had to be adjusted ever so often. Then came the relighting of Monsieur's cigar, and that, too, was quite a business; for Madame's fan would always give a suspicious little flirt every time the match was lighted; then a penalty had to be paid, and that, again, took time.

The aristocratic English family which was passing the summer at Saint-Germain was disturbed in its regulation walk by the passing of the gay little equipage. They raised their correct gray or blue eyes; there was neither contempt nor annoyance in their look—only the faintest shade of surprise. But the condor followed the carriage with its eyes, until it became a mere black speck at the vanishing-point of the straight-ruled interminable avenue.

"La joyeuse fête des Loges" is a genuine fair, with gingerbread cakes, sword-swallowers, and waffles piping hot. As the evening falls, colored lamps and Chinese lanterns are lighted around the venerable oak which stands in the middle of the fairground, and boys climb about among its topmost branches with maroons and Bengal lights.

Gentlemen of an inventive turn of mind go about with lanterns on their hats, on their sticks, and wherever they can possibly hang; and the most inventive of all strolls around with his sweetheart under a great umbrella, with a lantern dancing from each rib.

On the outskirts, bonfires are lighted; fowls are roasted on spits, while potatoes are cut into slices and fried in dripping. Each aroma seems to have its amateurs, for there are always people crowding round; but the majority stroll up and down the long street of booths.

Monsieur and Madame Tousseau had plunged into all the fun of the fair. They had gambled in the most lucrative lottery in Europe, presided over by a man who excelled in dubious witticisms. They had seen the fattest goose in the world, and the celebrated flea, "Bismarch," who could drive six horses. Furthermore, they had purchased gingerbread, shot at a target for clay pipes and soft-boiled eggs, and finally had danced a waltz in the spacious dancing-tent.

They had never had such fun in their lives. There were no great people there—at any rate, none greater than themselves. As they did not know a soul, they smiled to every one, and when they met the same person twice they laughed and nodded to him.

They were charmed with everything. They stood outside the great circus and ballet marquees and laughed at the shouting buffoons. Scraggy mountebanks performed on trumpets, and young girls with well-floured shoulders smiled alluringly from the platforms.

Monsieur Tousseau's purse was never at rest; but they did not grow impatient of the perpetual claims upon it. On the contrary, they only laughed at the gigantic efforts these people would make to earn—perhaps half a franc, or a few centimes.

Suddenly they encountered a face they knew. It was a young American whom they had met at the hotel in Paris.

"Well, Monsieur Whitmore!" cried Madame Tousseau, gayly, "here at last you've found a place where you can't possibly help enjoying yourself."

"For my part," answered the American, slowly, "I find no enjoyment in seeing the people who haven't money making fools of themselves to please the people who have."

"Oh, you're incorrigible!" laughed the young wife. "But I must compliment you on the excellent French you are speaking to-day."

After exchanging a few more words, they lost each other in the crowd; Mr. Whitmore was going back to Paris immediately.

Madame Tousseau's compliment was quite sincere. As a rule the grave American talked deplorable French, but the answer he had made to Madame was almost correct. It seemed as though it had been well thought out in advance—as though a whole series of impressions had condensed themselves into these words. Perhaps that was why his answer sank so deep into the minds of Monsieur and Madame Tousseau.

Neither of them thought it a particularly brilliant remark; on the contrary, they agreed that it must be miserable to take so gloomy a view of things. But, nevertheless, his words left something rankling. They could not laugh so lightly as before, Madame felt tired, and they began to think of getting homewards.

Just as they turned to go down the long street of booths in order to find their carriage, they met a noisy crew coming upward.

"Let us take the other way," said Monsieur.

They passed between two booths, and emerged at the back of one of the rows. They stumbled over the tree-roots before their eyes got used to the uncertain light which fell in patches between the tents. A dog, which lay gnawing at something or other, rose with a snarl, and dragged its prey further into the darkness, among the trees.

On this side the booths were made up of old sails and all sorts of strange draperies. Here and there light shone through the openings, and at one place Madame distinguished a face she knew.

It was the man who had sold her that incomparable gingerbread—Monsieur had half of it still in his pocket.

But it was curious to see the gingerbread-man from this side. Here was something quite different from the smiling obsequiousness which had said so many pretty things to her pretty face, and had been so unwearied in belauding the gingerbread—which really was excellent.

Now he sat crouched together, eating some indescribable mess out of a checked pocket-handkerchief—eagerly, greedily, without looking up.

Farther down they heard a muffled conversation. Madame was bent upon peeping in; Monsieur objected, but he had to give in.

An old mountebank sat counting a handful of coppers, grumbling and growling the while. A young girl stood before him, shivering and pleading for pardon; she was wrapped in a long water-proof.

The man swore, and stamped on the ground. Then she threw off the water-proof and stood half naked in a sort of ballet costume. Without saying a word, and without smoothing her hair or preening her finery, she mounted the little steps that led to the stage.

At that moment she turned and looked at her father. Her face had already put on the ballet-simper, but it now gave place to a quite different expression. The mouth remained fixed, but the eyes tried, for a second, to send him a beseeching smile. The mountebank shrugged his shoulders, and held out his hand with the coppers; the girl turned, ducked under the curtain, and was received with shouts and applause.

Beside the great oak-tree the lottery man was holding forth as fluently as ever. His witticisms, as the darkness thickened, grew less and less dubious. There was a different ring, too, in the laughter of the crowd; the men were noisier, the mountebanks leaner, the women more brazen, the music falser—so it seemed, at least, to Madame and Monsieur.

As they passed the dancing-tent the racket of a quadrille reached their ears. "Great heavens!—was it really there that we danced?" said Madame, and nestled closer to her husband.

They made their way through the rout as quickly as they could; they would soon reach their carriage, it was just beyond the circus-marquee. It would be nice to rest and escape from all this hubbub.

The platform in front of the circus-marquee was now vacant. Inside, in the dim and stifling rotunda, the performance was in full swing.

Only the old woman who sold the tickets sat asleep at her desk. And a little way off, in the light of her lamp, stood a tiny boy.

He was dressed in tights, green on one side, red on the other; on his head he had a fool's cap with horns.

Close up to the platform stood a woman wrapped in a black shawl. She seemed to be talking to the boy.

He advanced his red leg and his green leg by turns, and drew them back again. At last he took three steps forward on his meagre shanks and held out his hand to the woman.

She took what he had in it, and disappeared into the darkness.

He stood motionless for a moment, then he muttered some words and burst into tears.

Presently he stopped, and said: "Maman m'a pris mon sou!"—and fell to weeping again.

He dried his eyes and left off for a time, but as often as he repeated to himself his sad little history—how his mother had taken his sou from him—he was seized with another and a bitterer fit of weeping.

He stooped and buried his face in the curtain. The stiff, wrinkly oil-painting must be hard and cold to cry into. The little body shrank together; he drew his green leg close up under him, and stood like a stork upon the red one.

No one on the other side of the curtain must hear that he was crying. Therefore he did not sob like a child, but fought as a man fights against a broken heart.

When the attack was over, he blew his nose with his fingers, and wiped them on his tights. With the dirty curtain he had dabbled the tears all over his face until it was streaked with black; and in this guise, and dry-eyed, he gazed for a moment over the fair.

Then: "Maman m'a pris mon sou"—and he set off again.

The backsweep of the wave leaves the beach dry for an instant while the next wave is gathering. Thus sorrow swept in heavy surges over the little childish heart.

His dress was so ludicrous, his body so meagre, his weeping was so wofully bitter, and his suffering so great and man-like—

—But at home at the hotel—the Pavillon Henri Quatre, where the Queens of France condescended to be brought to bed there the condor sat and slept upon its perch.

And it dreamed its dream—its only dream—its dream about the snow-peaks of Peru and the mighty wing-strokes over the deep valleys; and then it forgot its rope.

It uplifted its ragged pinions vigorously, and struck two sturdy strokes. Then the rope drew taut, and it fell back where it was wont to fall—it wrenched its claw, and the dream vanished.—

—Next morning the aristocratic English family was much concerned, and the landlord himself felt annoyed, for the condor lay dead upon the grass.

TWO FRIENDS.

No one could understand where he got his money from. But the person who marvelled most at the dashing and luxurious life led by Alphonse was his quondam friend and partner.

After they dissolved partnership, most of the custom and the best connection passed by degrees into Charles's hands. This was not because he in any way sought to run counter to his former partner; on the contrary, it arose simply from the fact that Charles was the more capable man of the two. And as Alphonse had now to work on his own account, it was soon clear to any one who observed him closely, that in spite of his promptitude, his amiability and his prepossessing appearance, he was not fitted to be at the head of an independent business.

And there was one person who *did* observe him closely. Charles followed him step by step with his sharp eyes; every blunder, every extravagance, every loss he knew all to a nicety, and he wondered that Alphonse could keep going so long.

—They had as good as grown up together. Their mothers were cousins; the families had lived near each other in the same street; and in a city like Paris proximity is as important as relationship in promoting close intercourse. Moreover, the boys went to the same school.

Thenceforth, as they grew up to manhood, they were inseparable. Mutual adaptation overcame the great differences which originally marked their characters, until at last their idiosyncrasies fitted into each other like the artfully-carved pieces of wood which compose the picture-puzzles of our childhood.

The relation between them was really a beautiful one, such as does not often arise between two young men; for they did not understand friendship as binding the one to bear everything at the hands of the other, but seemed rather to vie with each other in mutual considerateness.

If, however, Alphonse in his relation to Charles showed any high degree of considerateness, he him self was ignorant of it; and if any one had told him of it he would doubtless have laughed loudly at such a mistaken compliment.

For as life on the whole appeared to him very simple and straightforward, the idea that his friendship should in any way fetter him was the last thing that could enter his head. That Charles was his best friend seemed to him as entirely natural as that he himself danced best, rode best, was the best shot, and that the whole world was ordered entirely to his mind.

Alphonse was in the highest degree a spoilt child of fortune; he acquired everything without effort; existence fitted him like an elegant dress, and he wore it with such unconstrained amiability that people forgot to envy him.

And then he was so handsome. He was tall and slim, with brown hair and big open eyes; his complexion was clear and smooth, and his teeth shone when he laughed. He was quite conscious of his beauty, but, as everybody had petted him from his earliest days, his vanity was of a cheerful, good-natured sort, which, after all, was not so offensive. He was exceedingly fond of his friend. He amused himself and sometimes others by teasing him and making fun of him; but he knew Charles's face so thoroughly that he saw at once when the jest was going too far. Then he would resume his natural, kindly tone, until he made the serious and somewhat melancholy Charles laugh till he was ill.

From his boyhood Charles had admired Alphonse beyond measure. He himself was small and insignificant, quiet and shy. His friend's brilliant qualities cast a lustre over him as well, and gave a certain impetus to his life.

His mother often said: "This friendship between the boys is a real blessing for my poor Charles, for without it he would certainly have been a melancholy creature."

When Alphonse was on all occasions preferred to him, Charles rejoiced; he was proud of his friend. He wrote his exercises, prompted him at examination, pleaded his cause with the masters, and fought for him with the boys.

At the commercial academy it was the same story. Charles worked for Alphonse, and Alphonse rewarded him with his inexhaustible amiability and unfailing good-humor.

When subsequently, as quite young men, they were placed in the same banker's office, it happened one day that the principal said to Charles: "From the first of May I will raise your salary."

"I thank you," answered Charles, "both on my own and on my friend's behalf."

"Monsieur Alphonse's salary remains unaltered," replied the chief, and went on writing.

Charles never forgot that morning. It was the first time he had been preferred or distinguished before his friend. And it was his commercial capacity, the quality which, as a young man of business, he valued most, that had procured him this preference; and it was the head of the firm, the great financier, who had himself accorded him such recognition.

The experience was so strange to him that it seemed like an injustice to his friend. He told Alphonse nothing of the occurrence; on the contrary, he proposed that they should apply for two vacant places in the Crédit Lyonnais.

Alphonse was quite willing, for he loved change, and the splendid new banking establishment on the, Boulevard seemed to him far more attractive than the dark offices in the Rue Bergère. So they removed to the Crédit Lyonnais on the first of May. But as they were in the chief's office taking their leave, the old banker said to Charles, when Alphonse had gone out (Alphonse always took precedence of Charles), "Sentiment won't do for a business man."

From that day forward a change went on in Charles. He not only worked as industriously and conscientiously as before, but developed such energy and such an amazing faculty for labor as soon attracted to him the attention of his superiors. That he was far ahead of his friend in business capacity was soon manifest; but every time he received a new mark of recognition he had a struggle with himself. For a long time, every advancement brought with it a certain qualm of conscience; and yet he worked on with restless ardor.

One day Alphonse said, in his light, frank way: "You are really a smart fellow, Charlie! You're getting ahead of everybody, young and old—not to mention me. I'm quite proud of you!"

Charles felt ashamed. He had been thinking that Alphonse must feel wounded at being left on one side, and now he learned that his friend not only did not grudge him his advancement, but was even proud of him. By degrees his conscience was lulled to rest, and his solid worth was more and more appreciated—

But if he was in reality the more capable, how came it that he was so entirely ignored in society, while Alphonse remained everybody's darling? The very promotions and marks of appreciation which he had won for himself by hard work, were accorded him in a dry, business manner; while every one, from the directors to the messengers, had a friendly word or a merry greeting for Alphonse.

In the different offices and departments of the bank they intrigued to obtain possession of Monsieur Alphonse; for a breath of life and freshness followed ever in the wake of his handsome person and joyous nature. Charles, on the other hand, had often remarked that his colleagues regarded him as a dry person, who thought only of business and of himself.

The truth was that he had a heart of rare sensitiveness, with no faculty for giving it expression.

158

Charles was one of those small, black Frenchmen whose beard begins right under the eyes; his complexion was yellowish and his hair stiff and splintery. His eyes did not dilate when he was pleased and animated, but they flashed around and glittered. When he laughed the corners of his mouth turned upward, and many a time, when his heart was full of joy and good-will, he had seen people draw back, half-frightened by his forbidding exterior. Alphonse alone knew him so well that he never seemed to see his ugliness; every one else misunderstood him. He became suspicious, and retired more and more within himself.

In an insensible crescendo the thought grew in him: Why should he never attain anything of that which he most longed for—intimate and cordial intercourse and friendliness which should answer to the warmth pent up within him? Why should everyone smile to Alphonse with out-stretched hands, while he must content himself with stiff bows and cold glances!

Alphonse knew nothing of all this. He was joyous and healthy, charmed with life and content with his daily work. He had been placed in the easiest and most interesting branch of the business, and, with his quick brain and his knack of making himself agreeable, he filled his place satisfactorily.

His social circle was very large—every one set store by his acquaintance, and he was at least as popular among women as among men.

For a time Charles accompanied Alphonse into society, until he was seized by a misgiving that he was invited for his friend's sake alone, when he at once drew back.

When Charles proposed that they should set up in business together, Alphonse had answered: "It is too good of you to choose me. You could easily find a much better partner."

Charles had imagined that their altered relations and closer association in work would draw Alphonse out of the circles which Charles could not now endure, and unite them more closely. For he had conceived a vague dread of losing his friend.

He did not himself know, nor would it have been easy to decide, whether he was jealous of all the people who flocked around Alphonse and drew him to them, or whether he envied his friend's popularity.

—They began their business prudently and energetically, and got on well.

It was generally held that each formed an admirable complement to the other. Charles represented the solid, confidence-inspiring element, while the handsome and elegant Alphonse imparted to the firm a certain lustre which was far from being without value.

Every one who came into the counting-house at once remarked his handsome figure, and thus it seemed quite natural that all should address themselves to him.

Charles meanwhile bent over his work and let Alphonse be spokesman. When Alphonse asked him about anything, he answered shortly and quietly without looking up.

Thus most people thought that Charles was a confidential clerk, while Alphonse was the real head of the house.

As Frenchmen, they thought little about marrying, but as young Parisians they led a life into which erotics entered largely.

Alphonse was never really in his element except when in female society. Then all his exhilarating amiability came into play, and when he leaned back at supper and held out his shallow champagne-glass to be refilled, he was as beautiful as a happy god.

He had a neck of the kind which women long to caress, and his soft, half-curling hair looked as if it were negligently arranged, or carefully disarranged, by a woman's coquettish hand.

Indeed, many slim white fingers had passed through those locks; for Alphonse had not only the gift of being loved by women, but also the yet rarer gift of being forgiven by them.

When the friends were together at gay supper-parties, Alphonse paid no particular heed to Charles. He kept no account of his own love-affairs, far less of those of his friend. So it might easily happen that a beauty on whom Charles had cast a longing eye fell into the hands of Alphonse.

Charles was used to seeing his friend preferred in life; but there are certain things to which men can scarcely accustom themselves. He seldom went with Alphonse to his suppers, and it was always long before the wine and the general exhilaration could bring him into a convivial humor.

But then, when the champagne and the bright eyes had gone to his head, he would often be the wildest of all; he would sing loudly with his harsh voice, laugh and gesticulate so that his stiff black hair fell over his forehead; and then the merry ladies shrank from him, and called him the "chimney-sweep."

—As the sentry paces up and down in the beleaguered fortress, he sometimes hears a strange sound in the silent night, as if something were rustling under his feet. It is the enemy, who has undermined the outworks, and to-night or to-morrow night there will be a hollow explosion, and armed men will storm in through the breach.

If Charles had kept close watch over himself he would have heard strange thoughts rustling within him. But he would not hear—he had only a dim foreboding that some time there must come an explosion.

—And one day it came.

It was already after business hours; the clerks had all left the outer office, and only the principals remained behind.

Charles was busily writing a letter which he wished to finish before he left.

Alphonse had drawn on both his gloves and buttoned them. Then he had brushed his hat until it shone, and now he was walking up and down and peeping into Charles's letter every time he passed the desk.

They used to spend an hour every day before dinner in a café on the great Boulevard, and Alphonse was getting impatient for his newspapers.

"Will you never have finished that letter?" he said, rather irritably.

Charles was silent a second or two, then he sprang up so that his chair fell over: "Perhaps Alphonse imagined that he could do it better? Did he not know which of them was really the man of business?" And now the words streamed out with that incredible rapidity of which the French language is capable when it is used in fiery passion.

But it was a turbid stream, carrying with it many ugly expressions, upbraidings and recriminations; and through the whole there sounded something like a suppressed sob.

As he strode up and down the room, with clenched hands and dishevelled hair, Charles looked like a little wiry-haired terrier barking at an elegant Italian greyhound. At last he seized his hat and rushed out.

Alphonse had stood looking at him with great wondering eyes. When he was gone, and there was once more silence in the room, it seemed as though the air was still quivering with the hot words. Alphonse recalled them one by one, as he stood motionless beside the desk.

"Did he not know which was the abler of the two?" Yes, assuredly! he had never denied that Charles was by far his superior.

"He must not think that he would succeed in winning everything to himself with his smooth face." Alphonse was not conscious of ever having deprived his friend of anything.

"I don't care for your *cocottes*," Charles had said.

Could he really have been interested in the little Spanish dancer? If Alphonse had only had the faintest suspicion of such a thing he would never have looked at her. But that was nothing to get so wild about; there were plenty of women in Paris.

And at last: "As sure as to-morrow comes, I will dissolve partnership!"

Alphonse did not understand it at all. He left the counting-house and walked moodily through the streets until he met an acquaintance. That put other thoughts into his head; but all day he had a feeling as if something gloomy and uncomfortable lay in wait, ready to seize him so soon as he was alone.

When he reached home, late at night, he found a letter from Charles. He opened it hastily; but it contained, instead of the apology he had expected, only a coldly-worded request to M. Alphonse to attend at the counting-house early the next morning "in order that the contemplated dissolution of partnership might be effected as quickly as possible."

Now, for the first time, did Alphonse begin to understand that the scene in the counting-house had been more than a passing outburst of passion; but this only made the affair more inexplicable.

And the longer he thought it over, the more clearly did he feel that Charles had been unjust to him. He had never been angry with his friend, nor was he precisely angry even now. But as he repeated to himself all the insults Charles had heaped upon him, his good-natured heart hardened; and the next morning he took his place in silence, after a cold "Good-morning."

Although he arrived a whole hour earlier than usual, he could see that Charles had been working long and industriously. There they sat, each on his side of the desk; they spoke only the most indispensable words; now and then a paper passed from hand to hand, but they never looked each other in the face.

In this way they both worked—each more busily than the other—until twelve o'clock, their usual luncheon-time.

This hour of déjeûner was the favorite time of both. Their custom was to have it served in their office, and when the old house-keeper announced that lunch was ready, they would both rise at once, even if they were in the midst of a sentence or of an account.

They used to eat standing by the fireplace or walking up and down in the warm, comfortable office. Alphonse had always some piquant stories to tell, and Charles laughed at them. These were his pleasantest hours.

But that day, when Madame said her friendly *"Messieurs, on a servi,"* they both remained sitting. She opened her eyes wide, and repeated the words as she went out, but neither moved.

At last Alphonse felt hungry, went to the table, poured out a glass of wine and began to eat his cutlet. But as he stood there eating, with his glass in his hand, and looked round the dear old office where they had spent so many pleasant hours, and then thought that they were to lose all this and imbitter their lives for a whim, a sudden burst of passion, the whole situation appeared to him so preposterous that he almost burst out laughing.

"Look here, Charles," he said, in the half-earnest, half-joking tone which always used to make Charles laugh, "it will really be too absurd to advertise: 'According to an amicable agreement, from such and such a date the firm of—'"

"I have been thinking," interrupted Charles, quietly, "that we will put: 'According to mutual agreement.'"

Alphonse laughed no more; he put down his glass, and the cutlet tasted bitter in his mouth.

He understood that friendship was dead between them, why or wherefore he could not tell; but he thought that Charles was hard and unjust to him. He was now stiffer and colder than the other.

They worked together until the business of dissolution was finished; then they parted.

A considerable time passed, and the two quondam friends worked each in his own quarter in the great Paris. They met at the Bourse, but never did business with each other. Charles never worked against Alphonse; he did not wish to ruin him; he wished Alphonse to ruin himself.

And Alphonse seemed likely enough to meet his friend's wishes in this respect. It is true that now and then he did a good stroke of business, but the steady industry he had learned from Charles he soon forgot. He began to neglect his office, and lost many good connections.

He had always had a taste for dainty and luxurious living, but his association with the frugal Charles had hitherto held his extravagances in check. Now, on the contrary, his life became more and more dissipated. He made fresh acquaintances on every hand, and was more than ever the brilliant and popular Monsieur Alphonse; but Charles kept an eye on his growing debts.

He had Alphonse watched as closely as possible, and, as their business was of the same kind, could form a pretty good estimate of the other's earnings. His expenses were even easier to ascertain, and he, soon assured himself of the fact that Alphonse was beginning to run into debt in several quarters.

He cultivated some acquaintances about whom he otherwise cared nothing, merely because through them he got an insight into Alphonse's expensive mode of life and rash prodigality. He sought the same cafés and restaurants as Alphonse, but at different times; he even had his clothes made by the same tailor, because the talkative little man entertained him with complaints that Monsieur Alphonse never paid his bills.

Charles often thought how easy it would be to buy up a part of Alphonse's liabilities and let them fall into the hands of a grasping usurer. But it would be a great injustice to suppose that Charles for a moment contemplated doing such a thing himself. It was only an idea he was fond of dwelling upon; he was, as it were, in love with Alphonse's debts.

But things went slowly, and Charles became pale and sallow while he watched and waited.

He was longing for the time when the people who had always looked down upon him should have their eyes opened, and see how little the brilliant and idolized Alphonse was really fit for. He wanted to see him humbled, abandoned by his friends, lonely and poor; and then—!

Beyond that he really did not like to speculate; for at this point feelings stirred within him which he would not acknowledge.

He *would* hate his former friend; he *would* have revenge for all the coldness and neglect which had been his own lot in life; and every time the least thought in defence of Alphonse arose in his mind he pushed it aside, and said, like the old banker: "Sentiment won't do for a business man."

One day he went to his tailor's; he bought more clothes in these days than he absolutely needed.

The nimble little man at once ran to meet him with a roll of cloth: "See, here is the very stuff for you. Monsieur Alphonse has had a whole suit made of it, and Monsieur Alphonse is a gentleman who knows how to dress."

"I did not think that Monsieur Alphonse was one of your favorite customers," said Charles, rather taken by surprise.

"Oh, *mon Dieu!*" exclaimed the little tailor, "you mean because I have once or twice mentioned that Monsieur Alphonse owed me a few thousand francs. It was very stupid of me to speak so. Monsieur Alphonse has not only paid me the trifle he was owing, but I know that he has also satisfied a number of other creditors. I have done *ce cher beau monsieur* great injustice, and I beg you never to give him a hint of my stupidity."

Charles was no longer listening to the chatter of the garrulous tailor. He soon left the shop, and went up the street quite absorbed in the one thought that Alphonse had paid.

He thought how foolish it really was of him to wait and wait for the other's ruin. How easily might not the adroit and lucky Alphonse come across many a brilliant business opening, and make plenty of money without a word of it reaching Charles's ears. Perhaps, after all, he was getting on well. Perhaps it would end in people saying: "See, at last Monsieur Alphonse shows what he is fit for, now that he is quit of his dull and crabbed partner!"

Charles went slowly up the street with his head bent. Many people jostled him, but he heeded not. His life seemed to him so meaningless, as if he had lost all that be had ever possessed—or had he himself cast it from him? Just then some one ran against him with more than usual violence. He looked up. It was an acquaintance from the time when he and Alphonse had been in the Crédit Lyonnais.

"Ah, good-day, Monsieur Charles!" cried he, "It is long since we met. Odd, too, that I should meet you to-day. I was just thinking of you this morning."

"Why, may I ask?" said Charles, half-absently.

166

"Well, you see, only to-day I saw up at the bank a paper—a bill for thirty or forty thousand francs—bearing both your name and that of Monsieur Alphonse. It astonished me, for I thought that you two—hm!—had done with each other."

"No, we have not quite done with each other yet," said Charles, slowly.

He struggled with all his might to keep his face calm, and asked in as natural a tone as he could command: "When does the bill fall due? I don't quite recollect."

"To-morrow or the day after, I think," answered the other, who was a hard-worked business man, and was already in a hurry to be off. "It was accepted by Monsieur Alphonse."

"I know that," said Charles; "but could you not manage to let *me* redeem the bill to-morrow? It is a courtesy—a favor I am anxious to do."

"With pleasure. Tell your messenger to ask for me personally at the bank to-morrow afternoon. I will arrange it; nothing easier. Excuse me; I'm in a hurry. Good-bye!" and with that he ran on—

—Next day Charles sat in his counting-house waiting for the messenger who had gone up to the bank to redeem Alphonse's bill.

At last a clerk entered, laid a folded blue paper by his principal's side, and went out again.

Not until the door was closed did Charles seize the draft, look swiftly round the room, and open it. He stared for a second or two at his name, then lay back in his chair and drew a deep breath. It was as he had expected—the signature was a forgery.

He bent over it again. For long he sat, gazing at his own name, and observing how badly it was counterfeited.

While his sharp eye followed every line in the letters of his name, he scarcely thought. His mind was so disturbed, and his feelings so strangely conflicting, that it was some time before he became conscious how much they betrayed—these bungling strokes on the blue paper.

He felt a strange lump in his throat, his nose began to tickle a little, and, before he was aware of it, a big tear fell on the paper.

He looked hastily around, took out his pocket-handkerchief, and carefully wiped the wet place on the bill. He thought again of the old banker in the Rue Bergère.

What did it matter to him that Alphonse's weak character had at last led him to crime, and what had he lost? Nothing, for did he not hate his former friend? No one could say it was his fault that Alphonse was ruined—he had shared with him honestly, and never harmed him.

Then his thoughts turned to Alphonse. He knew him well enough to be sure that when the refined, delicate Alphonse had sunk so low, he must have come to a jutting headland in life, and be prepared to leap out of it rather than let disgrace reach him.

At this thought Charles sprang up. That must not be. Alphonse should not have time to send a bullet through his head and hide his shame in the mixture of compassion and mysterious horror which follows the suicide. Thus Charles would lose his revenge, and it would be all to no purpose that he had gone and nursed his hatred until he himself had become evil through it. Since he had forever lost his friend, he would at least expose his enemy, so that all should see what a miserable, despicable being was this charming Alphonse.

He looked at his watch; it was half-past four. Charles knew the café in which he would find Alphonse at this hour; he pocketed the bill and buttoned his coat.

But on the way he would call at a police-station, and hand over the bill to a detective, who at a sign from Charles should suddenly advance into the middle of the café where Alphonse was always surrounded by his friends and admirers, and say loudly and distinctly so that all should hear it:

"Monsieur Alphonse, you are charged with forgery."

It was raining in Paris. The day had been foggy, raw, and cold; and well on in the afternoon it had begun to rain. It was not a downpour—

the water did not fall from the clouds in regular drops—but the clouds themselves had, as it were, laid themselves down in the streets of Paris and there slowly condensed into water.

No matter how people might seek to shelter themselves, they got wet on all sides. The moisture slid down the back of your neck, laid itself like a wet towel about your knees, penetrated into your boots and far up your trousers.

A few sanguine ladies were standing in the *portes cochères*, with their skirts tucked up, expecting it to clear; others waited by the hour in the omnibus stations. But most of the stronger sex hurried along under their umbrellas; only a few had been sensible enough to give up the battle, and had turned up their collars, stuck their umbrellas under their arms, and their hands in their pockets.

Although it was early in the autumn it was already dusk at five o'clock. A few gas-jets lighted in the narrowest streets, and in a shop here and there, strove to shine out in the thick wet air.

People swarmed as usual in the streets, jostled one another off the pavement, and ruined one another's umbrellas. All the cabs were taken up; they splashed along and bespattered the foot-passengers to the best of their ability, while the asphalte glistened in the dim light with a dense coating of mud.

The cafés were crowded to excess; regular customers went round and scolded, and the waiters ran against each other in their hurry. Ever and anon, amid the confusion, could be heard the sharp little ting of the bell on the buffet; it was la *dame du comptoir* summoning a waiter, while her calm eyes kept a watch upon the whole café.

A lady sat at the buffet of a large restaurant on the Boulevard Sebastopol. She was widely known for her cleverness and her amiable manners.

She had glossy black hair, which, in spite of the fashion, she wore parted in the middle of her forehead in natural curls. Her eyes were almost black and her mouth full, with a little shadow of a mustache.

Her figure was still very pretty, although, if the truth were known, she had probably passed her thirtieth year; and she had a soft little hand, with which she wrote elegant figures in her cash-book, and now and then a little note. Madame Virginie could converse with the young dandies who were always hanging about the buffet, and parry their witticisms, while she kept account with the waiters and had her eye upon every corner of the great room.

She was really pretty only from five till seven in the afternoon—that being the time at which Alphonse invariably visited the café. Then her eyes never left him; she got a fresher color, her mouth was always trembling into a smile, and her movements became somewhat nervous. That was the only time of the day when she was ever known to give a random answer or to make a mistake in the accounts; and the waiters tittered and nudged each other.

For it was generally thought that she had formerly had relations with Alphonse, and some would even have it that she was still his mistress.

She herself best knew how matters stood; but it was impossible to be angry with Monsieur Alphonse. She was well aware that he cared no more for her than for twenty others; that she had lost him—nay, that he had never really been hers. And yet her eyes besought a friendly look, and when he left the café without sending her a confidential greeting, it seemed as though she suddenly faded, and the waiters said to each other: "Look at Madame; she is gray to-night"—

—Over at the windows it was still light enough to read the papers; a couple of young men were amusing themselves with watching the crowds which streamed past. Seen through the great plate-glass windows, the busy forms gliding past one another in the dense, wet, rainy air looked like fish in an aquarium. Farther back in the café, and over the bililard-tables, the gas was lighted. Alphonse was playing with a couple of friends.

He had been to the buffet and greeted Madame Virginie, and she, who had long noticed how Alphonse was growing paler day by day, had—half in jest, half in anxiety—reproached him with his thoughtless life.

Alphonse answered with a poor joke and asked for absinthe.

How she hated those light ladies of the ballet and the opera who enticed Monsieur Alphonse to revel night after night at the gaming-table, or at interminable suppers! How ill he had been looking these last few weeks! He had grown quite thin, and the great gentle eyes had acquired a piercing, restless look. What would she not give to be able to rescue him out of that life that was dragging him down! She glanced in the opposite mirror and thought she had beauty enough left.

Now and then the door opened and a new guest came in, stamped his feet and shut his wet umbrella. All bowed to Madame Virginie, and almost all said, "What horrible weather!"

When Charles entered he saluted shortly and took a seat in the corner beside the fireplace.

Alphonse's eyes had indeed become restless. He looked towards the door every time any one came in; and when Charles appeared, a spasm passed over his face and he missed his stroke.

"Monsieur Alphonse is not in the vein to-day," said an onlooker.

Soon after a strange gentleman came in. Charles looked up from his paper and nodded slightly; the stranger raised his eyebrows a little and looked at Alphonse.

He dropped his cue on the floor.

"Excuse me, gentlemen, I'm not in the mood for billiards to-day," said he, "permit me to leave off. Waiter, bring me a bottle of seltzer-water and a spoon—I must take my dose of Vichy salts."

"You should not take so much Vichy salts, Monsieur Alphonse, but rather keep to a sensible diet," said the doctor, who sat a little way off playing chess.

Alphonse laughed, and seated himself at the newspaper table. He seized the *Journal Amusant*, and began to make merry remarks upon the illustrations. A little circle quickly gathered round him, and he was inexhaustible in racy stories and whimsicalities.

While he rattled on under cover of the others' laughter, he poured out a glass of seltzer-water and took from his pocket a little box on which was written, in large letters, "Vichy Salts."

He shook the powder out into the glass and stirred it round with a spoon. There was a little cigar-ash on the floor in front of his chair; he whipped it off with his pocket-handkerchief, and then stretched out his hand for the glass.

At that moment he felt a hand on his arm. Charles had risen and hurried across the room; he now bent down over Alphonse.

Alphonse turned his head towards him so that none but Charles could see his face. At first he let his eyes travel furtively over his old friend's figure; then he looked up, and, gazing straight at Charles, he said, half aloud, "Charlie!"

It was long since Charles had heard that old pet name. He gazed into the well-known face, and now for the first time saw how it had altered of late. It seemed to him as though he were reading a tragic story about himself.

They remained thus for a second or two, and there glided over Alphonse's features that expression of imploring helplessness which Charles knew so well from the old school days, when Alphonse came bounding in at the last moment and wanted his composition written.

"Have you done with the *Journal Amusant?*" asked Charles, with a thick utterance.

"Yes; pray take it," answered Alphonse, hurriedly. He reached him the paper, and at the same time got hold of Charles's thumb. He pressed it and whispered, "Thanks," then—drained the glass.

Charles went over to the stranger who sat by the door: "Give me the bill."

"You don't need our assistance, then?"

"No, thanks."

"So much the better," said the stranger, handing Charles a folded blue paper. Then he paid for his coffee and went.—

—Madame Virginie rose with a little shriek: "Alphonse! Oh, my God! Monsieur Alphonse is ill."

He slipped off his chair; his shoulders went up and his head fell on one side. He remained sitting on the floor, with his back against the chair.

There was a movement among those nearest; the doctor sprang over and knelt beside him. When he looked in Alphonse's face he started a little. He took his hand as if to feel his pulse, and at the same time bent down over the glass which stood on the edge of the table.

With a movement of the arm he gave it a slight push, so that it fell on the floor and was smashed. Then he laid down the dead man's hand and bound a handkerchief round his chin.

Not till then did the others understand what had happened. "Dead? Is he dead, doctor? Monsieur Alphonse dead?"

"Heart disease," answered the doctor.

One came running with water, another with vinegar. Amid laughter and noise, the balls could be heard cannoning on the inner billiard-table.

"Hush!" some one whispered. "Hush!" was repeated; and the silence spread in wider and wider circles round the corpse, until all was quite still.

"Come and lend a hand," said the doctor.

The dead man was lifted up; they laid him on a sofa in a corner of the room, and the nearest gasjets were put out.

Madame Virginie was still standing up; her face was chalk-white, and she held her little soft hand pressed against her breast. They carried him right past the buffet. The doctor had seized him under the back, so that his waistcoat slipped up and a piece of his fine white shirt appeared.

She followed with her eyes the slender, supple limbs she knew so well, and continued to stare towards the dark corner.

Most of the guests went away in silence. A couple of young men entered noisily from the street; a waiter ran towards them and said a few words. They glanced towards the corner, buttoned their coats, and plunged out again into the fog.

The half-darkened café was soon empty; only some of Alphonse's nearest friends stood in a group and whispered. The doctor was talking with the proprietor, who had now appeared on the scene.

The waiters stole to and fro making great circuits to avoid the dark corner. One of them knelt and gathered up the fragments of the glass on a tray. He did his work as quietly as he could; but for all that it made too much noise.

"Let that alone until by-and-by," said the host, softly.

—Leaning against the chimney-piece, Charles looked at the dead man. He slowly tore the folded paper to pieces, while he thought of his friend—

A GOOD CONSCIENCE.

An elegant little carriage, with two sleek and well-fed horses, drew up at Advocate Abel's garden gate.

Neither silver nor any other metal was visible in the harness; everything was a dull black, and all the buckles were leather-covered. In the lacquering of the carriage there was a trace of dark green; the cushions were of a subdued dust-color; and only on close inspection could you perceive that the coverings were of the richest silk. The coachman looked like an English clergyman, in his close-buttoned black coat, with a little stand-up collar and stiff white necktie.

Mrs. Warden, who sat alone in the carriage, bent forward and laid her hand upon the ivory door-handle; then she slowly alighted, drew her long train after her, and carefully closed the carriage door.

You might have wondered that the coachman did not dismount to help her; the fat horses certainly did not look as though they would play any tricks if he dropped the reins.

But when you looked at his immovable countenance and his correct iron-gray whiskers, you understood at once that this was a man who knew what he was doing, and never neglected a detail of his duty.

Mrs. Warden passed through the little garden in front of the house, and entered the garden-room. The door to the adjoining room stood half open, and there she saw the lady of the house at a large table covered with rolls of light stuff and scattered numbers of the *Bazar*.

"Ah, you've come just at the right moment, my dear Emily!" cried Mrs. Abel, "I'm quite in despair over my dress-maker—she can't think of anything new. And here I'm sitting, ransacking the *Bazar*. Take off your shawl, dear, and come and help me; it's a walking-dress."

"I'm afraid I'm scarcely the person to help you in a matter of dress," answered Mrs. Warden.

Good-natured Mrs. Abel stared at her; there was something disquieting in her tone, and she had a vast respect for her rich friend.

"You remember I told you the other day that Warden had promised me—that's to say"—Mrs. Warden corrected herself—"he had asked me to order a new silk dress—"

"From Madame Labiche—of course!"—interrupted Mrs. Abel. "And I suppose you're on your way to her now? Oh, take me with you! It will be such fun!"

"I am not going to Madame Labiche's," answered Mrs. Warden, almost solemnly.

"Good gracious, why not?" asked her friend, while her good-humored brown eyes grew spherical with astonishment.

"Well, you must know," answered Mrs. Warden, "it seems to me we can't with a good conscience pay so much money for unnecessary finery, when we know that on the outskirts of the town—and even at our very doors—there are hundreds of people living in destitution—literally in destitution."

"Yes, but," objected the advocate's wife, casting an uneasy glance over her table, "isn't that the way of the world? We know that inequality—"

"We ought to be careful not to increase the inequality, but rather to do what we can to smooth it away," Mrs. Warden interrupted. And it appeared to Mrs. Abel that her friend cast a glance of disapprobation over the table, the stuffs, and the *Bazars*.

"It's only alpaca," she interjected, timidly.

"Good heavens, Caroline!" cried Mrs. Warden, "pray don't think that I'm reproaching you. These things depend entirely upon one's individual point of view—every one must follow the dictates of his own conscience."

176

The conversation continued for some time, and Mrs. Warden related that it was her intention to drive out to the very lowest of the suburbs, in order to assure herself, with her own eyes, of the conditions of life among the poor.

On the previous day she had read the annual report of a private charitable society of which her husband was a member. She had purposely refrained from applying to the police or the poor-law authorities for information. It was the very gist of her design personally to seek out poverty, to make herself familiar with it, and then to render assistance.

The ladies parted a little less effusively than usual. They were both in a serious frame of mind.

Mrs. Abel remained in the garden-room; she felt no inclination to set to work again at the walking-dress, although the stuff was really pretty. She heard the muffled sound of the carriage-wheels as they rolled off over the smooth roadway of the villa quarter.

"What a good heart Emily has," she sighed.

Nothing could be more remote than envy from the good-natured lady's character; and yet—it was with a feeling akin to envy that she now followed the light carriage with her eyes. But whether it was her friend's good heart or her elegant equipage that she envied her it was not easy to say. She had given the coachman his orders, which he had received without moving a muscle; and as remonstrance was impossible to him, he drove deeper and deeper into the queerest streets in the poor quarter, with a countenance as though he were driving to a Court ball.

At last he received orders to stop, and indeed it was high time. For the street grew narrower and narrower, and it seemed as though the fat horses and the elegant carriage must at the very next moment have stuck fast, like a cork in the neck of a bottle.

The immovable one showed no sign of anxiety, although the situation was in reality desperate. A humorist, who stuck his head out of a garret window, went so far as to advise him to slaughter his horses on the spot, as they could never get out again alive.

177

Mrs. Warden alighted, and turned into a still narrower street; she wanted to see poverty at its very worst.

In a door-way stood a half-grown girl. Mrs. Warden asked: "Do very poor people live in this house?"

The girl laughed and made some answer as she brushed close past her in the narrow door-way. Mrs. Warden did not understand what she said, but she had an impression that it was something ugly.

She entered the first room she came to.

It was not a new idea to Mrs. Warden that poor people never keep their rooms properly ventilated. Nevertheless, she was so overpowered by the atmosphere she found herself inhaling that she was glad to sink down on a bench beside the stove.

Mrs. Warden was struck by something in the gesture with which the woman of the house swept down upon the floor the clothes which were lying on the bench, and in the smile with which she invited the fine lady to be seated. She received the impression that the poor woman had seen better days, although her movements were bouncing rather than refined, and her smile was far from pleasant.

The long train of Mrs. Warden's pearl-gray visiting dress spread over the grimy floor, and as she stooped and drew it to her she could not help thinking of an expression of Heine's, "She looked like a bon-bon which has fallen in the mire."

The conversation began, and was carried on as such conversations usually are. If each had kept to her own language and her own line of thought, neither of these two women would have understood a word that the other said.

But as the poor always know the rich much better than the rich know the poor, the latter have at last acquired a peculiar dialect—a particular tone which experience has taught them to use when they are anxious to make themselves understood—that is to say, understood in such a way as to incline the wealthy to beneficence. Nearer to each other they can never come.

Of this dialect the poor woman was a perfect mistress, and Mrs. Warden had soon a general idea of her miserable case. She had two children—a boy of four or five, who was lying on the floor, and a baby at the breast.

Mrs. Warden gazed at the pallid little creature, and could not believe that it was thirteen months old. At home in his cradle she herself had a little colossus of seven months, who was at least half as big again as this child.

"You must give the baby something strengthening," she said; and she had visions of phosphate food and orange jelly.

At the words "something strengthening," a shaggy head looked up from the bedstraw; it belonged to a pale, hollow eyed man with a large woollen comforter wrapped round his jaws.

Mrs. Warden was frightened. "Your husband?" she asked.

The poor woman answered yes, it was her husband. He had not gone to work to-day because he had such bad toothache.

Mrs. Warden had had toothache herself, and knew how painful it is. She uttered some words of sincere sympathy.

The man muttered something, and lay back again; and at the same moment Mrs. Warden discovered an inmate of the room whom she had not hitherto observed.

It was a quite young girl, who was seated in the corner at the other side of the stove. She stared for a moment at the fine lady, but quickly drew back her head and bent forward, so that the visitor could see little but her back.

Mrs. Warden thought the girl had some sewing in her lap which she wanted to hide; perhaps it was some old garment she was mending.

"Why does the big boy lie upon the floor?" asked Mrs. Warden.

"He's lame," answered the mother. And now followed a detailed account of the poor boy's case, with many lamentations. He had been attacked with hip-disease after the scarlet-fever.

"You must buy him——" began Mrs. Warden, intending to say, "a wheel-chair." But it occurred to her that she had better buy it herself. It is not wise to let poor people get too much money into their hands. But she would give the woman something at once. Here was real need, a genuine case for help; and she felt in her pocket for her purse.

It was not there. How annoying—she must have left it in the carriage.

Just as she was turning to the woman to express her regret, and promise to send some money presently, the door opened, and a well-dressed gentleman entered. His face was very full, and of a sort of dry, mealy pallor.

"Mrs. Warden, I presume?" said the stranger. "I saw your carriage out in the street, and I have brought you this—your purse, is it not?"

Mrs. Warden looked at it—yes, certainly, it was hers, with E. W. inlaid in black on the polished ivory.

"I happened to see it, as I turned the corner, in the hands of a girl—one of the most disreputable in the quarter," the stranger explained; adding, "I am the poor-law inspector of the district."

Mrs. Warden thanked him, although she did not at all like his appearance. But when she again looked round the room she was quite alarmed by the change which had taken place in its occupants.

The husband sat upright in the bed and glared at the fat gentleman, the wife's face wore an ugly smile, and even the poor wee cripple had scrambled towards the door, and resting on his lean arms, stared upward like a little animal.

And in all these eyes there was the same hate, the same aggressive defiance. Mrs. Warden felt as though she were now separated by an immense interval from the poor woman with whom she had just been talking so openly and confidentially.

"So that's the state you're in to-day, Martin," said the gentleman, in quite a different voice. "I thought you'd been in that affair last night.

Never mind, they're coming for you this afternoon. It'll be a two months' business."

All of a sudden the torrent was let loose. The man and woman shouted each other down, the girl behind the stove came forward and joined in, the cripple shrieked and rolled about. It was impossible to distinguish the words; but what between voices, eyes, and hands, it seemed as though the stuffy little room must fly asunder with all the wild passion exploding in it.

Mrs. Warden turned pale and rose, the gentleman opened the door, and both hastened out. As she passed down the passage she heard a horrible burst of feminine laughter behind her. It must be the woman— the same woman who had spoken so softly and despondently about the poor children.

She felt half angry with the man who had brought about this startling change, and as they now walked side by side up the street she listened to him with a cold and distant expression.

But gradually her bearing changed; there was really so much in what he said.

The poor-law inspector told her what a pleasure it was to him to find a lady like Mrs. Warden so compassionate towards the poor. Though it was much to be deplored that even the most well-meant help so often came into unfortunate hands, yet there was always something fine and ennobling in seeing a lady like Mrs. Warden—

"But," she interrupted, "aren't these people in the utmost need of help? I received the impression that the woman in particular had seen better days, and that a little timely aid might perhaps enable her to recover herself."

"I am sorry to have to tell you, madam," said the poor-law inspector, in a tone of mild regret, "that she was formerly a very notorious woman of the town."

Mrs. Warden shuddered.

She had spoken to such a woman, and spoken about children. She had even mentioned her own child, lying at home in its innocent cradle. She almost felt as though she must hasten home to make sure it was still as clean and wholesome as before.

"And the young girl?" she asked, timidly.

"No doubt you noticed her—her condition."

"No. You mean—"

The fat gentleman whispered some words.

Mrs. Warden started: "By the man!—the man of the house?"

"Yes, madam, I am sorry to have to tell you so; but you can understand that these people—" and he whispered again.

This was too much for Mrs. Warden. She turned almost dizzy, and accepted the gentleman's arm. They now walked rapidly towards the carriage, which was standing a little farther off than the spot at which she had left it.

For the immovable one had achieved a feat which even the humorist had acknowledged with an elaborate oath.

After sitting for some time, stiff as a poker, he had backed his sleek horses, step by step, until they reached a spot where the street widened a little, though the difference was imperceptible to any other eyes than those of an accomplished coachman.

A whole pack of ragged children swarmed about the carriage, and did all they could to upset the composure of the sleek steeds. But the spirit of the immovable one was in them.

After having measured with a glance of perfect composure the distance between two flights of steps, one on each side of the street, he made the sleek pair turn, slowly and step by step, so short and sharp that it seemed as though the elegant carriage must be crushed to fragments, but so accurately that there was not an inch too much or too little on either side.

Now he once more sat stiff as a poker, still measuring with his eyes the distance between the steps. He even made a mental note of the number of a constable who had watched the feat, in order to have a witness to appeal to if his account of it should be received with scepticism at the stables.

Mrs. Warden allowed the poor-law inspector to hand her into the carriage. She asked him to call upon her the following day, and gave him her address.

"To Advocate Abel's!" she cried to the coachman. The fat gentleman lifted his hat with a mealy smile, and the carriage rolled away.

As they gradually left the poor quarter of the town behind, the motion of the carriage became smoother, and the pace increased. And when they emerged upon the broad avenue leading through the villa quarter, the sleek pair snorted with enjoyment of the pure, delicate air from the gardens, and the immovable one indulged, without any sort of necessity, in three masterly cracks of his whip.

Mrs. Warden, too, was conscious of the delight of finding herself once more in the fresh air. The experiences she had gone through, and, still more, what she had heard from the inspector, had had an almost numbing effect upon her. She began to realize the immeasurable distance between herself and such people as these.

She had often thought there was something quite too sad, nay, almost cruel, in the text: "Many are called, but few are chosen."

Now she understood that it *could* not be otherwise.

How could people so utterly depraved ever attain an elevation at all adequate to the demands of a strict morality? What must be the state of these wretched creatures' consciences? And how should they be able to withstand the manifold temptations of life?

She knew only too well what temptation meant! Was she not incessantly battling against a temptation—perhaps the most perilous of all—the temptation of riches, about which the Scriptures said so many hard things?

She shuddered to think of what would happen if that brutish man and these miserable women suddenly had riches placed in their hands.

183

Yes, wealth was indeed no slight peril to the soul. It was only yesterday that her husband had tempted her with such a delightful little man-servant—a perfect English groom. But she had resisted the temptation; and answered: "No, Warden, it would not be right; I will not have a footman on the box. I dare say we can afford it; but let us beware of overweening luxury. I assure you I don't require help to get into the carriage and out of it; I won't even let the coachman get down on my account."

It did her good to think of this now, and her eyes rested complacently on the empty seat on the box, beside the immovable one.

Mrs. Abel, who was busy clearing away *Bazars* and scraps of stuff from the big table, was astonished to see her friend return so soon.

"Why, Emily! Back again already? I've just been telling the dress-maker that she can go. What you were saying to me has quite put me out of conceit of my new frock; I can quite well get on without one—" said good-natured Mrs. Abel; but her lips trembled a little as she spoke.

"Every one must act according to his own conscience," answered Mrs. Warden, quietly, "but I think it's possible to be too scrupulous."

Mrs. Abel looked up; she had not expected this.

"Just let me tell you what I've gone through," said Mrs. Warden, and began her story.

She sketched her first impression of the stuffy room and the wretched people; then she spoke of the theft of her purse.

"My husband always declares that people of that kind can't refrain from stealing," said Mrs. Abel.

"I'm afraid your husband is nearer the truth than we thought," replied Mrs. Warden.

Then she told about the inspector, and the ingratitude these people had displayed towards the man who cared for them day by day.

But when she came to what she had heard of the poor woman's past life, and still more when she told about the young girl, Mrs. Abel was so overcome that she had to ask the servant to bring some port-wine.

When the girl brought in the tray with the decanter, Mrs. Abel whispered to her: "Tell the dressmaker to wait."

"And then, can you conceive it," Mrs. Warden continued—"I scarcely know how to tell you"—and she whispered.

"What do you say! In one bed! All! Why, it's revolting!" cried Mrs. Abel, clasping her hands.

"Yes, an hour ago I; too, could not have believed it possible," answered Mrs. Warden, "But when you've been on the spot yourself, and seen with your own eyes—"

"Good heavens, Emily, how could you venture into such a place!"

"I am glad I did, and still more glad of the happy chance that brought the inspector on the scene just at the right time. For if it is ennobling to bring succor to the virtuous poor who live clean and frugal lives in their humble sphere, it would be unpardonable to help such people as these to gratify their vile proclivities."

"Yes, you're quite right, Emily! What I can't understand is how people in a Christian community—people who have been baptized and confirmed—can sink into such a state! Have they not every day—or, at any rate, every Sunday—the opportunity of listening to powerful and impressive sermons? And Bibles, I am told, are to be had for an incredibly trifling sum."

"Yes, and only to think," added Mrs. Warden, "that not even the heathen, who are without all these blessings—that not even they have any excuse for evil-doing; for they have conscience to guide them."

"And I'm sure conscience speaks clearly enough to every one who has the will to listen," Mrs. Abel exclaimed, with emphasis.

"Yes, heaven knows it does," answered Mrs. Warden, gazing straight before her with a serious smile.

When the friends parted, they exchanged warm embraces.

Mrs. Warden grasped the ivory handle, entered the carriage, and drew her train after her. Then she closed the carriage door—not with a slam, but slowly and carefully.

"To Madame Labiche's!" she called to the coachman; then, turning to her friend who had accompanied her right down to the garden gate, she said, with a quiet smile: "Now, thank heaven, I can order my silk dress with a good conscience."

"Yes, indeed you can!" exclaimed Mrs. Abel, watching her with tears in her eyes. Then she hastened in-doors.

ROMANCE AND REALITY.

"Just you get married as soon as you can," said Mrs. Olsen.

"Yes, I can't understand why it shouldn't be this very autumn," exclaimed the elder Miss Ludvigsen, who was an enthusiast for ideal love.

"Oh, yes!" cried Miss Louisa, who was certain to be one of the bridesmaids.

"But Sören says he can't afford it," answered the bride elect, somewhat timidly.

"Can't afford it!" repeated Miss Ludvigsen. "To think of a young girl using such an expression! If you're going to let your new-born love be overgrown with prosaic calculations, what will be left of the ideal halo which love alone can cast over life? That a man should be alive to these considerations I can more or less understand—it's in a way his duty; but for a sensitive, womanly heart, in the heyday of sentiment!—No, no, Marie; for heaven's sake, don't let these sordid money-questions darken your happiness."

"Oh, no!" cried Miss Louisa.

"And, besides," Mrs. Olsen chimed in, "your *fiancé* is by no means so badly off. My husband and I began life on much less.—I know you'll say that times were different then. Good heavens, we all know that! What I can't understand is that you don't get tired of telling us so. Don't you think that we old people, who have gone through the transition period, have the best means of comparing the requirements of to-day with those of our youth? You can surely understand that with my experience of house-keeping, I'm not likely to disregard the altered conditions of life; and yet I assure you that the salary your intended receives from my husband, with what he can easily earn by extra work, is quite sufficient to set up house upon."

Mrs. Olsen had become quite eager in her argument, though no one thought of contradicting her. She had so often, in conversations of this sort, been irritated to hear people, and especially young married women, enlarging on the ridiculous cheapness of everything thirty years ago. She felt as though they wanted to make light of the exemplary fashion in which she had conducted her household.

This conversation made a deep impression on the *fiancée*, for she had great confidence in Mrs. Olsen's shrewdness and experience. Since Marie had become engaged to the Sheriff's clerk, the Sheriff's wife had taken a keen interest in her. She was an energetic woman, and, as her own children were already grown up and married, she found a welcome outlet for her activity in busying herself with the concerns of the young couple.

Marie's mother, on the other hand, was a very retiring woman. Her husband, a subordinate government official, had died so early that her pension extremely scanty. She came of a good family, and had learned nothing in her girlhood except to Play the piano. This accomplishment she had long ceased to practise, and in the course of time had become exceedingly religious.—

—"Look here, now, my dear fellow, aren't you thinking of getting married?" asked the Sheriff, in his genial way.

"Oh yes," answered Sören, with some hesitation, "when I can afford it.

"Afford it!" the Sheriff repeated; "Why, you're by no means so badly off. I know you have something laid by—"

"A trifle," Sören put in.

"Well, so be it; but it shows, at any rate, that you have an idea of economy, and that's as good as money in your pocket. You came out high in your examination; and, with your family influence and other advantages at headquarters, you needn't wait long before applying for some minor appointment; and once in the way of promotion, you know, you go ahead in spite of yourself."

Sören bit his pen and looked interested.

"Let us assume," continued his principal, "that, thanks to your economy, you can set up house without getting into any debt worth speaking of. Then you'll have your salary clear, and whatever you can earn in addition by extra work. It would be strange, indeed, if a man of your ability could note find employment for his leisure time in a rising commercial centre like ours."

Sören reflected all forenoon on what the Sheriff had said. He saw, more and more clearly, that he had over-estimated the financial obstacles to his marriage; and, after all, it was true that he had a good deal of time on his hands out of office hours.

He was engaged to dine with his principal; and his intended, too, was to be there. On the whole, the young people perhaps met quite as often at the Sheriff's as at Marie's home. For the peculiar knack which Mrs. Möller, Marie's mother, had acquired, of giving every conversation a religious turn, was not particularly attractive to them.

There was much talk at table of a lovely little house which Mrs. Olsen had discovered; "A perfect nest for a newly married couple," as she expressed herself. Sören inquired, in passing, as to the financial conditions, and thought them reasonable enough, if the place answered to his hostess's description.

—Mrs. Olsen's anxiety to see this marriage hurried on was due in the first place, as above hinted, to her desire for mere occupation, and, in the second place, to a vague longing for some event, of whatever nature, to happen—a psychological phenomenon by no means rare in energetic natures, living narrow and monotonous lives.

The Sheriff worked in the same direction, partly in obedience to his wife's orders, and partly because he thought that Sören's marriage to Marie, who owed so much to his family, would form another tie to bind him to the office—for the Sheriff was pleased with his clerk.

After dinner the young couple strolled about the garden. They conversed in an odd, short-winded fashion, until at last Sören, in a tone which was meant to be careless, threw out the suggestion: "What should you say to getting married this autumn?"

Marie forgot to express surprise. The same thought had been running in her own head; so she answered, looking to the ground: "Well, if you think you can afford it, I can have no objection."

"Suppose we reckon the thing out," said Sören, and drew her towards the summer-house.

Half an hour afterwards they came out, arm-in-arm, into the sunshine. They, too, seemed to radiate light—the glow of a spirited resolution, formed after ripe thought and serious counting of the cost.

Some people might, perhaps, allege that it would be rash to assume the absolute correctness of a calculation merely from the fact that two lovers have arrived at exactly the same total; especially when the problem happens to bear upon the choice between renunciation and the supremest bliss.

In the course of the calculation Sören had not been without misgivings. He remembered how, in his student days, he had spoken largely of our duty towards posterity; how he had philosophically demonstrated the egoistic element in love, and propounded the ludicrous question whether people had a right, in pure heedlessness as it were, to bring children into the world.

But time and practical life had, fortunately, cured him of all taste for these idle and dangerous mental gymnastics. And, besides, he was far too proper and well-bred to shock his innocent lady-love by taking into account so indelicate a possibility as that of their having a large family. Is it not one of the charms of young love that it should leave such matters as these to heaven and the stork? [Note: The stork, according to common nursery legends, brings babies under its wing.]

There was great jubilation at the Sheriff's, and not there alone. Almost the whole town was thrown into a sort of fever by the intelligence that the Sheriff's clerk was to be married in the autumn. Those who were sure of an invitation to the wedding were already looking forward to it; those who could not hope to be invited fretted and said spiteful things; while those whose case was doubtful were half crazy with suspense. And all emotions have their value in a stagnant little town.

—Mrs. Olsen was a woman of courage; yet her heart beat as she set forth to call upon Mrs. Möller. It is no light matter to ask a mother to let her daughter be married from your house. But she might have spared herself all anxiety.

For Mrs. Möller shrank from every sort of exertion almost as much as she shrank from sin in all its forms. Therefore she was much relieved by Mrs. Olsen's proposition, introduced with a delicacy which did not always characterize that lady's proceedings. However, it was not Mrs. Möller's way to make any show of pleasure or satisfaction. Since everything, in one way or another, was a "cross" to be borne, she did not fail, even in this case, to make it appear that her long-suffering was proof against every trial.

Mrs. Olsen returned home beaming. She would have been balked of half her pleasure in this marriage if she had not been allowed to give the wedding party; for wedding-parties were Mrs. Olsen's specialty. On such occasions she put her economy aside, and the satisfaction she felt in finding, an opening for all her energies made her positively amiable. After all, the Sheriff's post was a good one, and the Olsens had always had a little property besides, which, however, they never talked about.

—So the wedding came off, and a splendid wedding it was. Miss Ludvigsen had written an unrhymed song about true love, which was sung at the feast, and Louisa eclipsed all the other bridesmaids.

The newly-married couple took up their quarters in the nest discovered by Mrs. Olsen, and plunged into that half-conscious existence of festal felicity which the English call the "honeymoon," because it is too sweet; the Germans, "Flitterwochen," because its glory departs so quickly; and we "the wheat-bread days" because we know that there is coarser fare to follow.

But in Sören's cottage the wheat-bread days lasted long; and when heaven sent them a little angel with golden locks, their happiness was as great as we can by any means expect in this weary world.

As for the incomings—well, they were fairly adequate, though Sören had, unfortunately, not succeeded in making a start without getting into debt; but that would, no doubt, come right in time.

—Yes, in time! The years passed, and with each of them heaven sent Sören a little golden-locked angel. After six years of marriage they had exactly five children. The quiet little town was unchanged, Sören was still the Sheriff's clerk, and the Sheriff's household was as of old; but Sören himself was scarcely to be recognized.

They tell of sorrows and heavy blows of fate which can turn a man's hair gray in a night. Such afflictions had not fallen to Sören's lot. The sorrows that had sprinkled his hair with gray, rounded his shoulders, and made him old before his time, were of a lingering and vulgar type. They were bread-sorrows.

Bread-sorrows are to other sorrows as toothache to other disorders. A simple pain can be conquered in open fight; a nervous fever, or any other "regular" illness, goes through a normal development and comes to a crisis. But while toothache has the long-drawn sameness of the tape-worm, bread-sorrows envelop their victim like a grimy cloud: he puts them on every morning with his threadbare clothes, and he seldom sleeps so deeply as to forget them.

It was in the long fight against encroaching poverty that Sören had worn himself out; and yet he was great at economy.

But there are two sorts of economy: the active and the passive. Passive economy thinks day and night of the way to save a half-penny; active economy broods no less intently on the way to earn a dollar. The first sort of economy, the passive, prevails among us; the active in the great nations—chiefly in America.

Sören's strength lay in the passive direction. He devoted all his spare time and some of his office-hours to thinking out schemes for saving and retrenchment. But whether it was that the luck was against him, or, more probably, that his income was really too small to support a wife and five children—in any case, his financial position went from bad to worse.

Every place in life seems filled to the uttermost, and yet there are people who make their way everywhere. Sören did not belong to this class. He sought in vain for the extra work on which he and Marie had reckoned as a vague but ample source of income. Nor had his good connections availed him aught. There are always plenty of people ready to help young men of promise who can help themselves; but the needy father of a family is never welcome.

Sören had been a man of many friends. It could not be said that they had drawn back from him, but he seemed somehow to have disappeared from their view. When they happened to meet, there was a certain embarrassment on both sides. Sören no longer cared for the things that interested them, and they were bored when he held forth upon the severity of his daily grind, and the expensiveness of living.

And if, now and then, one of his old friends invited him to a bachelor-party, he did as people are apt to do whose every-day fare is extremely frugal: he ate and drank too much. The lively but well-bred and circumspect Sören declined into a sort of butt, who made rambling speeches, and around whom the young whelps of the party would gather after dinner to make sport for themselves. But what impressed his friends most painfully of all, was his utter neglect of his personal appearance.

For he had once been extremely particular in his dress; in his student days he had been called "the exquisite Sören." And even after his marriage he had for some time contrived to wear his modest attire with a certain air. But after bitter necessity had forced him to keep every garment in use an unnaturally long time, his vanity had at last given way. And when once a man's sense of personal neatness is impaired, he is apt to lose it utterly. When a new coat became absolutely necessary, it was his wife that had to awaken him to the fact; and when his collars became quite too ragged at the edges, he trimmed them with a pair of scissors.

He had other things to think about, poor fellow. But when people came into the office, or when he was entering another person's house, he had a purely mechanical habit of moistening his fingers at his lips, and rubbing the lapels of his coat. This was the sole relic of "the exquisite Sören's" exquisiteness—like one of the rudimentary organs, dwindled through lack of use, which zoologists find in certain animals.—

Sören's worst enemy, however, dwelt within him. In his youth he had dabbled in philosophy, and this baneful passion for thinking would now attack him from time to time, crushing all resistance, and, in the end, turning everything topsy-turvy.

It was when he thought about his children that this befell him.

When he regarded these little creatures, who, as he could not conceal from himself, became more and more neglected as time went on, he found it impossible to place them under the category of golden-locked angels had sent him by heaven. He had to admit that heaven does not send us these gifts without a certain inducement on our side; and then Sören asked himself: "Had you any right to do this?" He thought of his own life, which had begun under fortunate conditions. His family had been in easy circumstances; his father, a government official, had given him the best education to be had in the country; he had gone forth to the battle of life fully equipped—and what had come of it all?

And how could he equip his children for the fight into which he was sending them? They had begun their life in need and penury, which had, as far as possible, to be concealed; they had early learned the bitter lesson of the disparity between inward expectations and demands and outward circumstances; and from their slovenly home they would take with them the most crushing inheritance, perhaps, under which a man can toil through life; to wit, poverty with pretensions.

Sören tried to tell himself that heaven would take care of them. But he was ashamed to do so, for he felt it was only a phrase of self-excuse, designed to allay the qualms of conscience.

These thoughts were his worst torment; but, truth to tell, they did not often attack him, for Sören had sunk into apathy. That was the Sheriff's view of his case. "My clerk was quite a clever fellow in his time," he used to say. "But, you know, his hasty marriage, his large family, and all that—in short, he has almost done for himself."

Badly dressed and badly fed, beset with debts and cares, he was worn out and weary before he had accomplished anything. And life went its way, and Sören dragged himself along in its train. He seemed to be forgotten by all save heaven, which, as aforesaid, sent him year by year a little angel with locks of gold—

Sören's young wife had clung faithfully to her husband through these six years, and she, too, had reached the same point.

The first year of her married life had glided away like a dream of dizzy bliss. When she held up the little golden-locked angel for the admiration of her lady friends, she was beautiful with the beauty of perfect maternal happiness; and Miss Ludvigsen said: "Here is love in its ideal form."

But Mrs. Olsen's "nest" soon became too small; the family increased while the income stood still.

She was daily confronted by new claims, new cares, and new duties. Marie set stanchly to work, for she was a courageous and sensible woman.

It is not one of the so-called elevating employments to have charge of a houseful of little children, with no means of satisfying even moderate requirements in respect of comfort and well-being. In addition to this, she was never thoroughly robust; she oscillated perpetually between having just had, and being just about to have, a child. As she toiled from morning to night, she lost her buoyancy of spirit, and her mind became bitter. She sometimes asked herself: "What is the meaning of it all?"

She saw the eagerness of young girls to be married, and the air of self-complacency with which young men offer to marry them; she thought of her own experience, and felt as though she had been befooled.

But it was not right of Marie to think thus, for she had been excellently brought up.

The view of life to which she had from the first been habituated, was the only beautiful one, the only one that could enable her to preserve her ideals intact. No unlovely and prosaic theory of existence had ever cast its shadow over her development; she knew that love is the most beautiful thing on earth, that it transcends reason and is consummated in marriage; as to children, she had learned to blush when they were mentioned.

A strict watch had always been kept upon her reading. She had read many earnest volumes on the duties of woman; she knew that her happiness lies in being loved by a man, and that her mission is to be his wife. She knew how evil-disposed people will often place obstacles between two lovers, but she knew, too, that true love will at last emerge victorious from the fight. When people met with disaster in the battle of life, it was because they were false to the ideal. She had faith in the ideal, although she did not know what it was.

She knew and loved those poets whom she was allowed to read. Much of their erotics she only half understood, but that made it all the more lovely. She knew that marriage was a serious, a very serious thing, for which a clergyman was indispensable; and she understood that marriages are made in heaven, as engagements are made in the ballroom. But when, in these youthful days, she pictured to herself this serious institution, she seemed to be looking into an enchanted grove, with Cupids weaving garlands, and storks bringing little golden-locked angels under their wings; while before a little cabin in the background, which yet was large enough to contain all the bliss in the world, sat the ideal married couple, gazing into the depths of each other's eyes.

No one had ever been so ill-bred as to say to her: "Excuse me, young lady, would you not like to come with me to a different point of view, and look at the matter from the other side? How if it should turn out to be a mere set-scene of painted pasteboard?"

Sören's young wife had now had ample opportunities of studying the set-scene from the other side.

Mrs. Olsen had at first come about her early and late, and overwhelmed her with advice and criticism. Both Sören and his wife were many a time heartily tired of her; but they owed the Olsens so much.

Little by little, however, the old lady's zeal cooled down. When the young people's house was no longer so clean, so orderly, and so exemplary that she could plume herself upon her work, she gradually withdrew; and when Sören's wife once in a while came to ask her for advice or assistance, the Sheriff's lady would mount her high horse, until Marie ceased to trouble her. But if, in society, conversation happened to fall upon the Sheriff's clerk, and any one expressed compassion for his poor wife, with her many children and her miserable income, Mrs. Olsen would not fail to put in her word with great decision: "I can assure you it would be just the same if Marie had twice as much to live on and no children at all. You see, she's—" and Mrs. Olsen made a motion with her hands, as if she were squandering something abroad, to right and left.

Marie seldom went to parties, and if she did appear, in her at least ten-times-altered marriage dress, it was generally to sit alone in a corner, or to carry on a tedious conversation with a similarly situated housewife about the dearness of the times and the unreasonableness of servant-girls.

And the young ladies who had gathered the gentlemen around them, either in the middle of the room or wherever they found the most comfortable chairs to stretch themselves in, whispered to each other: "How tiresome it is that young married women can never talk about anything but housekeeping and the nursery."

In the early days, Marie had often had visits from her many friends. They were enchanted with her charming house, and the little golden-locked angel had positively to be protected from their greedy admiration. But when one of them now chanced to stray in her direction, it was quite a different affair. There was no longer any golden-locked angel to be exhibited in a clean, embroidered frock with red ribbons. The children, who were never presentable without warning, were huddled hastily away—dropping their toys about the floor, forgetting to pick up half-eaten pieces of bread-and-butter from the chairs, and leaving behind them that peculiar atmosphere which one can, at most, endure in one's own children.

Day after day her life dragged on in ceaseless toil. Many a time, when she heard her husband bemoaning the drudgery of his lot, she thought to herself with a sort of defiance: "I wonder which of us two has the harder work?"

In one respect she was happier than her husband. Philosophy did not enter into her dreams, and when she could steal a quiet moment for reflection; her thoughts were very different from the cogitations of the poor philosopher.

She had no silver plate to polish, no jewelry to take out and deck herself with. But, in the inmost recess of her heart, she treasured all the memories of the first year of her marriage, that year of romantic bliss; and these memories she would furbish and furbish afresh, till they shone brighter with every year that passed.

But when the weary and despondent housewife, in all secrecy, decked herself out with these jewels of memory, they did not succeed in shedding any brightness over her life in the present. She was scarcely conscious of any connection between the golden-locked angel with the red ribbons and the five-year-old boy who lay grubbing in the dark back yard. These moments snatched her quite away from reality; they were like opium dreams.

Then some one would call for her from an adjoining room, or one of the children would be brought in howling from the street, with a great bump on its forehead. Hastily she would hide away her treasures, resume her customary air of hopeless weariness, and plunge once more into her labyrinth of duties and cares.

—Thus had this marriage fared, and thus did this couple toil onward. They both dragged at the same heavy load; but did they drag in unison? It is sad, but it is true: when the manger is empty, the horses bite each other.—

—There was a great chocolate-party at the Misses Ludvigsen's—all maiden ladies.

"For married women are so prosaic," said the elder Miss Ludvigsen.

"Uh, yes!" cried Louisa.

Every one was in the most vivacious humor, as is generally the case in such company and on such an occasion; and, as the gossip went the round of the town, it arrived in time at Sören's door. All were agreed that it was a most unhappy marriage, and a miserable home; some pitied, others condemned.

Then the elder Miss Ludvigsen, with a certain solemnity, expressed herself as follows: "I can tell you what was at fault in that marriage, for I know the circumstances thoroughly. Even before her marriage there was something calculating, something almost prosaic in Marie's nature, which is entirely foreign to true, ideal love. This fault has since taken the upperhand, and is avenging itself cruelly upon both of them. Of course their means are not great, but what could that matter to two people who truly loved each other? for we know that happiness is not dependent on wealth. Is it not precisely in the humble home that the omnipotence of love is most beautifully made manifest?—And, besides, who can call these two poor? Has not heaven richly blessed them with healthy, sturdy children? These—these are their true wealth! And if their hearts had been filled with true, ideal love, then—then—"

Miss Ludvigsen came to a momentary standstill.

"What then?" asked a courageous young lady.

"Then," continued Miss Ludvigsen, loftily, "then we should certainly have seen a very different lot in life assigned to them."

The courageous young lady felt ashamed of herself.

There was a pause, during which Miss Ludvigsen's words sank deep into all hearts. They all felt that this was the truth; any doubt and uneasiness that might perhaps have lurked here and there vanished away. All were confirmed in their steadfast and beautiful faith in true, ideal love; for they were all maiden ladies.

WITHERED LEAVES.

You *may* tire of looking at a single painting, but you *must* tire of looking at many. That is why the eyelids grow so heavy in the great galleries, and the seats are as closely packed as an omnibus on Sunday.

Happy he who has resolution enough to select from the great multitude a small number of pictures, to which he can return every day.

In this way you can appropriate—undetected by the custodians— a little private gallery of your own, distributed through the great halls. Everything which does not belong to this private collection sinks into mere canvas and gilding, a decoration you glance at in passing, but which does not fatigue the eye.

It happens now and then that you discover a picture, hitherto overlooked, which now, after thorough examination, is admitted as one of the select few. The assortment thus steadily increases, and it is even conceivable that by systematically following this method you might make a whole picture-gallery, in this sense, your private property.

But as a rule there is no time for that. You must rapidly take your bearings, putting a cross in the catalogue against the pictures you think of annexing, just as a forester marks his trees as he goes through the wood.

These private collections, as a matter of course, are of many different kinds. One may often search them in vain for the great, recognized masterpieces, while one may find a little, unconsidered picture in the place of honor; and in order to understand the odd arrangement of many of these small collections, one must take as one's cicerone the person whose choice they represent. Here, now, is a picture from a private gallery.—

There hung in a corner of the Salon of 1878 a picture by the English painter Mr. Everton Sainsbury. It made no sensation whatever. It was neither large enough nor small enough to arouse idle curiosity, nor was there a trace of modern extravagance either in composition or in color.

As people passed they gave it a sympathetic glance, for it made a harmonious impression, and the subject was familiar and easily understood.

It represented two lovers who had slightly fallen out, and people smiled as each in his own mind thought of those charming little quarrels which are so vehement and so short, which arise from the most improbable and most varied causes, but invariably end in a kiss.

And yet this picture attracted to itself its own special public; you could see that it was adopted into several private collections.

As you made your way towards the well-known corner, you would often find the place occupied by a solitary person standing lost in contemplation. At different times, you would come upon all sorts of different people thus absorbed; but they all had the same peculiar expression before that picture, as if it cast a faded, yellowish reflection.

If you approached, the gazer would probably move away; it seemed as though only one person at a time could enjoy that work of art—as though one must be entirely alone with it.—

In a corner of the garden, right against the high wall, stands an open summer-house. It is quite simply built of green lattice-work, which forms a large arch backed by the wall. The whole summer-house is covered with a wild vine, which twines itself from the left side over the arched roof, and droops its slender branches on the right.

It is late autumn. The summer-house has already lost its thick roof of foliage. Only the youngest and most delicate tendrils of the wild vine have any leaves left. Before they fall, departing summer lavishes on them all the color it has left; like light sprays of red and yellow flowers, they hang yet a while to enrich the garden with autumn's melancholy splendor.

The fallen leaves are scattered all around, and right before the summer-house the wind has with great diligence whirled the loveliest of them together, into a neat little round cairn.

The trees are already leafless, and on a naked branch sits the little garden-warbler with its rust-brown breast—like a withered leaf left hanging—and repeats untiringly a little fragment which it remembers of its spring-song.

The only thriving thing in the whole picture is the ivy; for ivy, like sorrow, is fresh both summer and winter.

It comes creeping along with its soft feelers, it thrusts itself into the tiniest chinks, it forces its way through the minutest crannies; and not until it has waxed wide and strong do we realize that it can no longer be rooted up, but will inexorably strangle whatever it has laid its clutches on.

Ivy, however, is like well-bred sorrow; it cloaks its devastations with fair and glossy leaves. Thus people wear a glossy mask of smiles, feigning to be unaware of the ivy-clad ruins among which their lot is cast.—

In the middle of the open summer-house sits a young girl on a rush chair; both hands rest in her lap. She is sitting with bent head and a strange expression in her beautiful face. It is not vexation or anger, still less is it commonplace sulkiness, that utters itself in her features; it is rather bitter and crushing disappointment. She looks as if she were on the point of letting something slip away from her which she has not the strength to hold fast—as if something were withering between her hands.

The man who is leaning with one hand upon her chair is beginning to understand that the situation is graver than he thought. He has done all he can to get the quarrel, so trivial in its origin, adjusted and forgotten; he has talked reason, he has tried playfulness; he has besought forgiveness, and humbled himself—perhaps more than he intended—but all in vain. Nothing avails to arouse her out of the listless mood into which she has sunk.

Thus it is with an expression of anxiety that he bends down towards her: "But you know that at heart we love each other so much."

"Then why do we quarrel so easily, and why do we speak so bitterly and unkindly to each other?"

"Why, my dear! the whole thing was the merest trifle from the first."

"That's just it! Do you remember what we said to each other? How we vied with each other in trying to find the word we knew would be most wounding? Oh, to think that we used our knowledge of each other's heart to find out the tenderest points, where an unkind word could strike home! And this we call love!"

"My dear, don't take it so solemnly," he answered, trying a lighter tone. "People may be ever so fond of each other, and yet disagree a little at times; it can't be otherwise."

"Yes, yes!" she cried, "there must be a love for which discord is impossible, or else—or else I have been mistaken, and what we call love is nothing but—"

"Have no doubts of love!" he interrupted her, eagerly; and he depicted in warm and eloquent words the feeling which ennobles humanity in teaching us to bear with each other's weaknesses; which confers upon us the highest bliss, since, in spite of all petty disagreements, it unites us by the fairest ties.

She had only half listened to him. Her eyes had wandered over the fading garden, she had inhaled the heavy atmosphere of dying vegetation—and she had been thinking of the spring-time, of hope, of that all-powerful love which was now dying like an autumn flower.

"Withered leaves," said she, quietly; and rising, she scattered with her foot all the beautiful leaves which the wind had taken such pains to heap together.

She went up the avenue leading to the house; he followed close behind her. He was silent, for he found not a word to say. A drowsy feeling of uneasy languor came over him; he asked himself whether he could overtake her, or whether she were a hundred miles away.

She walked with her head bent, looking down at the flower-beds. There stood the asters like torn paper flowers upon withered potato-shaws; the dahlias hung their stupid, crinkled heads upon their broken stems, and the hollyhocks showed small stunted buds at the top, and great wet, rotting flowers clustering down their stalks.

And disappointment and bitterness cut deep into the young heart. As the flowers were dying, she was ripening for the winter of life.

So they disappeared up the avenue. But the empty chair remained standing in the half-withered summer-house, while the wind busied itself afresh in piling up the leaves in a little cairn.

And in the course of time we all come—each in his turn—to seat ourselves on the empty chair in a corner of the garden and gaze on a little cairn of withered leaves.—

THE BATTLE OF WATERLOO.

Since it is not only entertaining in itself, but also consonant with use and wont, to be in love; and since in our innocent and moral society, one can so much the more safely indulge in these amatory diversions as one runs no risk of being disturbed either by vigilant fathers or pugnacious brothers; and, finally, since one can as easily get out of as get into our peculiarly Norwegian form of betrothal—a half-way house between marriage and free board in a good family—all these things considered I say, it was not wonderful that Cousin Hans felt profoundly unhappy. For he was not in the least in love.

He had long lived in expectation of being seized by a kind of delirious ecstasy, which, if experienced people are to be trusted, is the infallible symptom of true love. But as nothing of the sort had happened, although he was already in his second year at college, he said to himself: "After all, love is a lottery if you want to win, you must at least table your stake. 'Lend Fortune a helping hand,' as they say in the lottery advertisements."

He looked about him diligently, and closely observed his own heart.

Like a fisher who sits with his line around his forefinger, watching for the least jerk, and wondering when the bite will come, so Cousin Hans held his breath whenever he saw a young lady, wondering whether he was now to feel that peculiar jerk which is well known to be inseparable from true love—that jerk which suddenly makes all the blood rush to the heart, and then sends it just as suddenly up into the head, and makes your face flush red to the very roots of your hair.

But never a bite came. His hair had long ago flushed red to the roots, for Cousin Hans's hair could not be called brown; but his face remained as pale and as long as ever.

The poor fisherman was growing quite weary, when he one day strolled down to the esplanade. He seated himself on a bench and observed, with a contemptuous air, a squad of soldiers engaged in the invigorating exercise of standing on one leg in the full sunshine, and wriggling their bodies so as to be roasted on both sides.

"Nonsense!" [Note: The English word is used in the original] said Cousin Hans, indignantly; "it's certainly too dear a joke for a little country like ours to maintain acrobats of that sort. Didn't I see the other day that this so-called army requires 1500 boxes of shoe-blacking, 600 curry-combs, 3000 yards of gold-lace and 8640 brass buttons?—It would be better if we saved what we spend in gold-lace and brass buttons, and devoted our half-pence to popular enlightenment," said Cousin Hans.

For he was infected by the modern ideas, which are unfortunately beginning to make way among us, and which will infallibly end in overthrowing the whole existing fabric of society.

"Good-bye, then, for the present," said a lady's voice close behind him.

"Good-bye for the present, my dear," answered a deep, masculine voice.

Cousin Hans turned slowly, for it was a warm day. He discovered a military-looking old man in a close-buttoned black coat, with an order at his buttonhole, a neck-cloth twisted an incredible number of times around his throat, a well-brushed hat, and light trousers. The gentleman nodded to a young lady, who went off towards the town, and then continued his walk along the ramparts.

Weary of waiting as he was, Cousin Hans could not help following the young girl with his eyes as she hastened away. She was small and trim, and he observed with interest that she was one of the few women who do not make a little inward turn with the left foot as they lift it from the ground.

This was a great merit in the young man's eyes; for Cousin Hans was one of those sensitive, observant natures who are alone fitted really to appreciate a woman at her full value.

After a few steps the lady turned, no doubt in order to nod once again to the old officer; but by the merest chance her eyes met those of Cousin Hans.

At last occurred what he had so long been expecting: he felt the bite! His blood rushed about just in the proper way, he lost his breath, his head became hot, a cold shiver ran down his back, and he grew moist between the fingers. In short, all the symptoms supervened which, according to the testimony of poets and experienced prose-writers, betoken real, true, genuine love.

There was, indeed, no time to be lost. He hastily snatched up his gloves, his stick, and his student's cap, which he had laid upon the bench, and set off after the lady across the esplanade and towards the town.

In the great, corrupt communities abroad this sort of thing is not allowable. There the conditions of life are so impure that a well-bred young man would never think of following a reputable woman. And the few reputable women there are in those nations, would be much discomposed to find themselves followed.

But in our pure and moral atmosphere we can, fortunately, permit our young people somewhat greater latitude, just on account of the strict propriety of our habits.

Cousin Hans, therefore, did not hesitate a moment in obeying the voice of his heart; and the young lady, who soon observed what havoc she had made with the glance designed for the old soldier, felt the situation piquant and not unpleasing.

The passers-by, who, of course, at once saw what was going on (be it observed that this is one of the few scenes of life in which the leading actors are quite unconscious of their audience), thought, for the most part, that the comedy was amusing to witness. They looked round and smiled to themselves; for they all knew that either it would lead to nothing, in which case it was only the most innocent of youthful amusements; or it would lead to an engagement, and an engagement is the most delightful thing in the world.

While they thus pursued their course at a fitting distance, now on the same sidewalk and now on opposite sides of the street, Cousin Hans had ample time for reflection.

As to the fact of his being in love he was quite clear. The symptoms were all there; he knew that he was in for it, in for real, true, genuine, love; and he was happy in the knowledge. Yes, so happy was Cousin Hans that he, who at other times was apt to stand upon his rights, accepted with a quiet, complacent smile all the jostlings and shoves, the smothered objurgations and other unpleasantnesses, which inevitably befall any one who rushes hastily along a crowded street, keeping his eyes fixed upon an object in front of him.

No—the love was obvious, indubitable. That settled, he tried to picture to himself the beloved one's, the heavenly creature's, mundane circumstances. And there was no great difficulty in that; she had been walking with her old father, had suddenly discovered that it was past twelve o'clock, and had hastily said good-bye for the present, in order to go home and see to the dinner. For she was doubtless domestic, this sweet creature, and evidently motherless.

The last conjecture was, perhaps, a result of the dread of mothers-in-law inculcated by all reputable authors; but it was none the less confident on that account. And now it only remained for Cousin Hans to discover, in the first place, where she lived, in the second place who she was, and in the third place how he could make her acquaintance.

Where she lived he would soon learn, for was she not on her way home? Who she was, he could easily find out from the neighbors. And as for making her acquaintance—good heavens! is not a little difficulty an indispensable part of a genuine romance?

209

Just as the chase was at its height, the quarry disappeared into a gateway; and it was really high time, for, truth to tell, the hunter was rather exhausted.

He read with a certain relief the number, "34," over the gate, then went a few steps farther on, in order to throw any possible observer off the scent, and stopped beside a street-lamp to recover his breath. It was, as aforesaid, a warm day; and this, combined with his violent emotion, had thrown Hans into a strong perspiration. His toilet, too, had been disarranged by the reckless eagerness with which he had hurled himself into the chase.

He could not help smiling at himself, as he stood and wiped his face and neck, adjusted his necktie, and felt his collar, which had melted on the sunny side. But it was a blissful smile, he was in that frame of mind in which one sees, or at any rate apprehends, nothing of the external world; and he said to himself, half aloud, "Love endures everything, accepts everything."

"And perspires freely," said a fat little gentleman whose white waistcoat suddenly came within Cousin Hans's range of vision.

"Oh, is that you, uncle?" he said, a little abashed.

"Of course it is," answered Uncle Frederick. "I've left the shady side of the street expressly to save you from being roasted. Come along with me."

Thereupon he tried to drag his nephew with him, but Hans resisted. "Do you know who lives at No. 34, uncle?"

"Not in the least; but do let us get into the shade," said Uncle Frederick; for there were two things he could not endure: heat and laughter—the first on account of his corpulence, and the second on account of what he himself called "his apoplectic tendencies."

"By-the-bye," he said, when they reached the cool side of the street, and he had taken his nephew by the arm, "now that I think of it, I do know, quite well, who lives in No. 34; it's old Captain Schrappe."

"Do you know him?" asked Cousin Hans, anxiously.

"Yes, a little, just as half the town knows him, from having seen him on the esplanade, where he walks every day."

"Yes, that was just where I saw him," said his nephew. "What an interesting old gentleman he looks. I should like so much to have a talk with him."

"That wish you can easily gratify," answered Uncle Frederick. "You need only place yourself anywhere on the ramparts and begin drawing lines in the sand, then he'll come to you."

"Come to you?" said Cousin Hans.

"Yes, he'll come and talk to you. But you must be careful: he's dangerous."

"Eh?" said Cousin Hans.

"He was once very nearly the end of me."

"Ah!" said Cousin Hans.

"Yes, with his talk, you understand."

"Oh?" said Cousin Hans.

"You see, he has two stories," continued Uncle Frederick, "the one, about a sham fight in Sweden, is a good half-hour long. But the other, the battle of Waterloo, generally lasts from an hour and a half to two hours. I have heard it three times." And Uncle Frederick sighed deeply.

"Are they so very tedious, then, these stories? asked Cousin Hans.

"Oh, they're well enough for once in a way," answered his uncle, "and if you should get into conversation with the captain, mark what I tell you: If you get off with the short story, the Swedish one, you have nothing to do but alternately to nod and shake your head. You'll soon pick up the lay of the land."

"The lay of the land?" said Cousin Hans.

"Yes, you must know that he draws the whole manoeuvre for you in the sand; but it's easy enough to understand if only you keep your eye on A and B. There's only one point where you must be careful not to put your foot in it."

"Does he get impatient, then, if you don't understand?" asked Cousin Hans.

"No, quite the contrary; but if you show that you're not following, he begins at the beginning again, you see! The crucial point in the sham fight," continued his uncle, "is the movement made by the captain himself, in spite of the general's orders, which equally embarrassed both friends and foes. It was this stroke of genius, between ourselves, which forced them to give him the Order of the Sword, to induce him to retire. So when you come to this point, you must nod violently, and say: 'Of course—the only reasonable move—the key to the position.' Remember that—the key."

"The key," repeated Cousin Hans.

"But," said his uncle, looking at him with anticipatory compassion, "if, in your youthful love of adventure, you should bring on yourself the long story, the one about Waterloo, you must either keep quite silent or have all your wits about you. I once had to swallow the whole description over again, only because, in my eagerness to show how thoroughly I understood the situation, I happened to move Kellermann's dragoons instead of Milhaud's cuirassiers!"

"What do you mean by moving the dragoons, uncle?" asked Cousin Hans.

"Oh, you'll understand well enough, if you come in for the long one. But," added Uncle Frederick, in a solemn tone, "beware, I warn you, beware of Blücher!"

"Blücher?" said Cousin Hans.

"I won't say anything more. But what makes you wish to know about this old original? What on earth do you want with him."

"Does he walk there every forenoon?" asked Hans.

"Every forenoon, from eleven to one, and every afternoon, from five to seven. But what interest—?"

"Has he many children?" interrupted Hans.

"Only one daughter; but what the deuce—?"

"Good-bye, uncle!" I must get home to my books."

"Stop a bit! Aren't you going to Aunt Maren's this evening? She asked me to invite you."

"No, thanks, I haven't time," shouted Cousin Hans, who was already several paces away.

"There's to be a ladies' party—young ladies!" bawled Uncle Frederick; for he did not know what had come over his nephew.

But Hans shook his head with a peculiar energetic contempt, and disappeared round the corner.

"The deuce is in it," thought Uncle Frederick, "the boy is crazy, or—oh, I have it!—he's in love! He was standing here, babbling about love, when I found him—outside No. 34. And then his interest in old Schrappe! Can he be in love with Miss Betty? Oh, no," thought Uncle Frederick, shaking his head, as he, too, continued on his way, "I don't believe he has sense enough for that."

II.

Cousin Hans did not eat much dinner that day. People in love never eat much, and, besides, he did not care for rissoles.

At last five o'clock struck. He had already taken up his position on the ramparts, whence he could survey the whole esplanade. Quite right: there came the black frock-coat, the light trousers, and the well-brushed hat.

Cousin Hans felt his heart palpitate a little. At first he attributed this to a sense of shame in thus craftily setting a trap for the good old captain. But he soon discovered that it was the sight of the beloved one's father that set his blood in a ferment. Thus reassured, he began, in accordance with Uncle Frederick's advice, to draw strokes and angles in the sand, attentively fixing his eyes, from time to time, upon the Castle of Akerhuus.

The whole esplanade was quiet and deserted. Cousin Hans could hear the captain's firm steps approaching; they came right up to him and stopped. Hans did not look up; the captain advanced two more paces and coughed. Hans drew a long and profoundly significant stroke with his stick, and then the old fellow could contain himself no longer.

"Aha, young gentleman," he said, in a friendly tone, taking off his hat, "are you making a plan of our fortifications?"

Cousin Hans assumed the look of one who is awakened from deep contemplation, and, bowing politely, he answered with some embarrassment: "No, it's only a sort of habit I have of trying to take my bearings wherever I may be."

"An excellent habit, a most excellent habit," the captain exclaimed with warmth.

"It strengthens the memory," Cousin Hans remarked, modestly.

"Certainly, certainly, sir!" answered the captain, who was beginning to be much pleased by this modest young man.

"Especially in situations of any complexity," continued the modest young man, rubbing out his strokes with his foot.

"Just what I was going to say!" exclaimed the captain, delighted. "And, as you may well believe, drawings and plans are especially indispensable in military science. Look at a battle-field, for example."

"Ah, battles are altogether too intricate for me," Cousin Hans interrupted, with a smile of humility.

"Don't say that, sir!" answered the kindly old man. "When once you have a bird's-eye view of the ground and of the positions of the armies, even a tolerably complicated battle can be made quite comprehensible.— This sand, now, that we have before us here, could very well be made to give us an idea, in miniature, of, for example, the battle of Waterloo."

"I have come in for the long one," thought Cousin Hans, "but never mind! [Note: In English in the original.] I love her."

"Be so good as to take a seat on the bench here," continued the captain, whose heart was rejoiced at the thought of so intelligent a hearer, "and I shall try to give you in short outline a picture of that momentous and remarkable battle—if it interests you?"

"Many thanks, sir," answered Cousin Hans, "nothing could interest me more. But I'm afraid you'll find it terribly hard work to make it clear to a poor, ignorant civilian."

"By no means; the whole thing is quite simple and easy, if only you are first familiar with the lay of the land," the amiable old gentleman assured him, as he took his seat at Hans's side, and cast an inquiring glance around.

While they were thus seated, Cousin Hans examined the captain more closely, and he could not but admit that in spite of his sixty years, Captain Schrappe was still a handsome man. He wore his short, iron-gray mustaches a little turned up at the ends, which gave him a certain air of youthfulness. On the whole, he bore a strong resemblance to King Oscar the First on the old sixpenny-pieces.

And as the captain rose and began his dissertation, Cousin Hans decided in his own mind that he had every reason to be satisfied with his future father-in-law's exterior.

The captain took up a position in a corner of the ramparts, a few paces from the bench, whence he could point all around him with a stick. Cousin Hans followed what he said, closely, and took all possible trouble to ingratiate himself with his future father-in-law.

"We will suppose, then, that I am standing here at the farm of Belle-Alliance, where the Emperor has his headquarters; and to the north-fourteen miles from Waterloo—we have Brussels, that is to say, just about at the corner of the gymnastic-school.

"The road there along the rampart is the highway leading to Brussels, and here," the captain rushed over the plain of Waterloo, "here in the grass we have the Forest of Soignies. On the highway to Brussels, and in front of the forest, the English are stationed—you must imagine the northern part of the battle-field somewhat higher than it is here. On Wellington's left wing, that is to say, to the eastward—here in the grass—

we have the Château of Hougoumont; that must be marked," said the captain, looking about him.

The serviceable Cousin Hans at once found a stick, which was fixed in the ground at this important point.

"Excellent!" cried the captain, who saw that he had found an interested and imaginative listener. "You see it's from this side that we have to expect the Prussians."

Cousin Hans noticed that the captain picked up a stone and placed it in the grass with an air of mystery.

"Here at Hougoumont," the old man continued, "the battle began. It was Jerome who made the first attack. He took the wood; but the château held out, garrisoned by Wellington's best troops.

"In the mean time Napoleon, here at Belle-Alliance, was on the point of giving Marshal Ney orders to commence the main attack upon Wellington's centre, when he observed a column of troops approaching from the east, behind the bench, over there by tree."

Cousin Hans looked round, and began to feel uneasy: could Blücher be here already?

"Blü—Blü—" he murmured, tentatively.

"It was Bülow," the captain fortunately went on, "who approached with thirty thousand Prussians. Napoleon made his arrangements hastily to meet this new enemy, never doubting that Grouchy, at any rate, was following close on the Prussians' heels.

"You see, the Emperor had on the previous day detached Marshal Grouchy with the whole right wing of the army, about fifty thousand men, to hold Blücher and Bülow in check. But Grouchy—but of course all this is familiar to you—" the captain broke off.

Cousin Hans nodded reassuringly.

"Ney, accordingly, began the attack with his usual intrepidity. But the English cavalry hurled themselves upon the Frenchmen, broke their ranks, and forced them back with the loss of two eagles and several cannons. Milhaud rushes to the rescue with his cuirassiers, and the

Emperor himself, seeing the danger, puts spurs to his horse and gallops down the incline of Belle-Alliance."

Away rushed the captain, prancing like a horse, in his eagerness to show how the Emperor rode through thick and thin, rallied Ney's troops, and sent them forward to a fresh attack.

Whether it was that there lurked a bit of the poet in Cousin Hans, or that the captain's representation was really very vivid, or that—and this is probably the true explanation—he was in love with the captain's daughter, certain it is that Cousin Hans was quite carried away by the situation.

He no longer saw a queer old captain prancing sideways; he saw, through the cloud of smoke, the Emperor himself on his white horse with the black eyes, as we know it from the engravings. He tore away over hedge and ditch, over meadow and garden, his staff with difficulty keeping up with him. Cool and calm, he sat firmly in his saddle, with his half-unbuttoned gray coat, his white breeches, and his little hat, crosswise on his head. His face expressed neither weariness nor anxiety; smooth and pale as marble, it gave to the whole figure in the simple uniform on the white horse an exalted, almost a spectral, aspect.

Thus he swept on his course, this sanguinary little monster, who in three days had fought three battles. All hastened to clear the way for him, flying peasants, troops in reserve or advancing—aye, even the wounded and dying dragged themselves aside, and looked up at him with a mixture of terror and admiration, as he tore past them like a cold thunderbolt.

Scarcely had he shown himself among the soldiers before they all fell into order as though by magic, and a moment afterwards the undaunted Ney could once more vault into the saddle to renew the attack. And this time he bore down the English and established himself in the farm-house of La Haie-Sainte.

Napoleon is once more at Belle-Alliance.

"And now here comes Bülow from the east—under the bench here, you see—and the Emperor sends General Mouton to meet him. At half-past four (the battle had begun at one o'clock) Wellington attempts to drive Ney out of La Haie-Sainte. But Ney, who now saw that everything depended on obtaining possession of the ground in front of the wood—the sand here by the border of the grass," the captain threw his glove over to the spot indicated, "Ney, you see, calls up the reserve brigade of Milhaud's cuirassiers and hurls himself at the enemy.

"Presently his men were seen upon the heights, and already the people around the Emperor were shouting 'Victoire!'

"'It is an hour too late,' answered Napoleon.

"As he now saw that the Marshal in his new position was suffering much from the enemy's fire, he determined to go to his assistance, and, at the same time, to try to crush Wellington at one blow. He chose for the execution of this plan, Kellermann's famous dragoons and the heavy cavalry of the guard. Now comes one of the crucial moments of the fight; you must come out here upon the battle-field!"

Cousin Hans at once rose from the bench and took the position the captain pointed out to him.

"Now you are Wellington!" Cousin Hans drew himself up. "You are standing there on the plain with the greater part of the English infantry. Here comes the whole of the French cavalry rushing down upon you. Milhaud has joined Kellermann; they form an illimitable multitude of horses, breastplates, plumes and shining weapons. Surround yourself with a square!"

Cousin Hans stood for a moment bewildered; but presently he understood the captain's meaning. He hastily drew a square of deep strokes around him in the sand.

"Right!" cried the captain, beaming, "Now the Frenchmen cut into the square; the ranks break, but join again, the cavalry wheels away and gathers for a fresh attack. Wellington has at every moment to surround himself with a new square.

"The French cavalry fight like lions: the proud memories of the Emperor's campaigns fill them with that confidence of victory which

218

made his armies invincible. They fight for victory, for glory, for the French eagles, and for the little cold man who, they know, stands on the height behind them; whose eye follows every single man, who sees all, and forgets nothing.

"But to-day they have an enemy who is not easy to deal with. They stand where they stand, these Englishmen, and if they are forced a step backwards, they regain their position the next moment. They have no eagles and no Emperor; when they fight they think neither of military glory nor of revenge; but they think of home. The thought of never seeing again the oak-trees of Old England is the most melancholy an Englishman knows. Ah, no, there is one which is still worse: that of coming home dishonored. And when they think that the proud fleet, which they know is lying to the northward waiting for them, would deny them the honor of a salute, and that Old England would not recognize her sons—then they grip their muskets tighter, they forget their wounds and their flowing blood; silent and grim, they clinch their teeth, and hold their post, and die like men."

Twenty times were the squares broken and reformed, and twelve thousand brave Englishmen fell. Cousin Hans could understand how Wellington wept, when he said, "Night or Blücher!"

The captain had in the mean time left Belle-Alliance, and was spying around in the grass behind the bench, while he continued his exposition which grew more and more vivid: "Wellington was now in reality beaten and a total defeat was inevitable," cried the captain, in a sombre voice, "when this fellow appeared on the scene!" And as he said this, he kicked the stone which Cousin Hans had seen him concealing, so that it rolled in upon the field of battle.

"Now or never," thought Cousin Hans.

"Blücher!" he cried.

"Exactly!" answered the captain, "it's the old werewolf Blücher, who comes marching upon the field with his Prussians."

So Grouchy never came; there was Napoleon, deprived of his whole right wing, and facing 150,000 men. But with never failing coolness he gives his orders for a great change of front.

But it was too late, and the odds were too vast.

Wellington, who, by Blücher's arrival, was enabled to bring his reserve into play, now ordered his whole army to advance. And yet once more the Allies were forced to pause for a moment by a furious charge led by Ney—the lion of the day.

"Do you see him there!" cried the captain, his eyes flashing.

And Cousin Hans saw him, the romantic hero, Duke of Elchingen, Prince of Moskwa, son of a cooper in Saarlouis, Marshal and Peer of France. He saw him rush onward at the head of his battalions—five horses had been shot under him with his sword in his hand, his uniform torn to shreds, hatless, and with the blood streaming down his face.

And the battalions rallied and swept ahead; they followed their Prince of Moskwa, their savior at the Beresina, into the hopeless struggle for the Emperor and for France. Little did they dream that, six months later, the King of France would have their dear prince shot as a traitor to his country in the gardens of the Luxembourg.

There he rushed around, rallying and directing his troops, until there was nothing more for the general to do; then he plied his sword like a common soldier until all was over, and he was carried away in the rout. For the French army fled.

The Emperor threw himself into the throng; but the terrible hubbub drowned his voice, and in the twilight no one knew the little man on the white horse.

Then he took his stand in a little square of his Old Guard, which still held out upon the plain; he would fain have ended his life on his last battlefield. But his generals flocked around him, and the old grenadiers shouted: "Withdraw, Sire! Death will not have you."

They did not know that it was because the *Emperor* had forfeited his right to die as a French soldier. They led him half-resisting from the field;

and, unknown in his own army, he rode away into the darkness of the night, having lost everything. "So ended the battle of Waterloo," said the captain, as he seated himself on the bench and arranged his neck-cloth.

—Cousin Hans thought with indignation of Uncle Frederick, who had spoken of Captain Schrappe in such a tone of superiority. He was, at least, a far more interesting personage than an old official mill-horse like Uncle Frederick.

Hans now went about and gathered up the gloves and other small objects which the generals, in the heat of the fight, had scattered over the battle-field to mark the positions; and, as he did so, he stumbled upon old Blücher. He picked him up and examined him carefully.

He was a hard lump of granite, knubbly as sugar-candy, which almost seemed to bear a personal resemblance to "Feldtmarschall Vorwärts." Hans turned to the captain with a polite bow.

"Will you allow me, captain, to keep this stone. It will be the best possible memento of this interesting and instructive conversation, for which I am really most grateful to you." And thereupon he put Blücher into his coat-tail pocket.

The captain assured him that it had been a real pleasure to him to observe the interest with which his young friend had followed the exposition. And this was nothing but the truth, for he was positively enraptured with Cousin Hans.

"Come and sit down now, young man. We deserve a little rest after a ten-hours' battle," he added, smiling.

Cousin Hans seated himself on the bench and felt his collar with some anxiety. Before coming out, he had put on the most fascinating one his wardrobe afforded. Fortunately, it had retained its stiffness; but he felt the force of Wellington's words: "Night or Blücher"—for it would not have held out much longer.

It was fortunate, too, that the warm afternoon sun had kept strollers away from the esplanade. Otherwise a considerable audience would probably have gathered around these two gentlemen, who went on gesticulating with their arms, and now and then prancing around.

They had had only one on-looker—the sentry who stands at the corner of the gymnastic-school.

His curiosity had enticed him much too far from his post, for he had marched several leagues along the highway from Brussels to Waterloo. The captain would certainly have called him to order long ago for this dereliction of duty but for the fact that the inquisitive private had been of great strategic importance. He represented, as he stood there, the whole of Wellington's reserve; and now that the battle was over the reserve retired in good order northward towards Brussels, and again took up *le poste perdu* at the corner of the gymnastic-school.

III.

"Suppose you come home and have some supper with me," said the captain; "my house is very quiet, but I think perhaps a young man of your character may have no great objection to passing an evening in a quiet family."

Cousin Hans's heart leaped high with joy; he accepted the invitation in the modest manner peculiar to him, and they were soon on the way to No. 34.

How curiously fortune favored him to-day! Not many hours had passed since he saw her for the first time; and now, in the character of a special favorite of her father, he was hastening to pass the evening in her company.

The nearer they approached to No. 34, in the more life-like colors did the enchanting vision of Miss Schrappe stand before his eyes; the blonde hair curling over the forehead, the lithe figure, and then these roguish, light-blue eyes!

His heart beat so that he could scarcely speak, and as they mounted the stair he had to take firm hold of the railing; his happiness made him almost dizzy.

In the parlor, a large corner-room, they found no one. The captain went out to summon his daughter, and Hans heard him calling, "Betty!"

Betty! What a lovely name, and how well it suited that lovely being!

The happy lover was already thinking how delightful it would be when he came home from his work at dinner-time, and could call out into the kitchen: "Betty! is dinner ready?"

At this moment the captain entered the room again with his daughter. She came straight up to Cousin Hans, took his hand, and bade him welcome.

But she added, "You must really excuse me deserting you again at once, for I am in the middle of a dish of buttered eggs, and that's no joke, I can tell you."

Thereupon she disappeared again; the captain also withdrew to prepare for the meal, and Cousin Hans was once more alone.

The whole meeting had not lasted many seconds, and yet it seemed to Cousin Hans that in these moments he had toppled from ledge to ledge, many fathoms down, into a deep, black pit. He supported himself with both hands against an old, high-backed easy-chair; he neither heard, saw, nor thought; but half mechanically he repeated to himself: "It was not she—it was not she!"

No, it was not she. The lady whom he had just seen, and who must consequently be Miss Schrappe, had not a trace of blonde hair curling over her brow. On the contrary, she had dark hair, smoothed down to both sides. Her eyes were not in the least roguish or light blue, but serious and dark-gray—in short, she was as unlike the charmer as possible.

After his first paralysis, Cousin Hans's blood began to boil; a violent anguish seized him: he raged against the captain, against Miss Schrappe, against Uncle Frederick and Wellington, and the whole world.

He would smash the big mirror and all the furniture, and then jump out of the corner window; or he would take his hat and stick, rush downstairs, leave the house, and never more set foot in it; or he would at least remain no longer than was absolutely necessary.

Little by little he became calmer, but a deep melancholy descended upon him. He had felt the unspeakable agony of disappointment in his first love, and when his eye fell on his own image in the mirror, he shook his head compassionately.

The captain now returned, well-brushed and spick and span. He opened a conversation about the politics of the day. It was with difficulty that Cousin Hans could even give short and commonplace answers; it seemed as though all that had interested him in Captain Schrappe had entirely evaporated. And now Hans remembered that on the way home from the esplanade he had promised to give him the whole sham fight in Sweden after supper.

"Will you come, please; supper is ready," said Miss Betty, opening the door into the dining-room, which was lighted with candles.

Cousin Hans could not help eating, for he was hungry; but he looked down at his plate and spoke little.

Thus the conversation was at first confined for the most part to the father and daughter. The captain, who thought that this bashful young man was embarrassed by Miss Betty's presence, wanted to give him time to collect himself.

"How is it you haven't invited Miss Beck this evening, since she's leaving town to-morrow," said the old man. "You two could have entertained our guest with some duets."

"I asked her to stay, when she was here this afternoon; but she was engaged to a farewell party with some other people she knows."

Cousin Hans pricked up his ears; could this be the lady of the morning that they were speaking about?

"I told you she came down to the esplanade to say good-bye to me," continued the captain. "Poor girl! I'm really sorry for her."

224

There could no longer be any doubt.

"I beg your pardon—are you speaking of a lady with curly hair and large blue eyes?" asked Cousin Hans.

"Exactly," answered the captain, "do you know Miss Beck?"

"No," answered Hans, "it only occurred to me that it might be a lady I met down on the esplanade about twelve o'clock."

"No doubt it was she" said the captain. "A pretty girl, isn't she?"

"I thought her beautiful," answered Hans, with conviction. "Has she had any trouble?—I thought I heard you say—"

"Well, yes; you see she was engaged for some months"—

"Nine weeks," interrupted Miss Betty.

"Indeed! was that all? At any rate her *fiancé* has just broken off the engagement, and that's why she is going away for a little while—very naturally—to some relations in the west-country, I think."

So she had been engaged—only for nine weeks, indeed—but still, it was a little disappointing. However, Cousin Hans understood human nature, and he had seen enough of her that morning to know that her feelings towards her recreant lover could not have been true love. So he said:

"If it's the lady I saw to-day, she seemed to take the matter pretty lightly."

"That's just what I blame her for," answered Miss Betty.

"Why so?" answered Cousin Hans, a little sharply; for, on the whole, he did not like the way in which the young lady made her remarks. "Would you have had her mope and pine away?"

"No, not at all," answered Miss Schrappe; "but, in my opinion, it would have shown more strength of character if she had felt more indignant at her *fiancé's* conduct."

"I should say, on the contrary, that it shows most admirable strength of character that she should bear no ill-will and feel no anger; for a woman's strength lies in forgiveness," said Cousin Hans, who grew eloquent in defence of his lady-love.

225

Miss Betty thought that if people in general would show more indignation when an engagement was broken off, as so often happened, perhaps young people would be more cautious in these matters.

Cousin Hans, on the other hand, was of opinion that when a *fiancé* discovered, or even suspected, that he had made a mistake, and that what he had taken for love was not the real, true, and genuine article, he was not only bound to break off the engagement with all possible speed, but it was the positive duty of the other party, and of all friends and acquaintances, to excuse and forgive him, and to say as little as possible about the matter, in order that it might the sooner be forgotten.

Miss Betty answered hastily that she did not think it at all the right thing that young people should enter into experimental engagements while they keep a look out for true love.

This remark greatly irritated Cousin Hans, but he had no time to reply, for at that moment the captain rose from the table.

There was something about Miss Schrappe that he really could not endure; and he was so much absorbed in this thought that, for a time, he almost forgot the melancholy intelligence that the beloved one—Miss Beck—was leaving town to-morrow.

He could not but admit that the captain's daughter was pretty, very pretty; she seemed to be both domestic and sensible, and it was clear that she devoted herself to her old father with touching tenderness. And yet Cousin Hans said to himself: "Poor thing, who would want to marry her?"

For she was entirely devoid of that charming helplessness which is so attractive in a young girl; when she spoke, it was with an almost odious repose and decision. She never came in with any of those fascinating half-finished sentences, such as "Oh, I don't know if you understand me—there are so few people that understand me—I don't know how to express what I mean; but I feel it so strongly." In short, there was about Miss Schrappe nothing of that vagueness and mystery which is woman's most exquisite charm.

Furthermore, he had a suspicion that she was "learned." And everyone, surely, must agree with Cousin Hans that if a woman is to fulfil her mission in this life (that is to say, to be a man's wife) she ought clearly to have no other acquirements than those her husband wishes her to have, or himself confers upon her. Any other fund of knowledge must always be a dowry of exceedingly doubtful value.

Cousin Hans was in the most miserable of moods. It was only eight o'clock, and he did not think it would do to take his departure before half-past nine. The captain had already settled himself at the table, prepared to begin the sham-fight. There was no chance of escape, and Hans took a seat at his side.

Opposite to him sat Miss Betty, with her sewing, and with a book in front of her. He leaned forward and discovered that it was a German novel of the modern school.

It was precisely one of those works which Hans was wont to praise loudly when he developed his advanced views, colored with a little dash of free-thought. But to find this book here, in a lady's hands, and, what was more, in German (Hans had read it in a translation), was in the last degree unpleasing to him.

Accordingly, when Miss Betty asked if he liked the novel, he answered that it was one of the books which should only be read by men of ripened judgment and established principles, and that it was not at all suited for ladies.

He saw that the girl flushed, and he felt that he had been rude. But he was really feeling desperate, and, besides, there was something positively irritating in this superior little person.

He was intensely worried and bored; and, to fulfil the measure of his suffering, the captain began to make Battalion B advance "under cover of the night."

Cousin Hans now watched the captain moving match-boxes, penknives, and other small objects about the table. He nodded now and then, but he did not pay the slightest attention. He thought of the lovely Miss Beck, whom he was, perhaps, never to see again; and now and then he stole a glance at Miss Schrappe, to whom he had been so rude.

He gave a sudden start as the captain slapped him on the shoulder, with the words, "And it was this point that I was to occupy. What do you think of that?"

Uncle Frederick's words flashed across Cousin Hans's mind, and, nodding vehemently, he said: "Of course, the only thing to be done—the key to the position?"

The captain started back and became quite serious. But when he saw Cousin Hans's disconcerted expression, his good-nature got the upperhand, and he laughed and said:

"No, my dear sir! there you're quite mistaken. However," he added, with a quiet smile, "it's a mistake which you share with several of our highest military authorities. No, now let me show you the key to the position."

And then he began to demonstrate at large that the point which he had been ordered to occupy was quite without strategical importance; while, on the other hand, the movement which he made on his own responsibility placed the enemy in the direst embarrassment, and would have delayed the advance of Corps B by several hours.

Tired and dazed as Cousin Hans was, he could not help admiring the judicious course adopted by the military authorities towards Captain Schrappe, if, indeed, there was anything in Uncle Frederick's story about the Order of the Sword.

For if the captain's original manoeuvre was, strategically speaking, a stroke of genius, it was undoubtedly right that he should receive a decoration. But, on the other hand, it was no less clear that the man who could suppose that in a sham-fight it was in the least desirable to delay or embarass any one was quite out of place in an army like ours. He ought to have known that the true object of the manoeuvres was to let the opposing armies, with their baggage and commissariat wagons, meet at a given time and in a given place, there to have a general picnic.

While Hans was buried in these thoughts, the captain finished the sham-fight. He was by no means so pleased with his listener as he had been upon the esplanade; he seemed, somehow, to have become absent-minded.

It was now nine o'clock; but, as Cousin Hans had made up his mind that he would hold out till half-past nine, he dragged through one of the longest half-hours that had ever come within his experience. The captain grew sleepy, Miss Betty gave short and dry answers; Hans had himself to provide the conversation—weary, out of temper, unhappy and love-sick as he was.

At last the clock was close upon half-past nine; he rose, explaining that he was accustomed to go early to bed, because he could read best when he got up at six o'clock.

"Well, well," said the captain, "do you call this going early to bed? I assure you I always turn in at nine o'clock."

Vexation on vexation! Hans said good-night hastily, and rushed downstairs.

The captain accompanied him to the landing, candle in hand, and called after him cordially, "Good-night—happy to see you again."

"Thanks!" shouted Hans from below; but he vowed in his inmost soul that he would never set foot in that house again.—

—When the old man returned to the parlor, he found his daughter busy opening the windows.

"What are you doing that for?" asked the captain.

"I'm airing the room after him," answered Miss Betty.

"Come, come, Betty, you are really too hard upon him. But I must admit that the young gentleman did not improve upon closer acquaintance. I don't understand young people nowadays."

Thereupon the captain retired to his bedroom, after giving his daughter the usual evening exhortation, "Now don't sit up too long."

When she was left alone, Miss Betty put out the lamp, moved the flowers away from the corner window, and seated herself on the window-sill with her feet upon a chair.

On clear moonlight evenings she could descry a little strip of the fiord between two high houses. It was not much; but it was a glimpse of the great highway that leads to the south, and to foreign lands.

And her desires and longings flew away, following the same course which has wearied the wings of so many a longing—down the narrow fiord to the south, where the horizon is wide, where the heart expands, and the thoughts grow great and daring.

And Miss Betty sighed as she gazed at the little strip of the fiord which she could see between the two high houses.

—She gave no thought, as she sat there, to Cousin Hans; but he thought of Miss Schrappe as he passed with hasty steps up the street.

Never had he met a young lady who was less to his taste. The fact that he had been rude to her did not make him like her better. We are not inclined to find those people amiable who have been the occasion of misbehavior on our own part. It was a sort of comfort to him to repeat to himself, "Who would want to marry her?"

Then his thoughts wandered to the charmer who was to leave town to-morrow. He realized his fate in all its bitterness, and he felt a great longing to pour forth the sorrow of his soul to a friend who could understand him.

But it was not easy to find a sympathetic friend at that time of night.

After all, Uncle Frederick was his confidant in many matters; he would look him up.

As he knew that Uncle Frederick was at Aunt Maren's, he betook himself towards the Palace in order to meet him on his way back from Homan's Town. He chose one of the narrow avenues on the right, which he knew to be his uncle's favorite route; and a little way up the hill he seated himself on a bench to wait.

It must be unusually lively at Aunt Maren's to make Uncle Frederick stop there until after ten. At last he seemed to discern a small white object far up the avenue; it was Uncle Frederick's white waistcoat approaching.

Hans rose from the bench and said very seriously, "Good-evening!"

Uncle Frederick was not at all fond of meeting solitary men in dark avenues; so it was a great relief to him to recognize his nephew.

"Oh, is it only you, Hans old fellow?" he said, cordially. "What are you lying in ambush here for?"

"I was waiting for you," answered Hans, in a sombre tone of voice.

"Indeed? Is there anything wrong with you? Are you ill?"

"Don't ask me," answered Cousin Hans.

This would at any other time have been enough to call forth a hail-storm of questions from Uncle Frederick.

But this evening he was so much taken up with his own experiences that for the moment he put his nephew's affairs aside.

"I can tell you, you were very foolish," he said, "not to go with me to Aunt Maren's. We have had such a jolly evening, I'm sure you would have enjoyed it. The fact is, it was a sort of farewell party in honor of a young lady who's leaving town to-morrow."

A horrible foreboding seized Cousin Hans.

"What washer name?" he shrieked, gripping his uncle by the arm.

"Ow!" cried his uncle, "Miss Beck."

Then Hans collapsed upon the bench.

But scarcely had he sunk down before he sprang up again, with a loud cry, and drew out of his coat-tail pocket a knubbly little object, which he hurled away far down the avenue.

"What's the matter with the boy?" cried Uncle Frederick, "What was that you threw away?"

"Oh, it was that confounded Blücher," answered Cousin Hans, almost in tears.

—Uncle Frederick scarcely found time to say, "Didn't I tell you to beware of Blücher?" when he burst into an alarming fit of laughter, which lasted from the Palace Hill far along Upper Fort Street.

THE END.

Lightning Source UK Ltd.
Milton Keynes UK
UKHW021843170123
415517UK00008B/1015